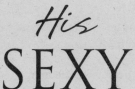

His
SEXY
Bad Habit

CHERIS HODGES

DAFINA BOOKS
Kensington Publishing Corp.
http://www.kensingtonbooks.com

DAFINA BOOKS are published by

Kensington Publishing Corp.
119 West 40th Street
New York, NY 10018

All Kensington Titles, Imprints, and Distributed Lines are available at special quantity discounts for bulk purchases for sales promotions, premiums, fund-raising, and educational or institutional use. Special book excerpts or customized printings can also be created to fit specific needs. For details, write or phone the office of the Kensington special sales manager: Kensington Publishing Corp., 119 West 40th Street, New York, NY 10018, attn: Special Sales Department, Phone: 1-800-221-2647.

Dafina and the Dafina logo Reg. U.S. Pat. & TM Off.

ISBN-13: 978-0-7582-4710-0
ISBN-10: 0-7582-4710-9

First Dafina mass market printing: January 2011

10 9 8 7 6 5 4 3 2 1

Printed in the United States of America

"Want a bite?" Antonio asked her.

"Not of that muffin," Serena said. "Tell me something, Antonio, what's your deal?"

"What do you mean?"

"Don't play coy with me," she said. "You know I want you, but you're sending mixed signals. If you're not married, then what's the problem?"

Antonio placed the other half of his muffin on top of the box and wiped his hands on his snug-fitting jeans. He took a step closer to her and Serena inhaled his scent of soap and masculinity. Her lips trembled as he brushed his fingertips across her cheek.

"Serena," he groaned. "There are some things that you should know about me and when you find them out, you might—"

She tilted her head up and planted a wet kiss on his lips. As she pressed her body against his, she didn't care what he needed to tell her. She just needed to taste his lips. Needed to feel the hardness of his body pressed against hers. Her tongue explored the sweetness of his mouth just as his did the same to her mouth. She could've kissed him all day, would've kissed him all day had they not heard a crash behind them.

Antonio pulled back from Serena. "Let me go check that out," he said. "What are you doing for lunch?"

"I'll be at home."

"Text me your address and I'll come over," he said.

Serena smiled and nodded. *He wants the same thing I want. Hot sex.*

Also by Cheris Hodges

JUST CAN'T GET ENOUGH

LET'S GET IT ON

MORE THAN HE CAN HANDLE

BETTING ON LOVE

NO OTHER LOVER WILL DO

Published by Dafina Books

This book is dedicated to anyone who's been hurt by love and decided to give it another try.

Acknowledgments

There are so many people that I'd like to thank. Each reader who has ever picked up one of my books, I sincerely thank you all. It's because of you that I continue to write these stories and I hope you continue to enjoy them.

To The Sistah-Friends Book Club in Columbia and Atlanta, thank you ladies for welcoming me into your "sistah hood."

To The Sistas Unlimited Book Club, thank you for your continuous support.

To The Prominent Women of Color Book Club, thank you ladies for your friendship and the spirited discussion in Jackonville.

To The Jax-African American Book Club for Women, it has been nice getting to know you ladies.

A big thank you to my agent, Sha-Shana Crichton, and my editor, Selena James. Your hard work is much appreciated.

And last but certainly not least, my loving parents and sister, Freddie and Doris Hodges and Adrienne Dease. I love you guys.

Chapter 1

Serena Jacobs looked down at her pink brides-maid dress and shook her head in disgust. Sure she'd agreed to be in her best friend Kandace Davis's wedding, but she had no idea that she'd be stuck in pink lace looking like a bottle of Pepto Bismol.

She hated the color pink. In her mind it made people think women were weak. And the last thing Serena Jacobs was was a weak woman. She scowled as she fluffed her honey brown curls.

"Will you smile?" Jade Goings asked as she adjusted the bodice of her strapless dress in the mirror.

"Why would Kandace choose pink and gold for her wedding colors?" Serena asked as she smoothed her hands down the sides of her dress. "She could've gotten away with slinky black dresses."

Alicia Michaels ran her fingers though her wavy black hair and shook her head. "Only you would associate black with a wedding. At least we're part of this one," she said, then shot a glance at Jade.

"Am I ever going to live that down? It was a spur of the moment deal," Jade said of her Las Vegas wedding that her friends hadn't participated in. She and her husband, James, met and got married in Las Vegas nearly two years ago. Still, her friends weren't happy that they hadn't been part of the ceremony.

Serena went silent, thinking back to the wedding she'd almost had that would've left her friends out in the cold, too. Five years ago, she'd left Atlanta to chase her dream of screenwriting. But the first person Serena'd met in Los Angeles, renowned filmmaker Emerson Bradford, had told her that her future wasn't behind the scenes.

"What do you mean?" Serena had asked as she ripped her screenplay from his hands. "You haven't even read my script."

"I'm sure it's good," he'd replied with a 10,000-watt smile that made Serena's anger go from boil to simmer. "But you have the face and body of a star."

"What makes you an authority?" she'd asked, placing her hand on her hip. "I've never even heard of you. For all I know you could be some poseur hanging around UCLA hoping all the wannabe screenwriters are so desperate to get their foot in the door that we'll just fall for the first line you offer."

Emerson had stood there with a smile on his face. "I have the perfect role for you. Do you have your SAG card?"

"For the last time, I'm a writer. Why do I need a Screen Actors Guild card?"

"Because, you're going to star in my next movie. We can discuss it over dinner," he'd said. And despite her apprehension at who Emerson had said he was, Serena had agreed to dinner with him. But before they'd met for dinner, she'd headed to Starbucks and did a Google search of Emerson Bradford. She'd been surprised and satisfied to find out that he was who he'd said he was. According to *Variety*, Emerson had just signed a deal with Warner Brothers for a sexy thriller that could be a star vehicle for the right actress. The magazine had quoted Emerson saying he'd wanted a fresh face for the movie. *So, he's not full of crap after all,* she'd thought as she reread the article and studied the picture of Emerson Bradford.

She'd taken him as a handsome man with a caramel complexion and an air of sophistication. His hazel eyes had seemed to sparkle in the picture and she'd allowed her curiosity to take over. She figured even if Emerson had been trying to run that Hollywood game on her, she'd at least get a free dinner out of it.

Serena had blown off her shift at M Grill and called Emerson to get the details on his dinner offer. He'd informed her that he'd send a car to pick her up and he'd wanted her to wear the sexiest thing she had in her closet.

* * *

"Hello," Jade said, snapping Serena out of her reverie. "We have to go check on the bride."

"Yeah, yeah," Serena said as she retouched her lipstick, then followed her girlfriends out of the dressing room into the bridal suite.

As Serena trailed her friends, she tried to shake her mind clear of Emerson. For so many years, she'd buried those memories, not even sharing them with her close friends. The fact that they returned in full force today bothered her.

She'd never been the type of woman who envied friends who got married. *You're being a fool. Marriage is for women like Jade and Kandace, not you. Don't let the wedding bells play with your head,* Serena thought as Jade opened the door to the suite.

"Hello," Jade said to Kandace, who was sitting at the vanity toying with her veil. "Are you ready?"

Kandace turned around with a nervous look on her face. "Where the hell have you all been?" she asked. "I had to put my mother out. She was just too much to deal with."

Jade walked over to Kandace and fixed her crooked veil. "Why would you put your mother out?"

"Knowing Miss Davis, she was crying, wasn't she?" Alicia asked as she admired Kandace's ivory Vera Wang dress with intricate beading work across the bodice.

Kandace nodded her head. "I didn't think you guys were ever going to come in here and save me. Oh my God, I'm so nervous. There have to be twenty cameras out there and a bunch of people I don't even know."

"What did you expect when you said you would marry Solomon Crawford?" Serena asked as she handed Kandace a tube of MAC lip gloss. "I'm pretty sure half of New York is out there."

Kandace shook her head. "I knew we should've just kept it simple," she said as she slowly rose from her seat.

Alicia pinched Serena's arm. "You know how she is, especially after everything that happened in Charlotte. Don't make her nervous about those cameras," she whispered. Jade followed Kandace as she paced back and forth.

"Kandace," Jade said as she stopped her friend from pacing. "Today is your day. The only thing that matters is that you and Solomon love each other. This is your day."

Kandace smiled and nodded. "All right. You're right, my day."

"And all of those cameras are for you," Serena added. "So, don't worry about them."

The three women surrounded Kandace and hugged her, being careful not to wrinkle her dress or mess up her makeup. "Let's get you down the aisle so you can become Mrs. Crawford," Jade said.

"Serena, are you sure you're okay with taking over for me in Charlotte?" Kandace asked once the women stopped hugging.

She smiled at her friend. "I'm fine with it. I have some unfinished business in the Queen City."

"Antonio Billups?" Alicia questioned.

"Hello, let's focus on the bride," Jade said. "Then we'll talk about Serena and our contractor."

Despite the fact that Kandace had been nervous before walking down the aisle, she was the picture of grace and love when she and hotel mogul Solomon Crawford exchanged their vows. Serena had to admit the ceremony was beautiful. She even felt a lone tear slide down her cheek as Kandace and Solomon kissed for the first time as husband and wife. As she linked arms with the groomsman she'd been paired with, all she could think about was the last conversation she'd had with Antonio Billups, the contractor who was going to revamp Hometown Delights after the horror that had occurred there last November.

Carmen De La Croix, or rather Chelsea Washington, had been obsessed with Solomon. When she'd seen that Solomon had fallen in love with Kandace, she'd stalked the couple and tried to kill Kandace in the restaurant. It was a messy scene and brought the wrong kind of attention from the media.

After Thanksgiving dinner, the women decided to redo the restaurant, which brought contractor Antonio Billups back into Serena's life since he'd been hired again, to oversee the renovations. Antonio intrigued her ever since they'd shared hot kisses in a room at the Westin hotel nearly two years ago. When he'd begun the initial work on the restaurant, Serena had thought she would've ended up in his bed by now, but Antonio pulled back. She felt as if he was hot and cold. Serena had done what she normally does when she doesn't get her way, tuned out emotionally—still, she wanted him and wondered what it would feel like to be wrapped up with Antonio.

Now that she would be in town she was going to get what she wanted from the sexy Mr. Billups. The thought of his naked body entwined with hers made her smile brightly as the photographer snapped a picture of the wedding party. She was definitely ready to head to Charlotte and oversee the renovation of the restaurant.

Antonio Billups yawned as he looked over the specs for Hometown Delights. He was set to start work on the restaurant when the owners returned from New York. Smiling, he thought about one of the owners in particular—Serena Jacobs. She had a killer body and lips that were soft like rose petals. But would she really fit into the life he had? He was a father first. Still, that didn't mean he wasn't a hot-blooded man who needed the comforts of a woman.

Could Serena offer him what he needed?

Looking out the window of his home office, Antonio thought back to the first moment he'd laid eyes on her.

She and Jade had met him at the property to talk about what renovations were needed before the restaurant could open. When Jade had gotten sick, Serena handled the meeting with him and Norman Engles, his business partner. Her deep brown eyes had struck him first. Then she'd smiled at him with a mix of seduction and desire dancing on her face as she'd extended her well-manicured hand and said, "I'm Serena Jacobs and I look forward to doing business with you gentlemen." Her voice had been melodic to his ears and his instant attraction to Serena had shocked him. It had been three years since he looked at a woman with lustful thoughts swirling in his head. Three years since his wife, Marian, had been killed in a collision with a drunk driver who was heading up the interstate going the wrong way.

But something in the way Serena Jacobs had looked at him awakened a dormant need. It had been a struggle for him to focus on business when he hadn't been able to tear his eyes away from her long shapely legs. It was as if something else had taken control of him when he'd said, "I can bring you the contracts for the project this evening and we can discuss them over a drink."

Norman had shot Antonio a stunned look. Asking a potential client out wasn't his partner's style, but he'd nodded approvingly at him when Serena had been talking to Jade on her cell phone.

"I was two seconds from doing that myself," Norman had whispered to Antonio. "She's a stone cold fox."

"And about twenty years younger than you," he'd replied to his partner as he patted the man's beer belly.

Norman sucked his teeth. "Just because it's snow on the roof don't mean the fireplace doesn't get hot. Just takes a little more time. I'm glad to see you coming out of the exile you put yourself in."

Antonio had shrugged his shoulders. "All I did was ask the woman out for a drink."

"I saw those looks you were giving her. This ain't about contracts or a drink," Norman had said.

Antonio had been about to deny what Norman had observed when Serena sauntered over to them and said, "I'll be ready at eight to discuss the contracts and have that drink." Her smile had caused an ache in his pants and swelling in his boxers.

"I look forward to it, Mrs. Jacobs," he'd said.

"Please, call me Serena. Mrs. Jacobs was my grandmother," she'd replied in a flirty tone.

Smiling, Antonio had nodded in reply. "All right, Serena. Where are we meeting?"

"I'm staying at the Westin down—I mean—Uptown. I hear they have a nice bar there," Serena had said.

"Then I'll see you at eight." After they left, Antonio had headed home and called his sister-in-law, Casey, to watch A.J.

"What's going on?" she'd asked him after agreeing to watch her nephew.

"I'm meeting with a client," he'd replied, not wanting to tell his sister-in-law that he was meeting a woman. Though his wife had been dead for three years, he hadn't been sure Casey would agree with him returning to the dating world.

Maybe she'd think he was betraying her sister and he hadn't wanted to have that conversation with her.

"I'd love to watch A. J. Should I come over there?" she'd inquired.

"Sure, he's getting ready to watch a movie on the Disney Channel. He's had his dinner and don't let him fool you into feeding him a bunch of ice cream before I get back."

"All right."

When Casey had arrived at his house, Antonio barely had said good-bye to her before he was out the door. His anticipation to see Serena had rendered him temporarily thoughtless. He'd sped from his northeast Charlotte home and arrived at The Westin in record time. The moment he'd stepped into the bar, Serena had met him, looking even more delicious in her black bandeau dress that skimmed her knees.

"It's pretty loud in here," she'd said. "Why don't we head up to my room and look over those contracts?"

"Are you sure?" he'd asked, not certain he'd be able to go into Serena's room and concentrate on business. Not the way she'd looked in that dress.

"Well, we can't talk over that music nor can we worry about spilling drinks on those important papers," she'd said, then ran her finger down his arm. Antonio had known Serena wanted to do more than talk business. Still, he'd followed her up to her room. Sure they'd gone over the contracts, but that took about twenty minutes, then she'd ordered drinks from room service and sat on the bed beside him. Their conversation had been light, talking about Charlotte's downtown area being called Uptown and how she got into the restaurant business.

She'd inched closer to him as he talked about how his company had worked on the Blake Hotel and helped turn the place into a boutique hotel that offered something different in the city. Serena had turned her head and their lips were inches from each other's. Antonio had expected her to turn her head away, but she'd pressed her lips against his and kissed him with a scorching passion that sent chills up and down his spine. He'd returned the kiss with fervor and zest that had allowed him to release years of pent up emotions, pent up desire and passion. She had melted against his chest and deepened the kiss. Their tongues danced against each other as Antonio had slipped his hand between her thighs.

Abruptly, he'd pulled back from her. "Whoa," he'd said, feeling like a teenager sneaking around with a girl. "This can't happen."

She'd raised her eyebrow and asked, "Why not? We're both adults."

"I can't do this. We're about to start working together."

Serena had risen to her feet and paced back and forth. "And? You're married, aren't you?"

Antonio held up his left hand. "I'm not married. But, like I said, we're about to start working together and I don't want to complicate matters with sex." He'd stood up and closed the space between them. He'd wanted to have sex with her, wanted to lift that little black dress above her head and see the splendor of her naked body.

Serena had seemed to notice his desire as she glanced down at the fly of his slacks. "I'm not a woman who plays games and I go after what I want," she'd said. "Since I know for sure this isn't one-sided, I'm telling you, again, we're adults."

"I know this," he'd replied. "But I have to try and be professional."

Serena had offered him a sly smile and pressed her body against his. "But I don't," she'd said and leaned in to kiss him again. Unable to resist, he'd cupped her bottom and started to inch up her dress. Before anything else could happen, the door had opened and Jade had walked in, causing them to break off the kiss.

That kiss still kept him up at night, even after all the time that had passed. It kept him yearning for more from Serena, but he couldn't get caught in her sexy web when he had A.J. and his business to run. Still, how much longer could he deny what he wanted?

Chapter 2

Two days after Kandace and Solomon were whisked away to Dundret in Sweden for their snow-filled honeymoon, Serena stood in the townhouse that Kandace used to rent, unpacking her things, since she was going to staying in Charlotte until the restaurant was redesigned. She was happy that she'd allowed movers to bring in all of the heavy items like her bedroom suite, her leather living room sectional, and her heavy bookcases. Had she been smarter, she would've allowed them to unpack her books and set up the entertainment center.

"Why did I bring all this crap?" she muttered as she looked around the maze of boxes. "It's not as if I'm going to live here forever." Serena plopped down on the edge of the sofa and reached for her cell phone to call Alicia and Jade. They could at least come over and help her unpack since they suggested she move into the townhouse, rather than take a suite at a hotel. Honestly,

Serena knew she needed a place of her own if she was going to enact her plan of cracking Antonio Billups.

Since the wedding, she'd only gotten a glimpse of him as he worked gutting the dining room of the restaurant. So far, Alicia and Jade had handled most of the business meetings because she'd been wrapping up her business in Atlanta. Now that she was in Charlotte she was ready to mix a lot of pleasure with a little business.

"Hello," Jade said when she picked up the phone.

"What are you doing?" Serena asked.

"I just tucked my son in for a nap. Are the movers done with you?"

"Yes. I'm calling so you and Alicia can come and help me unpack."

"Alicia's on her way back to Atlanta and Jaden just went to sleep, so it looks as if you're on your own right now," Jade said. "I'm actually surprised you're not at the restaurant."

Serena smiled. "You know, I will go over there and take a look at what's going on. By the time I get home, your son should be awake and you can come over."

"Serena, what's so special about Antonio Billups? I've never seen you go out of your way for a man. Hell, they normally fall at your feet. This is more than about you wanting to sleep with him."

"No, it isn't," Serena said. "Don't make it seem like I'm some man eater. He's different. I just can't put my finger on it right now. But I'm going to have fun trying to figure out just what's going on."

"Please be careful. He's the best contractor in town and the last thing we need is for you to give him a reason to quit on us," Jade cautioned.

"Trust me, what I want from Mr. Billups has nothing to do with our business," Serena said. "And since you're watching your sleeping baby, I'm going to the restaurant."

"What happens when a man sweeps you off your feet and you fall in love?"

"I don't believe in the whole fairy tale thing," Serena said. "I can stand on my own and I like my feet just where they are, firmly planted on the ground."

"That's what you say now," Jade said. "Maybe Antonio is what you need—a challenge."

"A challenge? What are you talking about? He's a man and soon enough, we'll do what both of us want to do. Had it not been for you, it would've happened already."

"How is your quasi-obsession with this man my fault?" Jade asked.

"We were close to sealing the deal that night when you walked in at the Westin," Serena said, closing her eyes and reliving that kiss.

"There have been other times for you to seal the deal. I swear, talking to you is just like talking to a man sometimes," Jade said in an exasperated tone.

"Please, I'm not as stupid as those so-called players you're always comparing me to. I don't believe in stringing people along," she said. *Been on the other end of that and I'm not trying do that to anyone else.*

"Just be careful and don't mess things up until we get the restaurant done," Jade said.

Serena sucked her teeth, then told her friend she'd see her later. After hanging up, she maneuvered through the boxes and headed upstairs to change into a pair of dark blue jeans, a fitted white T-shirt and a pair of red stilettos. She glanced at herself in the mirror and fluffed her hair. Serena knew her shoes weren't exactly the best ones to wear to a construction site, but she wasn't trying to be Miss Safety, she was trying to turn Antonio Billups into mush. Smiling, she grabbed her purse from the cluttered bed and headed downstairs.

"This was a perfectly good dining room," Norman complained as he loaded pieces of the stripped floor into the metal waste can. "Why are these women redoing it already?"

"They want a new start after everything that happened here," Antonio replied as he wiped his brow with the back of his hand. Part of him wondered if Serena would be involved in this renovation project. He looked for her every day he came to work, but he hadn't seen her yet. Since they'd already been at the restaurant for about six hours, he'd given up seeing her today.

"So, a beer after we finish up here?" Norman asked.

"No, I got to take A.J. out to dinner since I

missed his football practice yesterday," Antonio said, reaching down and grabbing another pile of debris. As he rose to his feet, he saw a pair of red shoes walking into the restaurant. When he saw those shoes were attached to curvy legs in tight jeans, his breath caught in his chest and he nearly dropped the debris from his hands.

"Hello, gentlemen," Serena said. The sound of her voice sent chills throughout his body. It had a husky quality he imagined was like that of the mythical sirens who seduced the sailors of ancient Greece.

Norman smiled at Serena like a Cheshire cat. "Well, hello," he said. "You'd better be careful walking in here in those shoes."

Looking at Antonio, she said, "I'm sure you guys can take care of me if I fall."

"That's a chance we don't want to take," Antonio said as he dropped the trash in the metal container. "Don't come any further. The floor is uneven."

"Okay," she said, then smiled at him. "It looks as if you guys are going to finish on schedule. That's good for our business."

"We aim to please," Norman said. "I'm going to step outside for a cigarette."

Antonio shot him a questioning look, but kept quiet. Norman didn't smoke.

When Norman was outside, Serena cautiously crossed over to Antonio. "It's good to see you again," she said.

"Good to see you, too," he replied as he inhaled

her scent. She smelled like roses and jasmine, intoxicating. "How was the wedding?"

Serena shrugged. "Good, if you're into those big affairs," she said.

Antonio folded his arms and shook his head. "Come on. You mean to tell me you're not one of those women who attends a wedding and starts dreaming of her own?"

She rolled her eyes and laughed. "Not at all. Maybe when you're finished here, you can help me in my townhouse," she said. "I could use a good pair of hands."

"Wish I could, but I have plans tonight," he said.

"Well, the entertainment center will hold, if you don't mind putting it together for me." Serena pouted and her lips looked so sexy.

His mind instantly flashed back to their kiss and he felt his desire growing in his pants. "So, you've moved to Charlotte?"

"For now. Jade isn't going to be able to be hands-on during the renovation, Kandace is on her honeymoon, and Alicia is putting together these business seminars trying to get Oprah's attention or something," she said. "So, you're stuck with me looking over your shoulder."

"That doesn't seem so bad," he replied with a smile. "Why don't you greet us with breakfast in the morning?"

"I could always serve you breakfast in bed," Serena said boldly.

"Is that so?" he said with a smirk on his face. "I'm going to take you up on that one day."

"Can I get a specific date on that?" Serena asked as she ran her index finger down his bare arm. Antonio took her hand in his and lifted it to his lips. Her skin was so soft. Silk had nothing on her.

"Make sure you wear sensible shoes in the morning," he said after letting her hand go. "I wouldn't want you to get hurt."

"Yes, sir. What time do you and your crew get here tomorrow?"

"Around six. Tomorrow is going to be a busy day because we're laying the floor," he said.

Serena took a step toward the door. "Then I'll see you at six," she said.

"All right, Miss Serena," he said as she walked out the door.

It wasn't until Serena was in her car that her breathing returned to normal. Antonio was now bald and his head would look perfect in her hands as he buried his face between her thighs. *Stop it,* she thought. *For all you know, his plans tonight could be with his girlfriend. I find it hard to believe that man is single.*

Serena started the car and headed back to her townhouse. As she pulled up, she saw Jade's car at the curb. "I'm going to have to get the key back from her," Serena said as she placed the car in park and hopped out. When she walked in, Jade was sitting on the cluttered sofa.

"Where's Jaden?" Serena asked.

"At home with his father," Jade said. "You obviously need a lot of help. Are you planning on leaving Atlanta for Charlotte?"

"Maybe," Serena said with a slick smile. "The restaurant is coming along great. They took the floor up today and the new one goes down tomorrow."

"And you walked in there in those shoes?" Jade said as she rose from the sofa and grabbed a box marked MOVIES.

"I was sure Antonio would've caught me if I had fallen," Serena replied, then took the box from Jade's hands. "My entertainment system isn't ready."

"So, what am I here to unpack?" She looked around at the boxes and shook her head. "Serena, what if you don't get what you want and have to go back to Atlanta?"

"Jade, darling, I'm going to get what I want. The first thing I want is your key," she said as she extended her hand to her friend. "Can't have you walking in when I get Mr. Billups in here to put my entertainment center together."

"Damn, you're fast," Jade said as she pulled the house key out of her pocket. "I hope he turns out to be the man to tame you."

"I'm not a horse and if I were, no man could tame me," she said. "Let's get busy." As the women opened boxes containing art, knickknacks, and books, Jade looked at her friend and shook her head.

"What's that look for?" Serena asked.

Jade sighed and Serena knew what her friend

was going to bring up. "Five years ago you weren't this bad," she said.

"Well, I'm a lot older and wiser. After seeing what all you guys have been through with men, why would I sign up for that?" Serena said, masking the real reason she'd closed her heart to love.

"Let's see, I'm happily married, Kandace is honeymooning with a man who loves her more than anything and—"

"And what? Two out of four aren't very good odds of love. I'd rather not take the chance," Serena said with finality in her voice.

"Sounds like someone has been hurt," Jade said as she placed an arrangement of pictures on the mantel above the fireplace.

"Whatever, Jade," Serena said as she began placing her books on the bookshelf. Even though she was over any feelings of love for Emerson Bradford, she didn't want to relive the way he crushed her heart as she stood at the altar waiting for him and he never showed up.

They'd wrapped filming on the movie the night before and Serena's final scene had been one where she was intimate with the lead character and his wife. It had been a sensual scene, once it was edited. Watching herself on screen had turned her on so much that when the crew had left the set, she'd planted herself in Emerson's lap.

"Who knew it took that much to get great sex

on the big screen," she'd said as she wrapped her legs around his waist.

"I just hope the scene actually stays in the movie," he'd replied as she'd untied her robe. "You are going to be a star, you know that."

Serena bit her bottom lip. "This was never my intention," she'd said. "I wanted to write scripts and let someone like you bring them to life."

"But I knew where you belonged," he'd said before taking her swollen nipples between his lips.

She'd moaned, ready to have some actual sex with her future husband, but Emerson had stopped teasing her taut nipples and gently removed her from his lap. "As much as I want you, I have to get this rough cut to the studio heads tonight. But after tomorrow we will have the rest of our lives to make love and hit movies," he'd said. "My beautiful muse."

"But Emerson," she'd protested, her voice sounding like a purr. "They don't need that movie right this second and I need you." Serena had dropped her robe and pressed her body against Emerson's. "And you need me."

The sound of glass breaking brought Serena back to reality. "Damn it," she muttered as she looked at the Tiffany lamp she'd smashed.

"Are you all right over there?" Jade asked.

"I need to pay more attention," she said. "I'll get the broom from the kitchen and clean this up."

"Stop thinking about seducing that man and

maybe you'll stop breaking things," Jade called out after her friend.

Antonio kicked off his boots at the front door then shook his head. *Some habits die hard,* he thought. Marian had always fussed about him tracking dust and dirt in the house, so to stave off an argument, Antonio just took his shoes off before walking inside. Though it had been three years since her death, he still did it.

"Daddy," A.J. called out when he heard the door close behind his father. "Are we going to have pizza? Aunt Casey said you were taking us for pizza. I want pepperoni and cheese."

"No on the pepperoni," Antonio said as he enveloped his son in his arms. "How about we get cheese, chicken, and green peppers?"

"All right," the boy said as he pouted. "But Aunt Casey said—"

"Aunt Casey didn't promise you anything," Casey Wallace said as she walked into the foyer. "You know your dad doesn't eat pork."

Antonio let his son go and told him to wash up so that he'd be ready to eat when the pizza arrived. "Thanks for staying with him today, Case," Antonio said.

"You know I don't mind," she said. "I thought you were going to take the boy out, though."

Antonio shook his head. "I'm wiped. The only person who showed up to work today was Norman and we had to take up the floor."

"Do you want me to keep A.J. overnight so you can get some rest?" she asked.

"Nah, I need to spend some time with my boy. You're welcomed to join us for dinner," he offered out of obligation, though part of him hoped Casey would go home. As much as he loved and appreciated her, he needed some quiet time with his son.

"Thanks," she said. "Why don't I go rent us a movie?"

"I think there's a baseball game on tonight, we're good on the movie," he said. "But you can order the pizza while I go take a shower."

"All right," she said with a smile.

Antonio dashed upstairs, shaking his head. Sometimes he wasn't sure if his sister-in-law was looking out for him and A.J. or if she was trying to move in. Casey had been devastated when Marian died and for six months, she didn't leave her sister's house. Antonio had moved out of the master bedroom so Casey could be closer to her sister's things. Norman had told him that Casey wasn't simply mourning the loss of her sister, she'd also been trying to take her sister's place in Antonio's life.

At first Antonio had just laughed it off, but he'd seen how Casey had been trying to do more things that his wife should've been doing before her death. He'd told her that she had to go home and give him and A.J. a chance to grieve their loss without worrying about how she would react. Her constant crying and sadness had scared A.J. and she hadn't been getting any better by living in a world of sorrow.

What he hadn't told Casey or anyone had been the fact that his marriage was over. Hidden in the foot locker that Marian had kept in the closet were divorce papers that she'd had drawn up two days before the accident. Antonio had known Marian had been unhappy. He'd been feeling the same way, but Antonio had kept his wedding vows. Marian had not. On the night of her accident, she'd been on her way to meet with the man she'd planned to leave Antonio for.

He shook his head and turned the shower spray off. He hated thinking about that night. Hated the fact that his son was without his mother and hated the guilt that he felt for not trying harder to make his marriage work.

Antonio knew he couldn't change the past, but he wasn't sure if he'd be able to move forward into the future.

With Serena?

"Where did that come from?" he mumbled as he toweled his body dry.

Antonio wrapped the towel around his waist and headed into the bedroom to slip into a pair of sweatpants and a T-shirt. By the time he'd arrived downstairs, Casey was opening the door for the Papa Johns pizza delivery man.

"Hey, I got that," Antonio said as he reached for his wallet from the coffee table.

Casey shook her head. "That's all right, Tonio, I'll pay for dinner," she said as she handed the pizza delivery driver a twenty dollar bill. "Keep the change."

When the pizza man left, Casey ushered A.J. into the kitchen so he could eat. Antonio followed them and stood in the doorway and watched his son sit at the table while his aunt placed paper plates on the table. "Casey," he said, "You're doing too much. We're just going to eat in front of the TV."

"Are you sure?" she asked. "He's been watching TV all day."

"Watching what you wanted to watch, Aunt Casey," A.J. said.

"Well, I'm the adult," she said as she placed a slice of pizza on A.J.'s plate. Antonio walked over to the table and picked up his son's plate and one of his own and grabbed two slices of pizza. "Go ahead and turn on the *Justice League* before the Braves' game," he told his son as he handed him his food. A.J. dashed into the den while taking bites of his food.

"Casey," Antonio said. "Thanks for dinner and everything, but you have to relax. A.J. and I have a routine."

"I'm not trying to interrupt your routine," she said.

"Just so we're clear," Antonio said.

"I guess I should leave, then," Casey said. "I was just trying to make sure we had a family meal."

"We do that on Sundays," he said. "Just ease up a little bit."

She folded her arms across her chest and

glared at him. "So, what am I, just the babysitter you call when you're in a pinch?"

"Remember, you volunteered for this. I don't want to argue with you, but I don't need you coming in here second-guessing how I raise my son."

"That's not what I'm doing," she protested.

"I can't tell," he said. "Casey, let's just agree to disagree, but this is my ship and I'm running it."

"Fine," Casey snapped. "I think I'm going to head home. I know when I'm not wanted." She turned swiftly on her heels, but Antonio stopped her.

"I don't want you to leave," he said. "A.J. expects you to stay for dinner and I'd appreciate it if you did."

She looked up at him and smiled dimly. "Thanks," Casey said as she turned to the table and picked up a slice of pizza. "I'm going to eat in here because I'm not interested in watching the *Justice League* or the Atlanta Braves."

Antonio gave Casey a smile and headed into the living room with his son.

Chapter 3

Serena woke up at five A.M. and didn't want to get out of her bed. She looked at the tangled sheets and wished they were evidence of a night with Antonio and not just her overactive imagination. All night she'd dreamed of him—his lips pressed against hers, his hardness buried deep in her hot, wet valley—giving her pleasure and passion she'd never felt before. Though it had just been a dream, Serena throbbed between her thighs as if she could feel the aftereffects of their lovemaking.

Groaning, she pounded her fist into the mattress, then threw her blanket off and crawled out of bed. Sure, she could've simply headed to Starbucks, picked up the coffee and muffins without dressing up in her typical fashion, but Serena wanted Antonio to see what he could've been waking up to. She took a quick shower, sprayed on her favorite jasmine body spray, and dressed in a pair of leggings, a fitted tunic, and a pair of four-inch black gladiator sandals that offered just enough of a glimpse of her toes to spark a foot fetish. Pulling her curly hair into a fluffy ponytail, she grabbed her keys and purse then headed for her baby blue Ford Mustang convertible.

It had taken her thirty minutes to get ready but only fifteen to collect a travel box of coffee from Starbucks, a dozen muffins, and cups for the coffee. She arrived at Hometown Delights at the same time as Antonio and his six-man crew.

The men walked into the restaurant and Antonio crossed over to Serena. "I can't believe you actually showed up," he said with a smirk on his luscious lips.

Serena sucked in a deep breath as she pulled out the box of muffins. "I'm a woman of my word," she said as she pressed the box against Antonio's chest. "I told you that I was going to bring you guys breakfast."

"I know they are going to appreciate this. Most of our employers only show up when they have a problem," he said as he took a peek in the box. "Looks good."

"The muffins?" she asked when she lifted the coffee and set it on the hood of the car. "Or something else?"

Antonio smiled and shook his head. "I don't know what to make of you," he said. "You know you look good."

"Just making sure you know," she said, then reached for the coffee.

Antonio beat her to it. "Wouldn't want you to break a nail," he quipped.

"My kind of man. Aware of the power of a man-icure," she said, then sauntered ahead of him, giving Antonio a prime look at her shapely back-side. When Serena entered the restaurant, all of the men stopped talking and stared at her as she set the coffee cups down on a table. One of the men started to say something, but stopped when Antonio walked in.

"Hey guys, Miss Jacobs brought us breakfast," he called out as he placed the muffins and coffee on the table next to the cups.

"That's really nice of you, Miss Jacobs," Norman said. Then he turned to the crew and said, "Why don't we go eat in the back, away from the dust."

Serena made a mental note of how much she liked Norman. He always made himself scarce when she and Antonio had a chance to be alone to-gether. Antonio picked up a muffin and broke it in half. "Want a bite?" he asked her.

"Not of that muffin," she said. "Tell me some-thing, Antonio. What's your deal?"

"What do you mean?"

Serena sighed and folded her arms across her chest as she watched him eat.

"My deal?" he said after he swallowed.

"Don't play coy with me," she said. "You know I want you, but you're sending mixed signals. If you're not married, then what's the problem?"

Antonio placed the other half of his muffin on top of the box and wiped his hands on his snug-fitting jeans.

Serena's eyes were drawn to his thighs. They looked so powerful and strong. She wanted to feel them on top of hers, wondered if he'd squeeze them around her. Blinking, she looked into his coffee brown eyes and swallowed.

"I haven't been dating since my wife died. I was married for eight years, so I don't know how this dating thing works now, and I have a lot of responsibilities. Believe me when I say this. I want you too."

"Well, what's the problem? How about we have dinner tonight and I can explain the whole dating thing to you?" she said with a seductive tilt to her voice.

Antonio took a step closer to her and Serena inhaled his scent of soap and masculinity. Her lips trembled as he brushed his fingertips across her cheek. "Serena," he groaned. "There are some things that you should know about me and when you find them out, you might—"

She tilted her head up and planted a wet kiss on his lips. As she pressed her body against his, she didn't care what he needed to tell her. She needed to taste his lips. Needed to feel the hardness of his body pressed against hers. Antonio pulled her closer and Serena gasped as she felt his bulge of desire pressing against her thighs. Her tongue explored the sweetness of his mouth just as his did the same to her mouth. She could've kissed him all day, would've kissed him all day had they not heard a crash behind them. Antonio pulled back from Serena. "Let me go check that out," he said. "What are you doing for lunch?"

"I'll be at home."

"Text me your address and I'll come over," he said.

Serena smiled and nodded. As she walked out to her car, she couldn't wait for lunch and thought about Jade's warning that Antonio could be different. The one who could make her fall in love. *Not going to happen,* she thought. *He wants the same thing I want. Hot sex.*

When Antonio found out the crash in the back of the restaurant had been a box of pots falling over and not something serious he wished he'd told Serena to wait. He needed to tell her about his son, his wife, and how their marriage had been falling apart before her death. Then maybe she'd understand that as much as he wanted her, he wasn't sure he had enough of himself to give.

"That sure was nice of Serena to bring breakfast over," Norman said as the men began to work. "You know that woman wants you."

"She told me," Antonio said as he lifted a bundle of flooring.

"What are you waiting on? Get her," he said. "She's a woman who's sending out all the right signals and you need to get back out there. How many dates have you turned down in the last three years?"

"I have a son to consider," Antonio said. "Most of the women around here want to jump directly into motherhood or don't want to be with me because I have A.J."

"Where does Serena rank on that scale?"

Antonio pulled his box cutter from his pocket and sliced open the flooring. "Well, she doesn't know about A.J."

"Why haven't you told her?" Norman asked.

Antonio began laying out the marble tiles and shook his head. "I don't know. It really hasn't come up and she doesn't seem like the motherly type."

"So, you like her, but you're afraid to let her in your life. What kind of sense does that make?" Norman said as he knelt down and started laying out the flooring. "No one said you have to marry her."

"I'm not afraid, but I'm too old for a meaningless fling and I don't want to teach my son to treat women as interchangeable bed buddies."

"See, you're a good man, too much of a good man. No one is saying invite your son on your dates or into your bedroom when it goes there. Who knows, Serena might be everything you've been looking for. More than anything else, you need to get some."

Antonio looked at his older friend, "What makes you think I'm not getting any?"

Norman shot him a knowing look and shook his head. "Please. The way you look at that woman whenever she's around proves you're longing. Stop overthinking it and get what you want. When the time comes, if you feel like she should meet your son, deal with it then. Right now, have some adult time with that sexy-ass woman. If I was five years younger, I would."

Antonio raised his eyebrow at Norman, who was easily knocking on sixty's door. "Five years?"

"Yes, five years," Norman said with a laugh. "But man, come on. Your wife would want you to move on with your life."

Inside Antonio bristled. His wife wouldn't have cared about his happiness. She certainly hadn't the last few years of the marriage. But that had been a secret Antonio had held close to his chest. Everyone had believed Antonio and Marian had been in love and their relationship would last forever.

"I guess I do need to move on with my life," Antonio finally said, shaking the thoughts of Marian from his head. "She invited me for lunch."

"I hope you plan on going," Norman said with a smile.

Antonio grinned. "I'm going to pretend I'm you, five years younger."

Norman laughed and the men returned to their work.

Serena entered her townhouse and realized she wasn't going to be able to go back to sleep. If she was going to have lunch with Antonio in her place, she was going to have to do something about the boxes she and Jade didn't get a chance to unpack. Kicking her shoes off at the door, Serena began grabbing the empty boxes, stuffing them inside each other. One thing she learned from her father, Dominic Jacobs, was that men didn't like messy women. Following the death of her mother, Serena had been raised by her father who'd used women to get what he'd wanted.

Dominic took care of his daughter with expert care, but he had help from the various women to whom he made promises he had no intention keeping. Growing up, it seemed as if there had been a new woman in the Jacobs house every week. Many of them had been under the impression that doting on Serena would win them favor with the handsome Dominic. It didn't work that way.

By the time Serena had become a teenager, she'd tried to warn them that their gifts were a waste of time and they'd do a lot better if they left Nic alone. They'd never listened to her, thinking she was just a kid not knowing what she was talking about. But they always end up with a broken heart.

Watching her father move though women the way he did had taught Serena she'd better play the game well or she'd end up like the heartbroken masses who her father dealt with. For a while, Serena had been able to save herself pain. In college, she'd earned the name of Ice Queen. Guys had been attracted to Serena's beauty and often they'd thought their childish games would be enough to get her into their bed since it had worked with other girls in the Atlanta University Center. But Serena hadn't fallen for it and they'd soon discovered no amount of money and smooth talk would get the Ice Queen.

When Serena had fallen in love, she'd fallen hard and for the wrong man. She still wore those scars. That was the reason she wouldn't allow herself to think of Antonio Billups as more than a fix for her passionate needs. How could she open herself up for anything more when she hadn't healed from her brush with love five years ago?

An hour later, Serena had gotten her house presentable and texted her address to Antonio. Since it was just a little after eight, she decided to take a seat on the sofa and watch a little bit of television. While she flipped through the channels, she decided she wouldn't hit Antonio with an all-out seduction. She had to get a feel for him first. What if he told her he was seeing someone or had given up on women since he wasn't married anymore?

As she flipped the channels, Serena stopped when she saw Emerson's face. Despite herself, she felt the same flutter in her heart she'd always felt when his hazel eyes looked at her. She pressed the volume button and listened intently to the story.

"What ever happened to Emerson Bradford?" *E! News* reporter Ryan Seacrest asked. "Once the toast of Hollywood, the famed director and producer has been MIA the last four years, after his previous film didn't garner the critical praise studio heads had expected. The sexual thriller bombed at the box office despite the fact that money had been invested in the film and some of Hollywood's brightest stars, including Halle

Berry, Denzel Washington, and Brad Pitt, had a role in the movie."

The camera cut to Emerson, who had aged well in Serena's opinion. His black wavy hair was sprinkled with grey at the temples, a few fine lines creased his caramel face, and his eyes had the same sparkle that had made Serena's heart melt all those years ago.

"That movie was not my original vision, so it's not surprising it didn't do as well as expected," Emerson said. Serena shook her head as she noticed his voice had taken on a more British sounding accent.

"He's from New England, not Britain," Serena muttered as the interviewer asked Emerson what he'd been doing over the last four years.

"Studying and getting the capital together to open my own studio where I will produce smart films people want to see," he said. "And I won't be constrained by the powers that be in Hollywood. I'll be able to put the best talent in roles that suit them."

Part of Serena wanted to see Emerson do well with his venture, but the hurt side of her prayed he'd fall on his face. When she thought about her wedding day and how she'd waited and waited for Emerson to arrive at the church, she changed the channel.

That is my past and I'm looking forward to the future, she thought as she headed up to the bathroom and began to run a bath because she'd gotten sweaty emptying boxes. As the water filled the garden tub, Serena's mind returned to her wedding day, or what should've been her wedding day.

The silence in the church meant something was wrong. Music should have been playing and Emerson was supposed to be waiting for her at the altar. Glancing down at her ivory dress that hugged her body close and skimmed her knees, she knew what was going on. He's not here, *she thought as she walked from the dressing room in the back of the church to the sanctuary. Inside, it was empty. They decided that their wedding ceremony would be just the two of them and one witness, the minister's wife. As Serena looked at the white lilies they'd picked out two weeks ago, they seemed more appropriate for a funeral than what was supposed to be a wedding. The signs had been as bright as the Hollywood sign glowing in the hills, but she'd ignored them until she stood at the altar alone with nothing but those damned lilies. Serena waited another hour, hoping that Emerson would show up. He said he wanted to marry her. He was the one who proposed and he had been the one to insist on a quick wedding.* The press, *she remembered.* I bet they are outside waiting to see us leave the church. I can't deal with this right now. *Tears spilled down her face and Serena wondered if she was being punished for her own misdeeds with men. Men she'd strung along like her father had done with countless women. Was this what love did to her? Was this all love had to offer—hurt and sadness?*

* * *

The drops of water on her feet broke into her thoughts and Serena shut the water off, averting a huge disaster of flooding the bathroom. "I don't have time to get caught up in the past," she said to herself as she let some of the water out of the tub. When the water was at an appropriate level, Serena stripped out of her clothes and climbed in. She hadn't expected the warm water to lull her to sleep.

As the day wore on Antonio fought the idea of going to Serena's for lunch. Though Norman had told him that lunch didn't mean anything, Antonio couldn't help but think about the things he wanted. He wasn't a casual type of guy and since he was the one responsible for A.J. learning how to treat women, he couldn't just jump into something with Serena, no matter how badly he wanted to. He had to take things slowly, but every time he was around her, slow was the last thing on his mind. Well, not exactly. Antonio wanted to make slow passionate love to Serena. Wanted to wrap her legs around his waist and grind against her until she exploded from the inside out. He wanted to hear her moan, feel the heat of her passion, and taste the sweetness of her lips.

"Isn't it about that time?" Norman asked at about eleven-fifteen.

"Yeah."

Norman frowned at his friend and partner. "Please don't tell me you've changed your mind. It's just lunch."

"I know. That's why I've decided to go."

Norman slapped his friend a high five. "Next time, I hope it is something more. She seems like the kind of woman who knows what she wants and we know you're part of what she wants."

That's what's making this so hard, because I want her, too, Antonio thought.

Chapter 4

When the doorbell sounded, Serena splashed herself with ice cold bath water as she realized she'd fallen asleep in the bathtub. "Damn it," she muttered, then jumped out of the tub and grabbed her terry-cloth robe. That was not how she'd planned to meet Antonio at the door. Looking at herself in the mirror as the doorbell chimed again, she saw that her hair had gotten wet while she'd slept. She didn't look her best, but it would have to do. Serena slowly walked downstairs and opened the front door.

"Am I early?" Antonio asked.

"No, I'm just late," she said with a smile. Part of her thought about allowing her belt to slip and give him a preview of what she had for him, but she decided to keep him waiting a little while longer. "Come in and have a seat. I'll be dressed in a minute."

A slight smile formed on Antonio's lips as he followed Serena inside. She didn't have to get dressed on his account, but he could tell that wasn't the lunch she'd planned.

"Why don't you point me to the kitchen and I'll start fixing us something to eat," he said.

"Are you serious?" she asked.

"I cook and though I'm no Devon Harris, you won't be disappointed," he said.

Serena smiled. "Well, aren't you full of surprises?" She pointed him to her kitchen, happy that she'd actually purchased some groceries and had something in there for him to cook. "I'll be down shortly."

Antonio nodded and began pulling pans from where they hung over the stove. Serena watched him briefly from the doorway as he made himself familiar with the kitchen and where the spices and meats were. As much as it pained her to say it, he looked as if he belonged there. Almost as if he'd make a good fit in her life.

Stop this nonsense. You're letting Jade get in your head and setting yourself up for failure, she thought as she tore herself away from the kitchen and headed upstairs to get dressed.

Though it would've been easy to put on the slinky black catsuit she'd meant to wear to answer the door, Serena pushed the sexy garment aside and opted for a pair of black leggings and a tunic-length tank top. She didn't put on any heels, just a pair of black socks. As she walked downstairs, she was met by the spicy smell of tomato sauce.

"You have it smelling good in here," she said, as she surveyed the simmering chicken and marinara sauce. "If that food is as good as it smells I may never let you go home."

Antonio turned around and smiled at her. "It's a simple chicken cacciatore dish that I make a lot." Serena crossed over to the stove where Antonio had a spoonful of the dish waiting for her to taste.

As Serena closed her lips around the spoon, Antonio watched those lips and wished he was that spoon. But it was the sound she made when she tasted the food that sent shivers down his spine. It was a moan that sounded like a woman in the throes of passion, getting totally satisfied. Antonio knew he could cook, but he doubted his food was that good. Still, she stroked his ego very well. "I guess you'd better sit down so I can fix you a plate," Antonio said.

"I guess I better," she said with a smile. "A man who can cook and doesn't get paid for it; that's a rare find."

Serena grabbed two plates, a set of glasses, and some silverware before taking a seat at the table. Antonio brought the pan over and spooned the food onto her plate.

"Now I owe you a meal," she said as he sat down across from her.

"Yes, you do," he said with a smile.

"I didn't plan this," Serena said. "But it couldn't have turned out better."

"Is that so?"

"This meal is wonderful," she said as she took a bite of the food. "So, how am I going to repay you for this?"

"I'll leave that up to you," he said.

Serena smiled and said, "A meal for a meal. Why don't we have dinner tonight? I'll cook."

"Tonight doesn't work for me," he said.

Serena's smile masked her questions. Masked the concern she had about what he actually did in the evenings when he wasn't working. "When's a good night for you?" she asked after a moment passed.

"What are you doing this weekend?" he asked. "We can meet for dinner or you can cook if you like."

"Friday night," she said. "And you don't have to worry about going out, I'll cook."

Serena rose to her feet and took their empty plates from the table and walked into the kitchen. Antonio followed her with the glasses and as he reached to place them in the sink, she turned around and faced him.

"Antonio," she said, her voice low and sultry. "Why are we acting as if there isn't electricity between us?"

He stroked her cheek gently. Yes, there was something there, something pulling him into her orbit, into her world. But was he ready for what came next?

"Serena," he moaned as she placed her hand against his chest.

Her fingers danced across his pecs and he lowered his head, capturing her lips in a scorching kiss that made her moan. She pressed her body against his hard one and he slipped his hands underneath her tunic. Serena's skin felt like the smoothest silk he'd ever touched. Her tongue tasted sweet and tangy like the meal they'd just finished. When she slipped her hand in his pocket, Antonio pulled back. He knew if she'd touched his throbbing erection he'd be a goner and wouldn't be able to control his sexual need for her.

"Serena," he said again.

"Antonio, you want me just as much as I want you. If you have someone else, tell me so I can stop torturing myself and you can save your relationship."

"There isn't anyone else. But there is something you should know about me."

"Please don't tell me you're gay," she groaned.

Antonio laughed. "I'm not gay. It's just that in the three years since my wife died, I haven't been with another woman. Losing her changed my life."

"Am I coming on too strong?" she said in a tone that didn't seem the least bit apologetic.

Her confidence was a major turn on. Antonio was hardened with desire and yearning. But he wanted to say something, wanted to tell her the truth about the end of his marriage. Wanted to tell her his obligation to his son was holding him back from playing the dating game. But when he opened his mouth, none of that came out. Instead, he covered Serena's mouth with his again, kissing her with urgency, heat, and passion.

Serena leaned into him. "If you kiss me like that again—"

He cut her off and kissed her with more fire

and passion as he backed her against the edge of the counter. In a quick motion, he pulled her leggings off. Antonio slipped his hands between the smoothness of her thighs. She shivered as his thumbs danced across the crotch of her satin and lace panties. Moaning, she called out his name as he slipped his finger in her panties and pressed it into her wetness. He eased inside her, making her squirm and grind against his touch. Dropping to his knees, Antonio replaced his finger with his hot tongue and Serena arched her back, pressing her pelvis into his mouth. He hungrily licked and sucked the sweetness of her essence until she screamed out in pleasure.

"Antonio, Antonio," she repeated as if it were a mantra as the waves of an orgasm washed over her. He continued his kiss, continued tasting her and lavishing her body with the attention he felt it deserved.

Serena screamed out in passion as his mouth closed around her throbbing desire. She threw her leg over his shoulder and Antonio got closer to her desire, lapping the juices. Pulling back, he looked up at the satisfied look on her face and smiled.

"Wow," she whispered. "That. Was—"

"Just the beginning," he said as he lifted her from the counter. "Where's your bedroom?"

"Upstairs," she said breathlessly. It seemed to take Antonio three steps to make it to the stairs and Serena's bedroom. She was glad she'd cleaned up and unpacked her room. He had a clear path to the bed and she couldn't wait to

find out what he would do to her to make her
feel even better than he already had. He laid her
on the bed, pulled off her tunic and stared down
at her body. It was just as beautiful as he'd imagined it would be.

Serena reached up and tugged at the buckle of
his belt, wanting to get his clothes off as quickly
as he'd taken hers off.

He grabbed her hand gently. "Let me look at
you for a moment," he said. "You're beautiful."

"Thank you," she replied. "Now, I want to see
how you look."

Antonio pulled his shirt off, revealing a
sculpted chest and washboard abs that made
Serena's mouth salivate. Inching toward the edge
of the bed, she wrapped her arms around his
waist and pulled him into her lips. She ran her
tongue up and down his abs and his knees went
weak. She unbuttoned and unzipped his pants
while stroking his erection that grew with every
touch. Antonio threw his head back as he felt the
heat of her breath at the tip of his manhood.
When she took him into her mouth, Antonio
gripped the edge of the bed. She took him
deeper into her mouth, reminding him how long
it had been since he'd felt passion and shared
such intimacy with a woman. She was doing
things to him his wife hadn't done in years.

Serena's tongue sent ripples of desire throughout his body. When she pulled her mouth away
from his swollen member, he wanted to dive
right between her creamy thighs and bury himself in her sticky sweetness. He remembered they

needed protection. "I don't have a condom," he said, feeling deflated.

"I got it covered," she said, then reached inside her nightstand drawer and held up a condom in a gold foil package.

Antonio smiled, thinking to himself that he should've known Serena would've been ready. Still, a part of him wondered if he wasn't moving too hastily by jumping into bed with her without telling her about his son. Those thoughts, no matter how important they were, floated from his mind as Serena opened the condom with one hand and stroked him with the other. As she slid the sheath in place, Antonio stroked her breasts until her nipples hardened like the tips of Hershey's Kisses.

Serena moaned as he replaced his thumbs with his tongue, kissing and sucking her breasts until she felt that she would explode. The things that man could do with his mouth had Serena bubbling with anticipation of what would come next. He didn't make her wait much longer as he tore his mouth from her breasts and lowered himself onto her. She wrapped her legs around his waist, drawing him into her wet valley.

Serena had been ready for Antonio for over a year, but the reality of having him grinding against her was proving to be better than any dream she'd ever had. He stroked her slowly, as if he was seeking her natural rhythm and teaching her his. As she squeezed her thighs around his hips, Serena felt as if she was going to climax and Antonio lavished in her body. As she thrust her hips forward, he matched her moves, her intensity. She now knew that he'd wanted the same things she'd longed for since their first kiss. Clutching his back, she rotated her hips, wanting desperately to ride him. Antonio caught the hint and held on to her hips as he rolled over onto his back.

Serena leaned into his chest as she took every inch of him inside her. Moaning, she ground against him. "You feel so good, so good," she cried as waves of her orgasm crashed against her.

"You feel even better," he said as he thrust forward. Antonio couldn't let that feeling end, he didn't *want* it to end. But as Serena stretched and arched her back, giving him all that he could handle, he filled the condom with his climax. She collapsed against his chest, both of them breathing as if they'd run the New York City Marathon. Antonio wrapped his arms around her lower back and held her tightly. He didn't think about the fact that he needed to get back to work or that he needed to tell her about his son. At that moment, he just wanted to bask in the afterglow.

Serena sighed with satisfaction in her tone. She was thankful Antonio hadn't disappointed her, but a thought crept into her mind—*what next?*

As she toyed with a curly hair on his chest, she pushed all rational thoughts out of her head and lay in his arms. If she was totally honest with herself, she'd admit that his strong arms felt great around her.

Before either of them knew it, they'd drifted off to sleep.

An hour later, Serena woke up with a start. Her mind was reeling from the man she'd dreamt of during her nap, and then she turned over in her bed and saw he was still there. It hadn't been a dream. She watched Antonio as he slept. His caramel-colored skin was as smooth as it was tasty, his body provided all the pleasure that it was built for. She ran her index finger down his strong bicep. *What's going on with him? Why am I letting Jade get inside my head anyway? We had great sex and that's all it's going to be. Neither one of us knows what tomorrow holds. And I'm not falling for him.*

As she looked down on his sleeping face, she felt an emotion she didn't usually feel—one she hadn't felt since the first time she and Emerson made love. "Lust," she mumbled.

Antonio stirred slightly before opening his eyes. "Wow, what time is it?" he asked as he rubbed his eyes.

"A little after four," she replied. "I guess it's a good thing you're the boss."

"But I better not let the ladies I'm working for find out about my four-hour lunch break," he quipped.

"Yes, because I hear they're pretty hardcore, stone cold, and will fire you if your shoes don't match your shirt," she joked.

Antonio rained kisses across her collarbone. "This is the part that I hate," he said.

"What's that?" she asked.

"Having to get out of this bed and go back to work."

"You hate your job?"

"Of course not. I hate leaving you," he said, then stroked her cheek. "I'm hoping this isn't a onetime thing."

Inside Serena smiled. Though she could tell her friends she was willing to have a quick fling with Antonio, there was something about him that made her think differently. She wasn't willing to say Antonio was the one, but she wanted to see where this thing would go. What would the ride be like? If it was anything like act one, Serena couldn't wait for more.

"This wasn't a onetime thing, but what about how your life has changed since your wife passed away? Are you sure you can handle more than one time?" she asked.

"I'm willing to take that chance," he said, wondering if Serena would be able to handle being second on his list of priorities. His son would always come first and he knew the women he'd date would have to understand that.

She shot him a sexy smile. "Good," she said. "Because I so want to do this again." When Serena pulled Antonio on top of her, he didn't think twice about going back to the job site.

Chapter 5

It was after six when Antonio pulled himself from Serena's arms and headed home. He had to cook dinner for his son, but as he drove home, his mind was focused on the erotic things he and Serena had done all afternoon. Her kisses were hot, sweet, and spine tingling. He gripped the steering wheel tighter as the image of Serena on top of him, with her luscious thighs clenching him flashed in his mind.

She's amazing, he thought. *But how is she going to react when she finds out I have a son and dating me isn't going to be exciting every day? I wonder if she even likes children?*

Antonio pulled into his driveway and saw A.J. running around the front yard chasing a butterfly while Casey watched from the porch with a glass of iced tea in her hand. He placed his truck in PARK and hopped out.

"Daddy," A.J. called out as he gave up his pursuit of the insect and rushed over to hug his father.

Antonio picked up his son and kissed his forehead.

"You had a long day," Casey said from the porch. "The restaurant should be reopening soon, huh?"

He turned to his sister-in-law. "Should be." "What do you want for dinner?" he asked A.J.

A.J. shrugged his shoulder. "Chicken and pasta."

"Sounds like chicken cacciatore to me," Casey piped up. "I'd be happy to help you cook. You look worn out."

Antonio smiled. He was worn out, but she had no idea how good he felt. "Thanks, Case, but I've taken up enough of your time today."

"I don't mind," she said as Antonio carried A.J. up the steps. "Besides, I don't have any dinner plans. Mom and Dad are still on vacation in Europe."

"You don't cook for yourself?" he asked as he walked into house and dropped A.J. on the sofa.

"Why should I cook when I have you and my parents?" she asked with a giggle. "Besides, no one cooks at home for one person any more."

"Maybe you need to find someone to cook for," he said as he headed into the kitchen. "When's the last time you've been on a date?"

"A date? Please, you wouldn't know how hard it is to date these days," she said. "Men are after one thing and I'm not going to give it up without a ring."

Antonio laughed as he began to take the

ingredients for the meal out of the refrigerator. As he placed the peppers and onions on the counter, he thought about the meal he'd cooked for Serena and smiled.

"What's with the sappy smile?" Casey asked as she hopped up on a barstool.

"Huh?"

"You seem really happy today," she said.

"I'm happy every day," Antonio said as he began chopping the vegetables. "But *you* need a life, Case."

"I have a life. It just happens to revolve around you and A.J. If I had a man, do you think I'd be able to babysit as much as I do? Most people don't like dating people with kids and I know A.J. isn't my son, but I take care of him as if he is. And I'm not complaining about it."

I'm seriously hoping she's wrong about that, he thought as he reached underneath the counter and pulled out a sauce pan. "It can't be that bad out there. You must be looking for love in all the wrong places," he said as he placed the pan on the stove and turned the heat on low.

"Maybe I'm just looking for something as wonderful as what my parents have and what you and my sister had," she said as she grabbed a piece of the pepper. "I've always admired your relationship with Marian. You were so good to her."

Antonio turned away from her and started seasoning the chicken breasts.

Casey continued talking. "Marian was so lucky to have a man like you. Every night, you were at home. You always took care of your son and worked hard to make sure every one was happy. My sister really loved you."

"Casey, do me a favor. Watch the veggies. I'm going to check on A.J.," he said. Antonio couldn't stand there and listen to Casey's fairy tale any longer. Hearing her talk so glowingly about the life she thought he and her sister had shared only confirmed to him that he'd done the right thing by not telling her how bad the marriage had been.

Serena stretched her arms above her head and yawned as Jade talked about the relaunch of the restaurant. "I'm sorry, am I boring you?" Jade asked as she shot a glance at her friend.

"No, I was listening. Bring in an R&B singer and make the reopening a festive event, got it," she said as she flipped her ponytail.

"What's that?" Jade said as she pointed to Serena's neck. "Is that a passion mark?"

Serena placed her hand on her neck covering the mark. "You don't miss anything, do you?"

"No, so you need to spill right now," Jade said as she crossed her legs. "How did you lure him over here?"

"I didn't lure him at all," Serena replied, unable to stop smiling. "All I did was invite him over for lunch and it was delicious."

"Wait a minute. I know you didn't cook," Jade said. "You never cook. You can't cook."

"I had every intention of cooking, but Antonio

took care of lunch," she said with a sparkle in her eyes.

"I can't believe you actually had food in the house," Jade said. "Was it everything you thought it would be?"

Serena crossed her legs tightly and beamed. "All of that and more. There's something special about that man and I can't wait to spend more time with him in my bed."

"That's all you want from him?" Jade asked with her eyebrow raised. "What if he wants more? What if he's not a 'hit it and quit it' man?"

"Jade, please. All men aren't looking for a wife and I'm sure Antonio isn't. He's been a widower for three years and he's probably just learning how to have fun again. And I'm the tour guide that he needs," Serena said. "Besides, once the restaurant is reopened, I'll be on my way back to Atlanta."

"I don't believe it."

"Believe what?" Serena asked. "I never said I would live in Charlotte. Remember that's why you moved here."

"And look at me now. I'm a mother, a wife, and head over heels in love. You could be next," Jade said.

Serena shook her head, her ponytail swinging furiously. "That's not going to happen. I gave up on fairy tales a long time ago. I'm all about my satisfaction."

"What about what Antonio wants? Since he's been married, he may want stability."

"Or he may be getting back into the dating

game and enjoying a no-strings-attached fling," Serena interjected. "Not everyone is seeking happily ever after."

Jade folded her arms across her chest and peered at her friend over her reading glasses. "I don't get you and why you're so bitter when it comes to relationships. Does this have anything to do with what happened while you were in L.A.?"

Serena closed her eyes and Emerson's face flashed in her mind. "Nothing happened in L.A. that I hadn't already known. I watched my father play women for years, watched those boys in college try to string women along, and let's not forget what I saw Stephen do to you."

Jade shuddered. "That seems like a lifetime ago. How is it that you take all the bad things into your memory, but throw out all of the good things that you're seeing now? Does that make sense?"

"Maybe not to you, but it does to me," Serena said. "One wonderful romp doesn't make a magical romance."

"Whatever, Serena. You should really stop pretending that you don't need anybody."

Serena rolled her eyes at her friend because on the surface, she didn't need anyone. She'd had an accomplished career in the computer industry. She'd worked at DVA Incorporated, the international computer company headquartered in Atlanta. But she'd taken a leave of absence from the company after she'd opened the restaurant with her friends. Serena didn't need a man to save her or to provide her anything. She'd done a good job of providing for herself. All she wanted a man for was to do just what Antonio had done earlier that day. At least, that's what she told herself.

Honestly, she would be open to love and what Jade and Kandace had if she wasn't afraid. Fear caused her to protect her heart with a bulletproof shell. She knew her heart was too fragile for her to risk—again. Maybe Serena would never get over what Emerson Bradford did and how he'd dismissed her because the studio hadn't given the green light to their movie. Had she just been his while the industry buzzed about his movie? Had their love only been a publicity stunt?

Serena had broken every rule when it came to Emerson and she'd been left with a broken heart. She had the scars to prove that everything she'd ever thought about love and dealing with the opposite sex had been true. She wasn't going to take that risk with Antonio to see if he was different, though she thought he could be. The way he made love to her, making sure she was pleased and satisfied while they were in bed made her think there was more to him.

"Hello, Serena," Jade said, once again interrupting Serena's thoughts. "Are you ordering dinner or what?"

"Actually, we should go out. It isn't often that James lets you out of the house these days," Serena joked. "Besides, we should scope out the competition and see what's going on in the restaurant world while we're closed."

"But let's not stay out too late," Jade said. "My son is finally sleeping through the night and his father and I have some things we need to go over in bed." The glee on Jade's face made Serena smile in spite of her cynical self. She knew it wouldn't be long before Jade and James added another baby to the Goings family.

Antonio tucked A.J. into bed and kissed his son of the forehead. "I love you, man," he whispered to his sleeping boy. Antonio had hoped that Casey would've left when A.J. went to sleep, but when he walked into the living room, she was still sitting on the sofa.

"Casey, you don't have to spend the night," he said as lightly as he could.

"I hadn't realized it was so late," she said as she yawned.

"Yeah. A.J. is sound asleep."

She smiled at Antonio but didn't move. Antonio sighed and took a seat on the love seat across from the sofa, focussing on the TV. "I guess I should get going," she finally said as she rose from the sofa. "Do you need me to watch A.J. tomorrow?"

"No," Antonio said. "He's going to a program at the library tomorrow and then we have evening plans."

"Oh," she said. "Then I guess I can get some laundry done."

Antonio stood up and walked Casey to the front door. "You deserve a break."

"I don't mind spending time with you two. It makes me feel closer to Marian."

"Casey," he said.

"I know it seems silly, but my sister loved you and her son. Being in her house and around you reminds me of her," she said, then hugged Antonio tightly. "Good night."

"Good night."

After she left, Antonio knew he was going to have be honest with his sister-in-law and let her know that the marriage she thought he'd shared with her sister wasn't as beautiful as she wanted to believe. Maybe she could get some closure and move on with her life. Finally, Antonio felt it was time for him to move forward with his life. And he could thank one person for that. Serena Jacobs.

From the first kiss they'd shared in the Westin to the afternoon they'd spent together, Antonio finally felt that he could be with another woman and not feel guilty about it. He'd never been the type of man to have meaningless affairs. He didn't know if Serena would be able to accept his family situation. He'd known two types of women. Women who would come and try to be A.J.'s mother and women who would run as soon as they heard he had a son.

Where would Serena fit in this situation? Antonio smiled, thinking that she didn't seem as if she would come in and try to be A.J.'s mother. But his smile faded when he thought she might not accept kids. That could be a deal breaker. Reaching for his cell phone, Antonio dialed Serena, ready to tell her about his son.

"Hello," she breathed when she answered the phone.

"Good evening, Serena. It's Antonio."

"Hi," she said, her voice sounding like the sweet notes of a sensual saxophone. "How are you?"

"I'm good. I was calling to confirm dinner plans tomorrow night," he said, feeling a bit awkward. Why was it so much easier when Serena was making all the moves?

"What time are you talking about?" she asked.

"Around seven-thirty. There's something I want to discuss with you," Antonio said.

"Sound serious," she said. "So, since I owe you a home cooked meal, why don't you come over to my place?"

"All right," he said.

"I really enjoyed lunch today," she said. "And I'm going to hold you to what you said about it not being a onetime thing."

"I never say something if I don't mean it," he said. "That's one thing you're going to learn about me."

"I'm looking forward to learning a lot about you," she purred. Her voice was making his libido rise like the sun. "What's your favorite meal?"

"Are you really a cook? Because I'm a man who likes to eat," he said with a laugh.

"All right then, I'm going to tell you what my signature dish is."

"What's that?"

"Chicken and broccoli," she said. "Anything else would come from my restaurant if Devon was still around."

Antonio laughed. "That's good to know and thanks for your honesty."

"So, now you know what we're having for dinner," she replied. "Are you a wine or beer drinker?"

"I don't drink much," he said.

"All right," she said. "Well, I have to hit the supermarket and get the ingredients for dinner. I'll see you tomorrow, as I have been charged with coming to the restaurant in the morning to check the progress of the renovations. For some reason, Jade thinks I've gotten you guys off schedule."

"You can reassure her that we are still running at the agreed pace," he said. "But I'm definitely not going to discourage you from checking on us tomorrow."

"I'll make sure the coffee is hot and the muffins are moist," she said.

"That sounds really good," he said, thinking about how moist she'd been when he'd tasted her.

"All right," she seemed to sing. "Six, right?"

"Six and please wear some sensible shoes. The floor is in really bad shape now," he said. "See you in the morning."

When Antonio hung up, he kicked his feet up on the sofa and smiled. There was something special about Serena and he was going enjoy peeling back every layer.

Chapter 6

Serena woke up at five-thirty ready to hop in the shower and get to the restaurant to see Antonio. Part of her had figured she'd stop dreaming about him after experiencing the real thing, but her dreams of Antonio had been so vivid she'd expected to find his heavenly body lying beside her when she opened her eyes. Now that she knew the feel of his lips, the way his hips moved when he was inside her, and the taste of his tongue, she was greedy and wanted more. That's why she was heading straight to Victoria's Secret as soon as she dropped off the coffee and muffins. She knew that tonight was going to be the stuff dreams were made of.

It was six-fifteen before she showered, got dressed, and made it to Starbucks. It took another fifteen minutes for her to make it to the restaurant. Serena smiled when she saw Antonio lifting a pile of tiles from the back of his truck. A warm feeling flowed from between her thighs up to her lips as she saw his muscular arms at work.

Serena pulled her car up beside his truck and beeped her horn. "Sorry I'm late," she said as she rolled her window down. "But I have coffee and muffins."

"Well, stop talking about it and feed us, woman," Antonio joked as he walked over to the passenger side of her car and opened the door. He grabbed the box of muffins as Serena balanced the coffee travel container and coffee cups. Before they headed inside, Antonio stopped Serena and kissed her gently on the lips.

"Do you always look this good this early in the morning?" he asked as he drank in her svelte body in a pair of dark blue jeans and a tight tank top.

"I guess you're going to have to spend the night and find out," she said with a wink as he opened the door to the restaurant.

The rest of the crew stopped their work when they saw Serena walk in. Norman smiled and walked over to her and took the coffee from her hands. "It's a pleasure to see you this morning, Miss Serena," he said with a huge grin on his face.

"Nice to see you too, Norman," she said.

"Thanks for the coffee and breakfast." He nodded at her.

"You're welcome." She watched as he set up the coffee. Norman fixed himself a cup of coffee and then walked over to the other men. Antonio turned to Serena and smiled at her.

"Norman likes you," he said.

"I like him too," she said. "You guys are close, huh?"

Antonio nodded as he fixed himself a cup of coffee. "Norman and my father were really close. Back when I was in school, he and my dad worked construction. I wanted to design buildings. I was halfway though architectural school when my father passed away. I came back to Charlotte and Norman taught me the business. He ran things until I got up to speed and he won't retire."

Serena wished she'd had people in her life like Norman when she was growing up. That's why she was so thankful for her friendship with Jade, Alicia, and Kandace. Her father did love his daughter, but his actions with other women left Serena with a bad taste in her mouth.

"It's good to have someone in your corner like that," she finally said. "I'll be in the office makeing sure all the arrangements for the grand opening are running smoothly. I'll be out of your hair."

"Until tonight," he said.

"A night you won't forget," she said, then sauntered down the hall.

When Serena was gone, Norman strode over to his friend and clasped his hand around his shoulder. "That was some energy between you two," he said. "Y'all seeing each other now?"

"We're getting to know each other. I don't know if we will be seeing each other when she knows about A.J."

"If you and this woman are getting to know each other, don't you think it's a little soon to introduce her to A.J.?" Norman asked.

"I think it's important she knows about my son so she can decide if this is something she wants to pursue. A.J. is the most important thing in my life."

"Yeah and that's rightly so, but what if things don't—"

"There's something special about Serena," he said. "I can feel it."

"For your sake, I hope you're right," Norman said. "I don't want to see you hurt again."

"I'm over that," he said wistfully. "It was the lies that got to me. I would've let Marian go without a fight had she been honest with me."

"I know you would've. Being with her was a battle from the beginning and she didn't—"

Antonio held up his hand. "I don't want to talk about it," he said. "It's finally time for me to move on."

"I'm happy you've taken yourself off the hook," Norman said. "It's not fair for you to continue to be a martyr."

"It's time," Antonio said as he opened a package of marble tiles.

"One question, though. What's your sister-in-law going to think about you dating?"

"What? It doesn't matter what Casey thinks," Antonio said.

"I told you that woman wants to replace her sister in your life and not just as a mother to your boy."

"Norman, you're wrong about that. She was close to her sister and spending time with me and A.J. makes her feel closer to Marian."

"I've been around a lot longer than you and I can tell you that woman is seeing to be the next Mrs. Billups."

Antonio shook his head, ignoring Norman's conspiracy theory, and started laying the tiles. He wasn't going to think about anything but Serena and how badly he wanted to walk into that office and dive between her thighs, tasting her sensual juices all over again.

"Hey, what are you doing?" Norman called out, breaking into Antonio's sexual fantasy. "Those tiles are backwards. I can guess where your mind is."

Antonio absentmindedly glanced down the hall as if he expected to see Serena saunter out of the office and beckon him inside. "I made a mistake," Antonio said, but the smile on his face confirmed what Norman had been thinking.

Serena struggled to keep her eyes open as she sat at the desk in the management office of the restaurant. She couldn't afford to go home and sleep the day away. She had a lot to do before Antonio came over for dinner, including buying what she needed to make her signature dish.

Clicking the computer mouse, she read a few articles about the restaurants in Charlotte that had opened since Hometown Delights closed for renovations. Nothing jumped out as immediate competition for the eatery when the doors re-opened. All of the reviews mentioned how no one was able to snag a celebrity chef like Devon Harris to work in their kitchens. Serena smiled as she sipped on her lukewarm coffee. It seemed as if Charlotte was waiting for Hometown Delights to reopen in two weeks. Kicking her feet up on the desk, Serena leaned back and allowed the sleep that she'd been fighting to take over.

An hour passed before Serena woke up to the sound of her cell phone ringing. Clearing her throat, she grabbed the phone and said, "Hello?"

"What are you doing?" Alicia asked. "And why aren't you at home?"

"I know you aren't calling me with questions. No one has seen you in a week," Serena said. "Are you still organizing this huge business summit?"

"See, you are so out of the loop. That's been put on hold. Having a bunch of millionaires talk to people about wealth in a recession doesn't seem to be a good idea. But I did talk to Jade and she told me about you and Mr. Contractor."

"You two really need a life if I'm the topic of your conversation."

"I thought you didn't mix business with pleasure?"

"Pleasure," she said in a near moan. "That's just what I'm thinking about until this restaurant reopens and we have to get back to business."

"What happens if something more develops between you and Mr. Billups? Knowing how you chew men up and spit them out, how are we going turn to him if we need his services again?"

"I'm so sick of you guys calling me this man-eater," Serena said. "Antonio and I are having fun. He's not looking for anything more than I am."

"Just what are you and Antonio looking for?"

"Great sex."

"And you know this because that's what he said? Everyone isn't like you," Alicia said. "Some people want a relationship. If Kandace can make Solomon Crawford commit, you never know what a man wants."

"Well, Antonio is no Solomon Crawford. He doesn't have a string of past booty calls or a psychotic stalker."

"Umm. Good point. But I hope you're not getting in over your head," Alicia said.

"How would I be doing that? He's single, I'm single, and we're adults. No one is making empty promises and no one's falling in love. It's a win-win for both of us. Please stop drinking Jade's Kool-Aid."

"I will as soon as you stop acting as if you're some guy who doesn't have emotions. Does this have anything to do with something that happened in L.A.?"

Serena cleared her throat. "The only thing that happened in L.A. was wasted time. I made a movie that was never released. Why do you guys think there is some big secret in L.A.? I tried screenwriting, got sucked into acting, and it didn't work. End of story."

"If you say so. I mean, you never talk about your time in L.A."

"Nothing to say. When do you plan to return to Charlotte?" Serena asked in an attempt to change the subject.

"I'll be back tomorrow," Alicia said. "And then you will have time to spend with your boyfriend."

"He's not my boyfriend, all right? But I have to go. There is something I need to get for my date tonight," she said.

"Leather or lace?" Alicia joked.

"I'm thinking black lace. But who knows, he may like a leather whip."

"You're sick. Don't turn that man out too much."

Serena hung up with her friend and looked at the clock. It was nine A.M. and the mall was now open. She shut down the computer and sauntered out of the office, heading for the front of the restaurant. Serena stopped as she saw Antonio on his knees laying the marble tiles. Watching him, all Serena could think about was how he worked out her body yesterday. Her knees went weak as memories flooded through her thighs and settled on her spine.

Serena tried to get her hormones under control before walking across the unfinished floor. As her heels clicked across the floor, Antonio lifted his head and caught a glimpse of her as the heel of her left shoe caught on a loose tile. He leaped up and grabbed her before she came close to the floor. Serena collapsed against Antonio's chest, smiling warmly as his hands gripped her waist.

"Sensible shoes," he admonished quietly.

"Great catch and you love my shoes," she said

as she kicked her leg out. Neither of them noticed the men were looking at them as Serena placed her hand against Antonio's chest and gently stroked him. She felt his desire growing between his thighs and pressing against her. She knew that feeling and wished they were alone so he could peel her clothes off and do all the things that he'd done to her yesterday. It was amazing how he made her body come alive by a simple touch. She hadn't felt that way since . . . ever.

Her breath caught in her chest as his hand moved up the small of her back. "I'd better go," she said as she felt her feet touch the floor.

"Yeah," he said, his voice low and deep. "But tonight, we're having dinner and I can't wait to see you."

Looking over his shoulder, Serena finally saw that their every move was being watched by Antonio's crew. She stepped back and smiled. "It seems as if you have a lot of explaining to do."

Antonio watched Serena's shapely backside as she sauntered out of the restaurant. When she was gone, his crew clapped enthusiastically.

"Way to go, Tonio," Leo Clarke called out.

"Shut up, Leo," Norman said.

"That woman is a brick house," Eddie Richardson said as he stopped hammering. "Good to know you're putting your name on that because I was tempted."

"You're a married man," Antonio said.

"But I ain't blind, dude," Eddie retorted. "Nobody should let all that fine go to waste."

"And that is a lot of fine," Leo said. "Good to see you living life again and in such a big way."

"Let's get back to work. It's the weekend and no one wants to be here all day," Antonio said. He wasn't going to share his private life with his crew and he wasn't going to feed into their fantasies about Serena because he had the real thing.

By the time the men took their lunch break, the buzz about Antonio and Serena had died down with everyone except Norman. He and Antonio sat on the back end of Antonio's truck munching on apple slices and turkey sandwiches.

"Got a question for you," Norman said in between bites. "After that little interlude in the dining room, do you really think you should take A.J. to meet Serena tonight?"

"You're right. I don't think it's time right now for them to meet."

"Uh-huh and I'm sure it has nothing to do with you finishing what you two got started."

Antonio laughed, unable to deny the truth in Norman's observation. "But, I don't have a sitter for A.J. and I've been leaning on Casey a little too much lately."

"You're in luck because I'm going to have my grandsons this weekend. We're going to Lake Norman for some fishing. A.J. is welcome to come along."

"Are you sure this isn't too much trouble?" Antonio asked, not wanting to pawn his son off on his friend.

"Those guys get along great and A.J.'s a good kid. I'd love for him to come along."

Antonio smiled. "Thanks, man."

"Maybe you can ease her into your son's life," Norman said.

Or ease right into her, Antonio thought as he took a bite of his sandwich.

Chapter 7

Serena held her pink and white Victoria's Secrets bags tightly as she ran to her car in the rain. She was totally drenched by the time she made it behind the wheel and wished she'd opted for valet parking. Before starting the car, Serena checked inside her bag to make sure the $200 worth of lace and satin she'd just purchased wasn't wet. She smiled when she saw that the paper in the top of the bag had protected her items. As she pulled out of the SouthPark mall parking deck, Serena's phone rang. She pressed the ANSWER button on the steering wheel. "Hello?"

"Serena, I heard you were working in our shut-down restaurant," Jade said as Jaden cooed in the background. "Just what kind of business were you conducting?"

"Why don't you feed your son and leave me alone?" Serena said with a laugh. "I was just surveying the work."

"Or the workers?" Jade asked. "I swear, you and Antonio are getting out of control."

"And? You know what? Antonio and I are having dinner tonight and I won't have to worry about you and Alicia questioning my motives because I have one thing in mind."

"I bet you do. Seriously, though, I went by the restaurant before picking up Jaden from James's office and it is looking really good in there. Norman said he thinks they're going to finish a week early."

"Great. So does that mean we're moving up the grand reopening?" Serena asked.

"No, Kandace called and she and Solomon are still on their honeymoon. She claims she's going to e-mail a list of her media contacts, but from all the moaning I heard while I was talking to her, I wouldn't look for that."

"I'm surprised she was able to make a phone call," Serena said. Not that she was upset that Kandace was enjoying her honeymoon with Solomon Crawford. He was a gorgeous man who loved her and though Serena wasn't the love conquers all type, she knew it was true for her friends. Especially Kandace. Her husband had quite a reputation as a love 'em and leave 'em man, but he fell head over heels for her and did what no one thought he'd ever do. Got married.

"Well, I talked to Devon and he's wondering if he can get back in the kitchen to start filming the new season of his show," Jade asked. "That's why I went to the restaurant today—to see where they were with the renovations. I must say, when I walked in, Antonio was disappointed to see me."

"What?"

"The door opened and everything stopped. When they saw it was me, the air pretty much left the building," Jade laughed. "The shoes should've given me away. I went in there with flats on, something I know you don't do."

"I have two pairs of flats and I don't like them," Serena said.

"Yeah, because heels make your butt look bigger, I remember," Jade said. "It must work since you and Antonio are hanging tough."

"Oh, shut up." Serena made a quick turn onto Fairview Road. "Are you at home?"

"Yes."

"I'll be over there after I leave Harris Teeter. I need to borrow your kitchen."

"You told that man you were cooking dinner for him? I thought you liked him."

"That's why I'm bringing the food to you," Serena said as she pulled into the parking lot of the grocery store.

"I think I'm starting to see why you were so eager to invest in a restaurant," Jade said. "But if I'm cooking, you are on diaper duty."

"Ugh, you can't do that to me."

"You need my help and I don't have a nanny, so yes, I can."

Serena laughed then hung up on her friend. She dashed inside the supermarket and quickly picked up the ingredients for her "signature dish," chicken and broccoli, which was actually Jade's concoction.

Serena did a lot of things in the kitchen, but cooking wasn't one of them. There had been a time when Serena wanted to cook and be domesticated. She'd purchased cookbooks and had been ready to play the dutiful wife.

But her dream of wedded bliss had come to a screeching halt when Emerson stood her up at the altar. No word of what had caused him to change his mind or anything. Serena stopped in the produce section and picked up a bunch of broccoli as she shook away the memories of her past. All she had to worry about was the present and that included Antonio Billups.

But what about your future? she heard Jade ask. *You can't keep hiding behind what happened in Los Angeles.*

"Get out of my head," she mumbled as she directed her cart to the dried foods aisle. She needed rice and seasonings, then she could head over to Jade's and spend some time with Jaden while his mother cooked. She liked kids well enough, but she never saw herself as a mother.

Serena was certain her motherly genes had never developed. The best part about hanging out with other people's children was the joy of returning them to their parents. It never failed though, whenever she held a baby, he or she either threw up on her or peed on her shoes. That's why she didn't want to spend a lot of time with Jaden. Being around that little boy always meant a trip to the cleaners.

Once she had all her groceries and had cleared the self-checkout line, she picked up some iced lattes at Starbucks for her and Jade, remembering to make her friend's drink a decaf since she was still nursing her son.

As she pulled into Jade and James's driveway, Serena thought about how quickly those two had become husband and wife and how happy they were. Jade deserved it after what she'd been through with her ex.

Don't you deserve happiness, too? How long are you going to hide behind relationships that go nowhere because you're afraid? Serena thought. *Maybe I should go into this thing with Antonio not expecting it to end.*

Serena shook her head as she got out of the car and grabbed her groceries. It was too soon to start thinking like that. She had to get Jade's happily ever after voice out of her head. She'd tried love once and that was enough.

"Knock, knock," Serena said as she opened the front door.

"In the den," Jade called out. Serena walked in and dropped the bags off in the kitchen, then headed for the den where Jade and Jaden were sitting on the floor playing with blocks.

Jade looked up and pointed at Serena. "Look Jaden, it's your godmommy Serena."

The little boy cooed and drool dripped down his chin. "Are you going to get that?" Serena asked.

Jade stood up, then lifted her son into her arms. "That's just sugar. It's not going to make you melt, Evilene." She placed Jaden in Serena's arms. Smiling, Serena kissed her godson then wiped his wet chin with the bottom of his shirt.

Jade shook her head as she headed into the kitchen with Serena on her heels.

"So," Serena said as she took a seat on a bar stool while Jaden attempted to pull her hoop earring. "Where's James?"

"He's in Huntersville looking at some property," she said. "The real estate market is crazy, but James and Maurice are planning to invest some money in a few stalled projects."

"Smart men," Serena said as she took her earring off and placed it out of Jaden's way. The little boy seemed to pout and Serena kissed his chubby cheek. "Do you think they're going to be able to save some of these stalled condo projects in Uptown?"

Jade shrugged her shoulders as she began to rinse the broccoli. "I hope so, because I am really tired of looking at these cranes. But James said he doesn't want to get involved in providing housing for people who can afford it. He thinks he and Maurice should do something to give back to the people who are suffering."

"But this is business, not charity."

Jade cut the stalks of the broccoli. "That's what they've been arguing about all day," she said as she shook her head. "James wants to do more mixed-income housing and Maurice wants to keep things upscale and expensive."

"I'm with Maurice on this one," Serena said as she bounced Jaden on her knee.

"Umm, I wouldn't do that," Jade said.

"What? Agree with . . . Ugh!" she exclaimed as her godson vomited on her blouse.

"Sorry. He just ate," Jade said as she handed her friend a paper towel.

Jaden looked up at his godmother and offered her a smile that made her forget she was going to have to make another trip to the cleaners.

She tweaked his nose. "Little man, you'd better make a lot of money when you grow up because I'm charging you for all my dry cleaning," she said then kissed his cheek.

The little boy laughed and Jade shook her head. "For someone who doesn't want kids, you're really good with him," she told Serena.

"That's because I know I can hand him right back to you."

"I'll get you a dry shirt," Jade said as she took Jaden from her arms. "And little guy, let's get you cleaned up." To Serena she said, "You might want to put some water in that pot on the stove so we can steam the broccoli."

"That's all right, I can wait," Serena said as she unbuttoned her blouse and took it off. She grabbed one of the empty grocery bags and stuffed her shirt inside. When she heard the front door open, she wished she could disappear.

"Look, man," she heard Maurice say. "We're trying to make money and I want to give back to people as much as you do, but—"

"Nah, Mo, you don't want to give back. If you

did, you'd get what I'm trying to do," James replied.

"I'm tired of arguing about this," Maurice said as they walked into the kitchen.

Serena grabbed a dish towel and attempted to cover her chest.

"Jade's cook . . . Serena, why are you topless?" James looked at her and furrowed his eyebrows. "Serena? What's going on?"

Jade and Jaden returned to the kitchen and when she saw her husband and her brother-in-law standing there, she burst out laughing, then quickly tossed Serena a white tank top.

"How about you two turn around," Jade said through her laughter. James and Maurice did as they were told.

"What are you two getting into?" James asked as he kissed Jade and took his son from her arms.

"And I know y'all aren't cooking for real," Maurice said.

"Shut up, Mo," Jade said as Serena signaled that she was decent. "We are cooking and it is for real."

"What time are we eating, then?" Maurice asked.

"This meal isn't for you guys," Serena said as she walked back to the bar stool. "I'm having dinner with a friend tonight."

James shook his head. "I didn't know you women still did this."

"Did what?" Jade asked.

"Tricking a man into thinking you could cook," Maurice chimed in.

Serena crossed her legs. "Trust me, I don't have to trick him. It's not my cooking that he's after."

"Wow," James said. "It's like listening to a female version of Maurice after the draft."

"I think I'm offended by that," Maurice said. "I never tricked those girls with food."

"And I'm not tricking Antonio," Serena said. "I just don't want to spend the night in the emergency room because I fed him raw chicken."

The trio of Goings laughed. "At least you're honest," James said as he took a seat at the table.

"Yeah, but what happens when your man wants you to cook for him in the morning?" Maurice asked as he pulled out his cell phone and punched in his wife, Kenya's, number. "Hey baby." He walked into the den to talk privately.

"I have muffins," she said. "Who said I'm going to allow him to spend the night?"

James nodded and pointed from Serena to Maurice, who'd returned to the kitchen. "I think you two are related."

"All right," Jade said, "stop giving my girl such a hard time. One day, she's going to be happy to cook."

"When is that day going to come for you, babe?" James asked his wife. Jaden laughed and tugged at his father's neck tie.

Jade shot James a sultry look over her shoulder. "We both know you didn't marry me for my cooking," she cooed.

James smiled at her shapely figure as she sauntered over to the stove. "Serena, you sure you can't just order out?"

"Sickening," Serena said.

Maurice laughed. "When are you going to join the club?" Maurice asked.

Serena folded her arms across her chest. "Not you too?"

"What?" Maurice asked. "As close as you and your girls are, I know you and Alicia are going to be walking down the aisle soon. That's how you women do."

Serena rolled her eyes. "Maurice, every woman's goal isn't to be Mrs. Somebody. I'm happy with my life. I don't need a husband."

Jade shook her head. "All right. We don't need to start this right now," she said.

Jaden fell asleep in his father's arms and James quietly rose from the table and took his son into the nursery.

"I wasn't trying to say you needed a man," Maurice said. "But everybody is happier when they have someone to share their life with."

Serena turned away from him, hating that for the second time that day thoughts of Emerson popped into her mind. What if they had gotten married? Would she be happy like James and Jade, Maurice and Kenya, and Solomon and Kandace?

No, he wasn't the one for you. Maybe you need to start hanging out with more single people, she thought.

Maurice's cell phone rang and he answered it as Serena headed over to the stove to watch what Jade was doing and to avoid further talk of marriage. "So," Jade said as she poured three cups of rice into a pot of boiling water. "You flashed everybody?"

"It's a good thing I had on a bra today," Serena joked.

"You're a trip and lucky that I'm an understanding friend."

"Please, neither one of those men have eyes for anyone but their lovely wives. I wouldn't have taken my shirt off had I known they were coming in," she said.

Jade nodded as she placed the broccoli in a pot then sprinkled a pinch of salt into the mix. "Girl, I know. What's amazing to me is that Maurice is telling you about the joys of marriage."

"Can we please talk about something else?" Serena asked after sucking her teeth.

Jade looked over Serena's shoulder and saw that Maurice was in deep conversation. "Can I ask you a question? About L.A.?"

"Jade," Serena cautioned.

"It's been five years and you never talk about it. One minute you're about to star in a movie and the next you're on your way back to Atlanta."

"I went to L.A., chased a dream, came up with nothing, and returned to reality," Serena said. "What more do you need to know?"

"You've been different. When you left, you weren't so cold to the idea of love," she said.

Serena yawned and rolled her eyes. "Do I need to cut up some chicken or something?"

Jade laughed. "Right. You, cooking? You *really* don't want to talk about L.A."

Maurice walked over to them and said, "Who's going to L.A.?"

"Nobody," Jade said.

"Well, I'm out of here. Kenya sends her best," he said as he strode over to Jade and gave her a brotherly peck on the cheek.

"Hey, keep your lips off my wife," James called from the doorway of the kitchen.

"Please," Maurice said as he headed for the door. "You've been kissing my wife for years."

Serena shook her head as she watched Jade stir the rice. "You people are just strange."

An hour later, Jade and Serena realized they'd cooked too much chicken and broccoli. "He's going to think I'm trying to fatten him up if I take all of this food home with me," Serena said.

James walked into the kitchen and saw how much food his wife had cooked up. "Are you having a party?" he asked.

"No," Serena said. "Obviously, someone didn't read the instructions on the rice."

James shook his head. "Restaurant owners who can't cook. It would be funny if it wasn't true."

Jade dipped her spoon into the rice and told James to open his mouth. "It won't be Devon Harris, but it's good."

James swallowed the rice and nodded. "Babe, I didn't know you had it in you. So, now dinner is on you."

"Great, then you guys keep half of this and I'll take the rest home for me and Antonio," Serena said. She glanced at her watch. "I have to get going."

Jade helped Serena pack half the food in plastic containers, then Serena took off for home so she could get ready for her date with Antonio and make it seem as if she'd spent time cooking their meal.

Chapter 8

Antonio and his crew packed up and called it a day around three-thirty since the floor needed to dry. Once the men installed the panels on the walls, the renovations on Hometown Delights would be complete. As distracted as he'd been, Antonio was surprised they'd gotten the work done. His distraction had a name. Serena.

He couldn't wait to see her and it didn't matter if dinner was good or not, as long as he got a chance to touch her, taste her, and get inside her again. He couldn't believe how hooked he'd gotten on Serena's body after just one time.

Antonio hadn't felt passion like he'd felt from Serena since he'd been a teenager. Smiling, he pulled out his cell phone and called Casey to let her know he'd be picking A. J. up early.

"Hey, Antonio," she said when she answered. "Is everything all right?"

"Everything is fine. I'm calling because I'm going to pick A.J. up early," he said.

"Okay, I was just about to make some Rice Krispies Treats. Maybe you can join us?" she said with a hopeful tone to her voice.

"No, I can't. A.J. has been invited on a fishing trip and I need to take him home and get him ready."

"That sounds like fun. So, you and A.J. are going fishing? I wish I could go, but I don't like being outside that much," Casey said as Antonio started his truck.

"Yeah," he said not revealing the truth of his plans.

"Mom and Dad will be back on Sunday and I was thinking we should get together and have a family dinner like we used to," she said.

"I'll let you know," Antonio said. "I'm going to hang up. Traffic is pretty bad right now. We'll talk more about this later."

"All right. I'll get A.J. ready."

When he hung up with Casey, he felt a little drained. Though he respected his former mother- and father-in-law, he didn't want to spend Sunday afternoon eating dinner with them and hearing more about how wonderful Marian was. Many times, though it seemed cruel, Antonio wanted to remind everyone that Marian had been human and she made mistakes. He wished they knew the truth about the direction the marriage had been heading before her death, but it seemed wrong to tell them now.

Antonio's cell phone rang again as he headed for Casey's house. "Yeah?" he said when he saw it was Norman.

"Hey man. You tore out of the parking lot so fast, I was just making sure everything was all right. Guess I know where your mind is," the older man said with a laugh.

"Yes, on picking up my son," Antonio said.

"Sure," he replied. "My grandsons should arrive at my place around five. We'll swing by and pick up A.J. afterwards. I'm going to pick up a few pizzas. Is there anything other than pork you don't want him to eat?"

"A.J. likes cheese pizzas. I'll be happy to chip in for dinner," Antonio said.

"No, that's not necessary. See you later, man."

"Hey, Norman, thanks for this and everything else."

"You know you're like a son to me, so you don't have to thank me."

When Antonio ended his call with Norman, he smiled and was thankful the older man was a part of his life and his son's life. Antonio's father had died when Marian had been pregnant with A.J. One of his biggest regrets in life was that his son hadn't a chance to meet his father. Keith Billups had been a good man. He raised Antonio alone after his mother died and never put anything or anyone ahead of his son. He'd taught Antonio to follow his dreams and how to be a good man. The lessons he'd learned as a child, he tried to pass on to his son.

Antonio pulled into Casey's driveway and hopped out of the car. He knocked on the front door and waited for Casey to answer. She opened the door dressed in a pair of spandex shorts and a tight T-shirt. "Hey, Tonio," she said. "A.J.'s in the living room."

"Thanks for watching him today. Next week he'll be in a day camp program at Discovery Place," he said as he headed for the living room.

"I'm going to miss him. I've enjoyed hanging out with you guys."

"And I appreciate it, but we've intruded on you enough," Antonio said as he entered the living room and kissed his sleeping son.

A.J.'s eyes fluttered open. "Daddy," he said excitedly.

"What's up, Sport? Are you ready to go?"

The little boy nodded. "We're going camping, right?"

"Well, you are. Mr. Norman and his grandsons invited you to go fishing and hang out with them this weekend."

"And you're going to be by yourself?" A.J. asked. "I don't want to go and have fun if you're lonely."

"I'll be working," he said, then kissed his son's forehead.

Casey walked into the living room and sat on the sectional and looked at Antonio and A.J. "While A.J. is camping, why don't I bring you dinner?"

"That's all right, Case," he said. "I plan to spend most of the evening in bed."

She smiled and nodded. "I bet you are tired. You work so hard."

Antonio looked down at his son. "Ready to go, Champ?"

"Yeah," the little boy said as he leaped from the sofa.

"Don't forget to grab your things from the kitchen," Casey called out. "I made him some Rice Krispies Treats to take home."

A.J. dashed into the kitchen to get his treats, leaving Antonio and Casey in the living room alone. "What are you doing tomorrow?" she asked. "Will A.J. be back in time for Sunday dinner?"

"Case, I'm going to rest tomorrow and I'm sure A.J. will see his grandparents, but I'm not going to guarantee we'll make it for dinner," he said as he rose to his feet.

"Okay. They're going to be disappointed," Casey said. "I already told them we'd all have dinner together."

"We'll stop by to see them next week. A.J., let's go," Antonio said.

Casey stood up and crossed over to Antonio. "Did I do something wrong?" she asked as she stood across from him. "Sometimes, you act like you can't wait to get away from me."

"Casey, you know I love you and appreciate everything you do for me and A.J., but sometimes you come on a little too strong. I understand your parents want to spend time with their grandson, but they are rarely in town and they know A.J. is available to them anytime. I don't need you making a schedule for us."

"I'm sorry," she said. "It's just that you and A.J. are the last connections I have to my sister."

Immediately, he felt bad about admonishing her. He knew Casey was still having a hard time processing her sister's death. But how would she feel if she knew the truth about where things had been heading with him and Marian?

"It's all right, Casey. I'll try to make dinner," he said as A.J. bounded into the living room with a Ziploc bag filled with dessert bars. "Ready, son?"

"Yes, sir," he replied, then rushed over to his aunt and gave her a hug.

"Have fun, nephew," she said, then placed a kiss on his forehead. "Catch a fish for me."

Antonio and A.J. waved good-bye to Casey and headed out the door. "Did you have fun with your aunt today?"

"It was all right, but I'm ready to go to day camp so I can play with other kids," A.J. said. "Do I get to go to school this year?"

"Yes," Antonio said, happy that his son was excited about going to school. "We're going to get you enrolled next week."

The little boy pumped his fist excitedly. When they arrived at home, Antonio helped A.J. pack his camping and fishing gear. He watched how excited his son was about hanging out in the woods for the weekend and Antonio made a mental note to take his son camping more often.

"Are you sure you're going to be okay without me, Dad?" A.J. asked after zipping his backpack. "Are you and Aunt Casey going to play together?"

"No, I'm going to play with a new friend tonight," Antonio said with a smile. "And Sunday, we're going to have dinner with your grandparents."

"I thought they were at that rope place."

"Rope place? You mean Europe? They're

coming back tonight," he said with a laugh. "Maybe they brought you some ropes to play with." Antonio tickled his son's stomach.

"What am I going to do with ropes?" A.J. asked. "Maybe they brought me a game or something I can build my own restaurant with."

"What are you trying to do, put me out of business already?"

Moments later, Norman and his grandsons arrived at the Billups's house. A.J. barely allowed Norman and his three grandsons, Kamir, DaJon, and Fredrick to come inside.

"Slow down, homeboy," Norman said. "I need to talk to your dad for a second. DaJon, help A.J. load his stuff in the truck."

"Yes, sir," the eight year old said as if he was happy for the responsibility.

When the four boys were outside, Antonio turned to Norman. "Are you sure you can handle all four of them? I can pack a bag and come along."

"What are you trying to do, look for an excuse not to see Miss Serena? If you want to trade places, I'd be happy to."

"Not on your life. But those four are going to be a handful and I feel kind of guilty adding A.J. to the mix so I can go out on a date."

"Listen, I volunteered for this. Trust me, you're going to be thanking me come Monday morning."

"All right. Regardless, I'm a cell phone call away."

"I won't need you, but that's good to know. Of

course, you got my number if you plan to call and check on A.J."

Antonio smiled. No matter what he had planned for the weekend, he would call and check on his son.

Two hours later, Antonio was on his way to Serena's for dinner. He still wasn't sold on her cooking dinner. She didn't look like the kind of woman who spent much time in the kitchen at the stove. Though he knew where some of her talents in the kitchen were. Antonio took a quick detour to Amelie's French Bakery to pick up some petit fours for dessert. Then he went to the Midwood Flower Shop and purchased a half-dozen red roses for Serena as a thank you in advance for dinner.

Looking around the kitchen, Serena felt as if she had everything in place. She'd heated the precooked dinner without making the rice stick to the pot. A first. At some point, Serena figured she'd give actual cooking a chance. She dashed into the dining room and made sure the table was set properly. Then she lit the two candles in the center of the table and dimmed the lights. Next, she adjusted the straps on her little black dress and tugged at the cups of her teddy, thinking that when Antonio took her dress off, he was going to like what was underneath.

Her mind wandered back to Maurice's comments at Jade's house. *Everybody is happier when they have somebody to share their life with.*

"Easy for him to say," she mumbled. "I've tried to share my life. Now all I want is instant gratification."

With that thought in the air, Serena pulled her dress off and ran upstairs to hang it in her closet. She hadn't really invited Antonio over to eat . . . dinner. But if he wanted to, it was there. Serena smiled at her sultry complexion in the mirror. The red teddy set off her creamy complexion and added blush to her cheeks that no amount of makeup could. She grabbed a bit of cocoa butter and smoothed it across her breasts. As soon as she finished, she heard the doorbell chime.

For a second, she considered putting her dress back on, but when the doorbell chimed again, she decided against it. Serena bounded down the stairs and opened the door.

"Hello," she said. Antonio's mouth flew open and he nearly dropped the bouquet of roses and box of sweets.

"Well, I guess I'm early, because you didn't finish getting dressed."

"You don't like my outfit?" she asked as she spun around.

He stepped inside and closed the door behind him. "Oh, I like," he said.

Serena took the flowers and the box from his hands and set them on the table near the door. With his hands free, Antonio was able to pull Serena against his chest. She felt the hardness of his manhood pressing against her thigh and instantly moisture pooled between her legs.

"What about dinner?" she asked as his hands stroked her back.

"You have a microwave, right?" he asked, pulling her closer. "Dinner will keep."

Serena lifted her head and Antonio captured her lips in a searing kiss that sent jolts of desire though her system. She parted her lips and drew his tongue deeper into her mouth. Soft moans filled the air as he slipped his hands between her thighs and stroked her with his thumb. He could feel the pool of her desire through the crotch of her lingerie. Just the thought of her wetness and the sweet taste of it, made him harder. In a quick motion, he lifted her into his arms and carried her upstairs into her bedroom.

Once they crossed the threshold of the bedroom, Antonio laid her across the bed and drank in the image of her sexy body in red satin and lace. His mouth craved her taste and when she uncrossed her long, lean legs, he licked his lips then dove between her thighs. With the flat of his hand, he stroked her through the lingerie. Serena's body was under his control as his fingers slipped between the satin and into her wet valley.

Her breath caught in her chest as his finger brushed against her pounding bud of desire. She was so wet, hot, and ready to feel him deep inside her. But Antonio had other plans for her. He had to taste her sweetness. He unsnapped the crotch of her teddy and lifted her hips to his lips. As she felt the heat from his breath against the folds of her flesh, her body tingled with anticipation, desire, and yearning. She wiggled her hips as if she was silently begging him to put the fire out that he'd lit inside her.

Heeding her silent pleas, Antonio slowly licked her wetness until she quivered in delight.

Serena's moans penetrated the silence, reaching its crescendo when she climaxed. "Need. You," Serena cried. "Now."

Antonio pulled his mouth away from her, licking her juices from his lips as he unbuttoned his jeans and kicked out of them while Serena pulled his shirt over his head and tossed it on the floor. Rolling onto his back, Antonio pulled Serena on top of him and covered her mouth with his. He could feel the heat of her desire as they kissed and she ground against him. He wanted to dive inside her, take her then and there. But they needed protection. As Serena straddled him, he heard the rattle of a condom wrapper.

"You think of everything," he said as she slid the condom down his erection. Serena smiled a sexy smile then leaned in and brushed her lips against his. Antonio ran his tongue across her full bottom lip and she arched her back like a cat lounging in the sun. He felt her heat and gripped her hips, bring her opening to the tip of his erection. She took the length of him inside her, moaning in pleasure as he raised his hips while she ground against him. Serena gripped his shoulders as he pressed deeper, seemingly trying melt into him. Her hips moved with the rhythm of a cadence drum. Antonio fell in stride with her, meeting her strokes and stirring her juices until she cried out as another orgasm attacked her senses.

Wrapping his arm around her waist, he flipped her over onto her back, taking total control of their encounter. Antonio covered her taut nipple with his mouth as she rotated her hips underneath his. He sucked her nipple, gently biting her as he felt his climax building. Serena wrapped her legs around his waist and squeezed her thighs tightly around him as his lips and tongue danced across her chest.

Unable to hold back his desire, Antonio exploded inside her. He held her against his chest as he collapsed onto the bed. Sweat covered their bodies as they both released satisfied sighs. "Amazing," he murmured as he nuzzled against Serena's neck.

"That's what I was going to say about you," she whispered as her head rested on his chest. Serena stroked his arm and smiled. "So, are you ready to eat?"

"Woman, I can't even move," Antonio said.

"Good, because I can't either," she replied with a laugh.

Antonio closed his eyes and Serena smiled at him, feeling so comfortable in his arms. The comfort she felt with him was a shock to her system. *This is just about pleasure, remember,* she silently told herself. *Don't read more into this.*

"What are you thinking about over there?" Antonio asked when he opened his eyes and caught Serena's gaze.

"Nothing," she replied, offering him a sweet smile.

Antonio reached up and stroked her cheek. "I can tell you what's on my mind," he said. "I like being around you. I haven't felt like this since I was a teenager."

"Well, I've had a thing for you since our first kiss," she said honestly.

"Really, I couldn't tell," he joked. "But I'm sure you've noticed the feeling is mutual. So what happens next?"

Serena sighed. Next was the problem. She didn't want to think about next. Next meant the chance she'd be hurt again. "I don't know."

"We've pretty much passed the taking it slow part. And I don't really do casual," he said.

"Let's just take it one day at a time," she said as she pressed her hand against his chest. Antonio propped up on his elbow and looked down at her.

"It's been a while since I've done this, so I probably should've asked sooner. Is there someone else in Atlanta?" he asked.

"No, there's not. But, honestly," she said, "I can't plan my future right now because I don't know how long I'm going to be in Charlotte. I just know I want to spend many nights just like this—with you and no one else."

Antonio fell silent and Serena wondered if she'd laid it on a little too thick. She couldn't open up to him right then. She was afraid. If it had been anyone else, she would've laughed.

"Well, let's take it one day at a time until you're ready," he said.

"Until I'm ready? What about you?"

"I haven't dated much since my wife died. I've had other obligations and things to focus on. But seeing you last year, I knew it was time. When I kissed you, I knew I had to have you."

"I couldn't tell. You bolted out of the hotel like you had a colony of fire ants in your pants," she said with a laugh. Then she slipped her hands underneath the blanket and stroked his penis, bringing it back to life. "But now, I know just what is in your pants."

It didn't take them long to forget about the cold dinner downstairs and start making love all over again.

Chapter 9

It was three A.M. before Serena and Antonio made it to the kitchen for dinner. Though the meal Jade had cooked was still in the pots on the stove, Serena fixed their plates and popped them in the microwave, afraid that she'd scorch the food if she tried to heat it up on the stove.

"Tell me again how you got into the restaurant business?" Antonio asked when she took the plates out of the microwave.

"I know what food should taste like. It doesn't mean I'm chained to the stove cooking it," Serena said as she set his plate in front of him.

"Chains, interesting choice of words," he quipped. Antonio dug into his meal and smiled after taking the first bite. "Not bad."

"Glad you like it," she said as she took a bite of the food.

"I can tell that it isn't frozen, so I'm really impressed," Antonio said.

"So," Antonio said. "Now that I know you can master dinner, what's for breakfast?"

Serena grinned. "I have oat bran flakes."

"Why don't I cook you breakfast?" he asked. "That is if I'm invited to spend the night."

"It's already morning, so I'd say you've already spent the night," she said.

Antonio reached across the table and stroked the back of Serena's hand. "You're right. But as long as it's dark, it's still nighttime in my book. Since I don't have to trek into the restaurant, I can return to bed."

"That sounds good to me," she said as she rose from her chair and sauntered over to him. Serena eased onto his lap and locked her legs around his waist. "But we don't have to go straight to bed."

Antonio wrapped his arms around her waist. "That's fine with me," he said as Serena brought her lips down on his neck. His desire grew against her thighs, causing Serena to moan when she felt his hardness against her. Traveling down his neck to his chest, she took one of his nipples between her teeth and he thrust his hips into hers. She wanted him right then as she ground against his hardness, becoming wetter and wetter as he matched her sensual movements. In one quick motion, Antonio rose from the chair holding on to Serena tightly.

"Now it's time for bed," he said as he rushed toward the stairs. Her hot kisses made each step up the staircase excruciating. Antonio's erection throbbed relentlessly as he took the final step and crossed the threshold of the bedroom.

As he placed Serena on the edge of the bed, she grasped his hips pulling him against her lips. She blazed a trail with her tongue from his navel to the tip of his erection. Antonio's knees trembled as she took the length of him into her mouth.

"Oh, Serena," he moaned as her fingers danced up and down the length of his erection while she worked her mouth. Antonio buried his hands in her curly hair as he felt the grips of his climax coming. Serena pulled back from him and slipped out of her robe. He pounced on to her, ready to taste every inch of her tantalizing body, starting with her diamond-hard nipples. As Antonio's tongue alternated between her breasts, Serena moaned in delight. His journey took him down her flat belly to the V of her thighs. Slowly, he kissed her upper thighs, parting her legs and slipping his finger between the wet folds of her flesh. Serena arched her back into Antonio's touch. His finger stroked her desire until she felt as if the Atlantic Ocean was running between her legs, but when he replaced his finger with his tongue, Serena exploded.

She gripped the sheets and cried out loudly as Antonio lapped her juices like a man dying of thirst. "Antonio, Antonio," she called out as she felt her fourth orgasm coming down.

Pulling back from her, he looked at the satisfied look on Serena's face and smiled. She was beautiful. She was quickly becoming a sweet addiction he couldn't get enough of.

She opened her eyes and met Antonio's gaze. "What's wrong?" she asked.

"I was simply admiring the view," he said as he reached for a condom from the nightstand. "You're a beautiful woman."

"You're not so bad yourself," she replied as she watched him roll the sheath in place. Antonio eased on top of her, melting into her body, making her moan as they became one. Slowly, they rocked back and forth, their bodies in sync as well as their heartbeats. Serena locked her legs around his waist as Antonio pumped his hips into hers like a smooth jazz beat.

"Serena, damn baby," he whispered as their pace quickened and he felt the build up of his climax.

Her response was to tighten herself around him and close her mouth on his neck. The heat from her kiss pushed him over the edge and Antonio spilled his desire, then collapsed on top of her. They shifted against each other until Serena's head ended up resting on his chest. He brushed his lips across her forehead as they looked up at the glass ceiling watching the sky change from inky black to dawn's faint pink. It didn't take long for the couple to drift off to sleep.

The ringing of a phone woke Serena and Antonio around nine A.M. Serena started to reach for her phone, then realized the generic ringtone wasn't hers. She tapped Antonio on the shoulder when he didn't move. "Are you going to get that?"

"I'd better," he groaned as he reached for his pants to retrieve his phone. Looking at the CALLER ID, Antonio shook his head. It was Casey.

"Yeah?" he said when he answered.

"Where are you?" Casey asked. "I figured we could have breakfast together since A.J. is camping. I even picked up some shrimp and grits but you're not at home. Are you on a job site?"

"No, Casey. I'm sorry you went to the house. You should've called first," he said.

"I did, but when you didn't answer, I figured you were sleeping in."

Antonio sighed and sat up in the bed. "Why don't I call you later? A.J. and I will see you on Sunday." He snapped his phone shut just as Serena sprinted from the bed.

She closed herself up in the bathroom feeling angry and confused as she turned the water on and sighed. Yes, she'd heard a female voice on the phone but what right did she have to be jealous? She'd said she wanted a brief fling with him—which meant she had no claim on him nor could she get upset about who called him.

"Get it together," she whispered as she splashed water on her face. "He isn't your man." Still the green-eyed monster had Serena in her cold grip. *If that's his woman then fine. I've gotten what I've wanted and I can go right back to Atlanta as soon as the restaurant relaunches.*

A soft knock on the door brought Serena out of her thoughts. "Yes?" she said trying to keep her voice cool and detached.

"Are you all right in there?"

Say yes, say yes, she told herself. But instead of responding, Serena shut the water off and opened the door. "I was just giving you space to talk to your woman," she said, all of the coolness drained from her voice. *So much for being cool, moron,* Serena thought.

When Antonio smirked at her, Serena felt a surge of anger course through her system. "Well, don't let me hold you up from your woman," she snapped. "If you need to leave you know your way to the door."

"That wasn't my woman. I told you I'm single. That was my sister-in-law."

Serena folded her arms across her chest as she looked at him. Part of her could understand why his dead wife's sister would want to remain close to him. She probably felt a connection with him because of her sister, but Serena wondered how deep that connection went. What if they were more than just family? Suppose he and his sister-in-law had started something that was more than familial?

"Whatever," she said. "It doesn't matter what you and your sister-in-law do."

"We don't do anything. Casey stays close to me because she wants to continue to have a connection with her sister and she has that through my son," Antonio said.

Serena blinked in rapid succession. "Son?"

He nodded. "I have a five-year-old son, which has a lot to do with why you think I was running hot and cold with you when we first met."

"Wow," she said quietly. "A son. I had no idea that you were . . . That's a lot of responsibility."

Antonio nodded. "But I wouldn't have it any other way. I love my son and he's the most important thing in my life."

Serena leaned against the wall, her head reeling from the fact that Antonio wasn't seeing another woman, but was a father. "So, where's your son now?"

"Camping with Norman and his grandsons."

"Why didn't you tell me sooner that you had a son?" she asked as she ran her hand across her face.

He shrugged his shoulders. "I know that some women run as soon as they find out I have a son or they immediately think I'm trying to make them A.J.'s new mother. I had no idea what was between us but from the look on your face, I'm thinking you're a runner."

"This is a bit more than I expected, but I'm not a runner."

"Good, because I like you, and when the time is right, I'd like to introduce you to my son."

Serena offered a small smile. Though she said she wasn't a runner, she wasn't ready to be a stepmommy either. It wasn't that she didn't like kids. She just preferred liking them from a distance. She sighed inwardly. Her thoughts were selfish, but she wondered how Antonio's son would change what they had. Should she run? Finally, she said, "That would be nice, one day."

"So, are you ready for breakfast?" he asked, cocking his eyebrow.

"Just coffee. I actually have to go and see Jade in a little bit," she said as she looked at the clock on the nightstand. "I didn't realize how late it was." Serena felt horrible lying to him, but she didn't know if she could handle dealing with a man who had the responsibility of raising a son.

Antonio bit down on his lower lip. "All right," he said suspiciously. "Are you sure you're not running?" he asked as he reached for his pants.

"Antonio, I'm sorry. I don't even know why I'm acting like this," Serena said.

"I'm not going to force my son on you, but if you're going to be a part of my life we come as a package. Tell me if you can't deal with that and we can say good-bye right now." Antonio slipped his pants on and waited for Serena's reply. When she didn't say anything, he nodded.

"Then I guess I have my answer." He kissed her cheek as he walked out of the room with his shirt clenched in his hands.

Standing in the middle of her bedroom, Serena tried to tell herself that saying good-bye would be the best thing. She'd be saving his son from a childhood like hers, where random women had popped in and out of her dad's life. She'd gotten what she wanted—her curiosity had been satisfied and she could move on.

But a small voice inside her that wouldn't be ignored told her to go downstairs and stop Antonio from leaving. For once, Serena listened to that voice and tore off after him.

"Antonio," she said as he reached for the doorknob. She closed the space between them and grabbed his hand. "Don't go."

"Why should I stay?" He looked into her eyes and Serena felt a jolt from her heart. A feeling she hadn't experienced since L.A.

"Because," she said as she squeezed his hand. "I . . . I . . ."

"Let me guess. You've never dated a man with a child?"

She nodded, but didn't say anything for a moment. "There's something you should know about me. I was raised by a single father," she said as they headed over to the sofa. "Dominic Jacobs is a great father, but he was a bit of a player."

"What does that have to do with me?"

"I had a flashback for a second and I was transported back to my childhood, and that wasn't fair to you."

Antonio took her hand into his. "Since my wife died, I haven't dated seriously. When I met you and felt a spark between us, I tried to fight it because I don't want to be that father who brings too many people in and out of his son's life. A.J. is the most important person to me, but I see that I can open myself again to find someone I can spend adult time with. I'd like that person to be you, but you have to accept every part of me and that includes my son."

"I can do that," she said. "But it's going to be a process."

Antonio nodded. "I know that. Like I said, I won't be bringing A.J. around until I know where we're going."

"I wish my father would've had that same attitude," she said. "He loved my mother so much that when she died, he hardened his heart and treated women as if they were disposable tissues." Shaking her head, Serena realized she had never told that story to a man before. She normally shared her past only with her girlfriends or her diary.

The screenplay she'd been working on when she was in L.A. five years ago was loosely based on her father. Though she hadn't thought about it in years, she wondered if she should revamp it and try to make her dream of getting it on the big screen come true.

"That must have been hard to watch, especially since you're a woman," he said.

Serena smiled, "I learned a lot."

"Uh-oh," he said. "So does that mean I have to reteach you how a man treats a woman?"

"Yes," she said. "And just how are you going to do that?"

He winked at her. "I'm the teacher and you're the student. Just get ready for some great lessons. First, we're going to start with breakfast." Antonio rose from the sofa and headed into the kitchen. Serena smiled as she followed him.

Chapter 10

After breakfast, Antonio decided he and Serena needed to do something that didn't involve the bed—as much as he wanted to take her upstairs and feast on her some more. But hearing about her view of men and how she watched her father use women for his pleasure, he knew he had to show her something else.

They headed to Freedom Park to take a walk and talk. Antonio smiled as they pulled into the parking lot. He couldn't remember the last time he'd had a simple date like this. Maybe in high school when he and Marian had started seeing each other.

"This place is pretty," Serena said.

"I keep forgetting you're not from Charlotte," he said. "I'm going to have to give you a tour of some of Charlotte's best kept secrets."

"Sounds fun," she said. "And one day we're going to have to hit Atlanta."

"Works for me," he said as they climbed out of

his truck. Antonio held Serena's hand and they walked along the cement path leading to the pond. Antonio pointed out the soundstage where there were free concerts in the summer and the places where people played on the lawns.

"This place is huge," she said as they finally made it to the pond.

"You should see it during Festival in the Park—in September. A.J. and I come out here and eat junk food for a few hours and look at art that he doesn't like."

Serena stroked his forearm. "That sounds like fun. You seem like a wonderful father."

"I try," he said.

"Do you mind if I ask you a personal question?"

Antonio turned to her and nodded. "Seems like that's the tone of the day."

"How did your wife die?"

He felt his heart drop to his stomach. Sure, he knew that question would come up one day, but today?

"Car accident on I-485," he said. "She was hit by a drunk driver going the wrong way."

"Oh my goodness," she said. "What happened to the driver?"

"He died about two days later in the hospital, but Marian was killed instantly."

She shook her head and said, "That must have been so hard to lose her like that."

"It was extremely hard because we were having some problems and . . ." Antonio's voice trailed off.

Serena squeezed his hand. "Wow," she said

quietly. "That had to be more than hard." Part of her wondered if he and his wife were going to work on their problems before her death. Was that why he'd shut himself off from other women after all of this time? Serena knew about shutting down after heartbreak, but losing his wife—was that something he was truly over?

"The worst part is that her family had no idea what was going on and as much as I mourned the loss of my wife, I had to put up this front of everything being all right. That's why Casey is so clingy to me. She thinks I need her to be Marian's replacement sometimes."

They fell into an uncomfortable silence as they walked around the pond.

Antonio sighed. "I thought about telling Marian's family what was really going on, but I didn't want to sully her memory."

"That's very honorable, but how would the truth sully her memory?"

"Let's change the subject," he said as they headed over to a bench.

Serena nodded as they took a seat. She leaned against Antonio's broad shoulder and said, "Well, since today is about honesty and sharing, I have something else I should tell you."

"What's that? You have husband in Atlanta?"

"No, silly, I don't have a husband in Atlanta." She poked him with her elbow. "I really can't cook," she said hoping to inject levity into their conversation. "Dinner was actually cooked at my best friend's house and I brought it home and heated it up."

Antonio laughed, pulled Serena against his chest, and kissed her forehead. "We're going to have to work on your cooking skills," he said.

"Who said I want to improve?" she joked.

"I'm a true southern boy and I like a home-cooked meal every now and then. Besides, I'll teach you. If I can learn to cook, trust me you can, too."

Serena relaxed in Antonio's arms, feeling good about being with him and looking forward to seeing where things would go. She hadn't felt like that since Emerson, and in the back of her mind, she was afraid. But she brushed those feelings aside and enjoyed the sunlight and Antonio's touch.

They sat on the bench in a comfortable silence watching a flock of ducks floating in the pond, then a jogger stopped in front of them. Antonio and Serena looked up at the woman.

"Antonio, what's going on here?" she asked.

"Casey," he said. "Hello to you, too."

She placed her hands on her hips as sweat poured down her face. Cocking her head to the side, Casey gave Serena a hostile once-over and Serena raised her eyebrow at Antonio's sister-in-law.

"So, who's your friend?" Casey asked.

Antonio sighed. "Casey, this is Serena Jacobs."

Neither woman attempted to shake hands with the other. "So," Casey said. "I guess that's why we couldn't have breakfast this morning. Is she the reason you sent A.J. camping this weekend?"

"Do I need to give you two some privacy?" Serena asked as she rolled her eyes.

"No," Antonio said. "Casey, you're out of line."

"I apologize," she said insincerely. "I guess I knew this day would come, but I'm not used to seeing you with someone other than *my sister.* It was nice to meet you, Serena." Casey offered them a weak smile and jogged off.

"Your sister-in-law seems a bit possessive," Serena said when Casey was out of earshot. "Are you sure you're not married to another one of her sisters?"

Antonio sighed. "I don't know what's going through her head at times," he said. "But I'll handle it. She has no right to be rude to you."

"It's no big deal," Serena said. "What do you say you show me some more of this park?"

"I have an even better idea," he said as they rose from the bench. "Let's get started on your tour of Charlotte."

Serena nodded. "Sounds like a good plan and then I'll spring for lunch."

"No, then we're going to Trader Joe's. We'll go back to your place and you can get your first cooking lesson."

"All right," she said. "I guess I'm ready to learn."

"You have to do more than guess," he said as they headed for his truck. When Antonio glanced over his shoulder, he saw Casey watching him and Serena walk away. Suddenly, he heard Norman's voice in his head telling him that Casey wanted more than to stay connected with her sister by being around him.

He would definitely have to have a talk with her and let her know that his life was his own and he was going to date.

As Serena and Antonio headed to Marshall Park in Uptown Charlotte—the beginning of her tour—Serena's cell phone rang. She looked down at the screen and saw that it was Alicia calling.

"I have to take this," she told Antonio before answering the phone. "Nice of you to call," she said into the phone.

"Oh stop it. From what I hear, you're not missing me," Alicia said with a laugh. "I'm going to be back in Charlotte next week. But I need you to tell me how the work is coming along with the contractor. Have you cracked that nut?"

"I can't get into that right now, but the restaurant looks great."

"Oh my goodness, you're with him. Please tell me you're not going to spit him out before we get everything we need for the reopening."

Serena sighed and swiftly changed the subject. "How's the seminar coming along?"

"Oh, you must be really close to him because I told you about that yesterday. Are you in bed or out of bed? That was a silly question, you wouldn't have picked up if you were in bed with that man."

Serena gripped her cell phone wishing she'd rolled her nosy friend into voicemail instead of answering.

"Serena?" Alicia asked. "Are you still there?"

"I thought you wanted something important," Serena said in an irritated tone.

Antonio glanced over at her and smiled, then said, "We're here."

"Alicia, I have to go. We'll talk later." She hung up the phone and climbed out of the truck.

"Business?" Antonio asked as they walked toward the park.

Serena nodded. "The best thing about being business partners with your friends is that you can hang up on them without worrying about hurting their feelings."

Antonio smiled. "So, that conversation was more about your personal life than the restaurant?"

"You got it."

"What do your friends know about us?"

Serena ran her fingers through her hair and smiled. "That I wanted you from the moment I saw you and I usually get what I want. They just want to make sure I don't mess up your working relationship with the restaurant."

Antonio stopped walking and turned to Serena with a smirk on his lips. "From the moment you saw me? Was it worth the wait?"

"Definitely."

"Just so you know, it wasn't a one-sided thing."

Serena took his face in her hands and laid a searing kiss on him that made their knees shake. Pulling back, Antonio thought about piling into the truck and going back to her place and taking that kiss to another level. She'd awakened a desire in him he'd thought died the moment he found out his wife was having an affair. Serena made him feel wanted, made him feel as if he was desired and needed.

"If you do that again, we're never going to finish this tour," he said when he caught his breath.

"All right," she said, then slipped her hand in his. "I'll try to be good."

"Don't try too hard," he said, then brushed his lips against her neck.

They walked over to a patch of grass near the man-made waterfall in the center of the park. Antonio reached into his pocket and pulled out two pennies. He handed one to Serena and said, "Make a wish."

She closed her eyes and tossed the penny into the water, then laughed. "You're bringing the kid out in me," she said after Antonio tossed his coin in.

"Everybody needs to take some time and have fun every now and then."

"I haven't had fun in a while. Maybe it's time that we change that."

"Yes, it is time to change that. Let's go," he said, then they headed to his truck.

Serena expected that Antonio would drive to Trader Joe's, but he headed back to her place. She looked at him with questions dancing in her eyes.

Antonio smiled. "I know you have a swimsuit up there."

"Yes, but what do I need it for?"

"For the next phase of the tour," he said with a

sly smile. "Tick tock, we still have to go to Trader Joe's so you can get your cooking lesson."

Serena pressed her chest against Antonio's and asked, "Are you sure you're not just trying to get me all wet? Because you don't have to take me to water to do that."

He slipped his hand around her waist and grinned at her. "Um, keep talking like that and the tour might end right here. Or you could go upstairs and change and we can see just how wet you can get later." Antonio brushed his lips against hers then stepped back. "Now, go get that swimsuit."

Serena headed upstairs and fished her purple bandeau bathing suit out of her dresser drawer. She changed out of the strapless romper she'd been wearing and put the suit on. Looking at herself in the mirror, Serena thought about Antonio's smile and the fun they'd been having all day, but in the back of her mind reality tugged at her thoughts. It wasn't always going to be like this. His sister-in-law's reaction to her made her feel as if there would be problems. She pushed those thoughts to the back of her mind as she pulled her romper over her swimsuit and headed to the closet to grab a couple towels.

"All right. I'm ready," she called from the top of the stairs.

Antonio smiled at her. "Let's go."

Serena walked downstairs and linked arms with him. As they walked to the truck, she sighed and turned Antonio and took his face in her hands and kissed him gently.

"What was that for?" he asked when she broke the kiss.

"For all the fun we're having," she said. "For you being such a nice guy."

"A nice guy? That isn't a bad thing, is it? Women don't normally go for the 'nice guy.'"

Serena squeezed his cheek. "Most nice guys aren't built like you either," she joked. "Besides, at some point, bad boys get old and boring."

"So, nice guys are a consolation prize?" he asked as he playfully swatted her bottom.

"Not at all," she said. "It's just that some women, myself included, take a while to recognize just how fun a nice guy can be."

Antonio let her go and opened the passenger door for Serena. "Got to keep up the good guy image," he said as she slipped into the truck.

As he started the truck, Serena snapped her seat belt on, then asked, "So, where are we going?"

"First, to my place so I can grab some swim trunks, then we're going to my favorite place," he said.

"And that place is?"

"Even if I told you, you wouldn't know, so sit back and enjoy the ride."

Serena raised her hand in mock salute. "All right. I'm going to sit back and let you take me away."

About ten minutes later, they pulled into the driveway of Antonio's two-story home. Serena was struck by the beauty of the woodwork on the outside of the house. The front door was adorned with wood-carved flowers that reminded her of work she'd seen in art books. They got out of the truck and walked up to the front door. Before Antonio unlocked it, Serena ran her hand across the smooth wood.

"Did you do this?" she asked.

"Yeah," he said wistfully as if her question struck a nerve.

Serena dropped her hand and stepped aside so Antonio could unlock the door. She watched him as he cast a glance at the door and wondered what the significance of the door was.

"The place is a little messy," he said as he pushed the door open. Serena shook her head as she took a glance at the foyer. It wasn't messy, just lived in. Dusty work boots were lined near the door and a few pairs of small sneakers. A winding staircase led upstairs and a crystal chandelier hung in the center of the high ceiling. The walls were painted a chocolate brown but there were telltale signs of a child living there—a few nicks and smudges on the walls.

The house had a comfortable feel to it and Serena could almost hear the sound of a little boy laughing. Warmth and love seemed to radiate from the walls. She smiled at Antonio and said, "This house is nice."

"Let me give you a quick tour," he said, then led her into the living room. The open space room had a huge sectional sofa in the center of the room, a plasma screen TV hanging on the wall and creamy beige carpet covering the floor with a few spots of fruit juice sprinkled here and there. There were two TV trays at the ends of the sofa. Serena assumed that Antonio and his son ate many meals watching television.

"And through here," he said as he led her to the kitchen, "is a room you probably wouldn't have much use for."

"Ha, ha," she said as she playful slapped him on the shoulder. Serena looked around the ultra modern kitchen with its stainless steel appliances and marble island in the center of the room. Pots hung from the ceiling. "You're serious about this cooking thing, huh?"

"Me and my son have to eat and it costs too much to eat out every night. No offense," Antonio said with a grin. "And A.J. would want McDonald's every night."

Serena crinkled her nose. "I can't remember the last time I've eaten at McDonald's," she said. "Though I will admit for a while when I was in L.A., that was all I could afford."

"You lived in Los Angeles?"

Serena ran her hand through her hair. "A long time ago. I had dreams of being a screenwriter."

"Now, that is a surprise. I would've never taken you for the showbiz type."

"What does that mean?"

He cocked his head to the side and looked at her. "Don't take this the wrong way, but you seem all business and being a screenwriter isn't a job or a career I would associate with you. I could believe that you were an actress, though."

Serena shivered inwardly but kept a smile on her face. "Well," she said. "I tried acting. It didn't work out and I stepped back into reality."

"Did you ever make a movie?" he asked as he led her out of the kitchen and into the enclosed back porch.

"It didn't work out. Just a pipe dream," she said, struggling to keep her voice even. The last thing Serena wanted to think about were her years in Los Angeles or the movie she'd made with Emerson—the man she had expected to marry and with whom she'd thought she'd rise to the heights of Hollywood royalty.

"Well," Antonio said. "I'm sure you would've been a great actress and would've filled the big screen with grace. But I'm not going to say I'm disappointed. If you were a big-time actress, I never would've met you."

She smiled and hoped they'd never talk about her failed acting career again. "So, what's this?" she asked as she looked around the porch. "Seems real cozy."

"It is," Antonio said. "Some nights, A.J. and I sit out here until we fall asleep."

"Did you build this?" she asked as she took note of the structure and the woodwork on the column.

Antonio nodded and smiled. "I did a lot of the work on this place after Marian died to keep myself from going crazy. It gave me a chance to put a new stamp on the house for me and my son."

"It must have been really hard after your wife died."

Antonio's face went totally blank and he led her back into house. "I'm going upstairs to get my shorts," he said.

While he headed upstairs, Serena silently

kicked herself as she walked into the den. *Way to go, talking about his dead wife,* she thought as she looked at the pictures on the top of a wooden bookshelf. Serena was surprised to see there weren't any pictures of Antonio and his wife— just photographs of him and his son. She picked up a picture of Antonio holding the little boy who looked just like him while the little boy held a fish that was longer than his arm. Antonio's bright smile radiated from behind the frame and the little boy looked just as happy as his father.

"You know, you're welcome to come on the next trip," Antonio said from behind her.

Serena returned the picture to the bookshelf, then turned around and faced Antonio. "That's all right. The thought of touching worms and gutting fish just creeps me out." She glanced down at his bright orange board shorts and smiled. "Nice shorts."

He laughed. "Ok, you've seen my suit, but where's yours?"

Serena smirked at him, then pulled off her romper revealing her purple bandeau suit.

Antonio appreciatively drank in her image in the strapless suit. He closed the space between them and wrapped his arms around her waist. "I think orange and purple go well together," he said, then brushed his lips across her shoulders.

"Really?" she said. "Why don't we slip out of these suits and find out?"

"Oh no," he said. "That comes later. Right now, we're going to get wet." Antonio placed a sweet kiss on her lips.

Serena groaned and almost told him she was already wet, but she pulled her romper back on and followed Antonio outside. "Wherever we're going better be worth it," she said as she climbed in the truck.

"It will be," he said, starting the engine.

Serena studied Antonio as he drove. The man was as close to perfection as she'd ever seen. From the shape of his jaw to the cleft in his chin, he oozed sexuality. Now that she'd had a taste of him, she was sure she couldn't walk away even though he had a child and the responsibility that came with being a single father.

There was also the issue of his dead wife. If what Serena and Antonio had turned out to be more than a fling, would she be in competition with Marian's memory?

Hold up! Relationship? You have been hanging around Jade too long. This is just sex and when I go back to Atlanta, we can call it quits, she thought.

Chapter 11

Los Angeles, California

Emerson Bradford sat at his desk with his feet kicked up flipping through the *Los Angeles Times*. As he came to the entertainment section, his blood began to boil. WHATEVER HAPPENED TO EMERSON BRADFORD?

He'd hoped that his appearance on *E! News* would've killed the *LA Times* story. But it was obvious that the slanderous reporters at the paper wanted to throw more mud on his name. Ever since his last movie, *Style,* flopped at the box office and Thomas Kinney, the movie critic from the *Times* lambasted the film, Emerson had a hate/hate relationship with the paper. He never commented on stories when they called him and he'd even tried to get Thomas Kinney black-balled from movie premieres in the city. It hadn't worked. No one gave a damn about what Emerson Bradford thought anymore.

As he read the byline on the article and saw that Kinney had written it, Emerson groaned and read what he knew would be another attack on him and his craft.

> *Once the toast of Hollywood, director Emerson Bradford seems to be a has-been. The last two movies he's brought to the big screen have flopped in a major way. It's a far cry from the days of* Sultry Summer, *his biggest hit to date.*
>
> *"Emerson Bradford was supposed to be the next big thing," said Hadley Washington, former head of Warner Bros. "We wanted to sign him to a multi picture deal when* Sultry Summer *made the big time. But his second film, which was supposed to be a sexy thriller like* Basic Instinct, *didn't cut the mustard. We passed and withdrew our offer."*
>
> *For a while, or at least for two other films, Warner Brothers looked silly for passing up on Bradford. New Line Cinema wasn't going to make the same mistake and signed Bradford to a $100 million dollar movie deal.*
>
> *New Line Cinema has yet to break even.*

Emerson tossed the paper across the room. "Damned hack. What the hell does he know about filmmaking?" He rose to his feet and kicked the bottom of his desk. Emerson knew he was in trouble. Whenever people in Hollywood started asking "whatever happened to" you might as well be dead. But he wasn't going to give up right away. Emerson knew he had an ace in the hole and it was time to play it.

Stalking back to his phone, Emerson pressed the intercom button.

"Yes, sir?" Annette Peterson, his assistant, said.

"I have a mission for you. Go to the archives and find my film *De Chocolat.*"

"What year was it filmed?" she asked.

"Five years ago. I think it's time to see if I can get this film on the big screen. I'm going to prove to the world that I haven't lost anything."

"Yes, sir."

Emerson sat down and pulled up his Internet browser and typed in Serena's name. He hadn't thought about her in years and wondered what she'd been doing. Had she continued acting? No, he would've known about it—unless she was acting in New York. He hoped she was a Broadway star and he could cash in on her success. Of course, he'd have to do some additional editing before the movie was released, to make it seem new and current.

He looked at the screen and was surprised to see the first article about Serena was on a business Web site. "Restaurant?" he muttered as he clicked on the link. His eyes grew with excitement when he saw NFL superstar Maurice Goings in a picture with Serena and three other women. Those would be the friends she'd always talked about.

"Well, well," he said. "Looks like my little muse is in with the NFL. Maybe I should take a trip to Charlotte and see if she still wants to be famous. This might work out for both of us." Emerson pressed the intercom button again, and then remembered he'd sent his assistant to look for the print of the film. He focused on Serena's features. She was still as sexy as when he'd first met her. But the innocence he'd been attracted to was gone. A part of him knew he'd been the one who'd jaded her. Maybe, he reasoned, releasing the movie would make things right.

Emerson folded his hands underneath his chin and pondered what would've happened had he married Serena. He'd been wrong to leave her at the altar without telling her why. He'd felt as if he'd failed her. He'd wanted nothing more than to make his beautiful muse a star. But when the studio had balked on releasing the film, his spirit had been crushed and he wondered if he'd made a mistake casting Serena in the lead. There had been no way he could marry her when he felt she'd been the reason his career had began to sputter. It was supposed to be the film that put him on the level with Spike Lee in his early days, or even Martin Scorsese.

The script was fresh and original, nothing like your typical African-American film, thanks to Serena and her crisp writing skills. Emerson had known he was taking a real risk, but it had been a risk he'd wanted to take to elevate what studios thought about black films. He'd grown tired of the social movies. He'd wanted to do something sexy. Hollywood hadn't been ready and that crushed his spirit—until his next movie, which made box office history.

Though he'd tried to find Serena two months after leaving her at the altar, when he'd arrived at her apartment in East Los Angeles, she was gone with no forwarding address. Emerson didn't look for her any further. His life became filled with being the hottest director in Hollywood. Sometimes he wondered if she had seen his success . . . and if she'd watched his epic fall. As he returned to his Internet search of Serena and read the recent headlines her restaurant had made, he began to wonder if she would be the key to his return to the top.

Serena wiped her face with a towel as she sat on the bench beside Antonio at Latta Park. They'd spent the last hour running through the sprinklers at the park in the blazing sun. She smiled. "This was really fun." she said.

"I know. I'm surprised this place isn't crawling with kids. A.J. and I come here all the time," he said, drinking from a water bottle. "Only he's not as easy to get out of the water as you were."

"I'm just resting. Getting ready for round two," she joked as she reached down and dried her feet. Antonio set his water aside and took over drying her feet. As he massaged her feet, Serena tossed her head back engrossed in the pleasure of his hands against her skin.

"We still have to cook lunch," he said as he slowly moved up her calf and stopped at her knee. "And I can't wait to peel that suit off you."

"Then lunch can wait."

"No, ma'am. I'm hungry and you need to learn

how to cook," he said as he ran his fingers across her thighs.

Serena moaned quietly as her body tingled from his touch. "All right, but if you teach me to cook, then it's only fair that I get to teach you a lesson later."

Antonio leaned in and kissed her cheek. "I'm all for learning new things."

Smiling seductively, Serena wrapped her towel around Antonio's neck and brought his lips to hers.

Before she could kiss him, a group of parents and their kids walked by. "Get a room," one of the mothers hissed.

Serena dropped her head on Antonio's shoulder. "I guess we'd better go."

"Yeah," he said as they rose to their feet. Antonio grabbed their clothes and they headed to the parking lot. Once inside his truck, Antonio stroked Serena's thigh and smiled at her. "Ready?" he asked.

"Depends on what you're asking about," she said as she leaned over and kissed him with a fiery passion that made his head spin.

Pulling back, Antonio looked at Serena with desire flickering in his eyes. "You know, we can order a pizza," he said. "Papa Johns delivers."

"What about the cooking lesson?" she asked, batting her eyelashes seductively.

"Dinner, I can teach you how to cook dinner," Antonio replied, then started the engine and headed for his house.

Arriving at Antonio's place, he and Serena

leaped from the truck and rushed inside. He enveloped her in his arms and kissed her with the fire that had built up inside him since their kiss at the park. Pushing Serena against the wall, he broke off the kiss and slowly peeled her swimsuit from her sensual body.

Serena placed her hand on his chest. "I want you out back," she moaned as she slipped her hand inside his shorts and stroked his growing erection until his knees quaked.

Antonio could only nod his head as he began walking toward the enclosed porch.

Once they were on the porch, Serena pushed him back onto one of the plush wicker chairs. Wrapping her legs around his waist, she ground against him enjoying his hardness against her wetness. Reaching down, she tugged at the waistband of his shorts until they were around his ankles. Unwrapping her legs from his waist, Serena eased down his body until her lips hovered over his erection. She drew him into her mouth, making him moan in delight.

He gripped the arms of the chair as Serena sucked and took him to the heights of pleasure. His legs shook as the grips of an orgasm touched his system.

Serena locked eyes with Antonio as she ran her tongue up and down his shaft.

"Damn," he moaned as he pushed her back. "I have to get a condom. I need to be inside you."

She nodded, her lips curved into a sultry smile as Antonio rushed inside to grab some protection.

Moments later, he was back with his erection
sheathed, ready to take her. He closed the space
between them and lifted Serena into his arms,
kissing her until he felt her body shiver. As they
fell back onto a larger lounge chair, Serena
mounted his erection, tossing her head back in
ecstasy as he swam in her wetness. Her body
throbbed with pleasure as she ground against
him slowly. They fell into a sensual rhythm, sending ripples of desire between them that sizzled
like electricity as they reached their peak. Antonio held on to her as he exploded. Serena
brushed her lips across his neck as she collapsed
against his sweaty chest.

He ran his hands up and down her smooth
back and smiled as he felt his passion growing
again inside her valley. Antonio rotated his hips,
hitting her G-spot, making her scream out his
name.

"I can't get enough of you, I can't get enough
of you," he moaned as their bodies melted into
each other.

Serena opened her mouth to say the same
thing, but words failed her as her senses were
short-circuited by her fifth orgasm. She closed
her eyes as Antonio lifted her and laid her on the
wicker sofa.

He joined her on the oversized chair and held
her tightly.

Serena placed her hand on the flat of his chest.
"Wow," she whispered.

"Wow is one way to describe it."

Serena looked up and saw the sun was setting. "Looks like we missed lunch."

"It was well worth it," he replied as he stroked her arm.

"It feels good out here," she said as she shifted in his arms.

"Would you like to spend the night? We can put a log in the fire pit and roast marshmallows. Think you can handle that much cooking?" he asked with a laugh.

She playfully slapped his shoulder. "Not funny. Don't you think it's a little warm for a fire, though?"

"It's always hot with you. But around midnight, it will be considerably cooler out here."

"All right. But I'm going to need some drier clothes."

"I have a T-shirt you can put on for now, then we can head to your place and the grocery store so we can at least try to cook dinner."

Serena stroked his cheek and yawned. "You're so sweet, but I'm so over cooking," she said with a grin. "I'd be more than happy to watch you."

"That doesn't sound fair. The only way you get to watch is if you pack one of those little lacy numbers you like so much."

"Done."

While Antonio got up and headed inside to get her a T-shirt, Serena sat up and stretched her legs.

"Antonio," a female voice called out, then the back door opened.

Serena covered her breasts with her arms as she looked into Casey's face.

"Oh my God," Casey exclaimed, then slammed out the back door.

Serena scrambled to find her clothes and burst inside. She was surprised to see Casey walking in the *front* door.

"Antonio," the women called out in concert.

What is Casey doing here? Antonio thought as he sped down the stairs with a T-shirt in his hand. Casey and Serena looked up at him and Antonio shook his head. "Casey, what are you doing here?" he asked as he glanced at Serena, who was dressed in her damp romper, looking very uncomfortable.

"Well, there's no need for me to ask you what you're doing. And in my sister's house," Casey snapped.

"Wait a damned minute," he said.

"No. What if A.J. had come home and found this tramp naked on the back porch!?"

Serena threw up her hands and said, "You don't know me and out of respect for this grown man, I'm going to let your insult slide. But you should think about the next words that come out of your mouth."

Casey placed her hand on her hip and looked up at Antonio. "So, is this why you sent A.J off with Norman? So you could—"

"Casey, you need to give me back my key and then leave, since you can't respect my privacy," Antonio said as he crossed over to his sister-in-law. "I don't understand what's going on with you."

"How can you spit on my sister's memory like this?" Casey exclaimed, then slammed out of the house.

"Do you need to go after her?" Serena asked as Antonio handed her the shirt.

He shook his head. "I'm sorry about that. I had no idea she was going to show up here."

"Is there something going on with the two of you that I should know about? She's not worried about her sister's memory or your son finding us."

"There is nothing going on with me and Casey, but I'm beginning to think that Norman was right."

"Right about what?"

"Casey wanting more than just a connection to her sister."

"She acts like a jealous lover," Serena snapped. "Is that the cause, because I don't share."

"There is nothing going on between me and Casey," he said. "I was married to her sister and that would be a little too incestuous."

"Maybe we should call it a night." Serena said as she pulled Antonio's T-shirt over her head, then slipped out of her romper.

Antonio pulled her into his arms. "I don't think so," he said. "I have plans for you and we're not going to let Casey ruin them."

"Too late for that," she said as she patted his arm.

Antonio brushed his lips against hers. "Come on, babe," he said. "You still have to eat."

Serena smiled and Antonio knew she was going

to agree to come back for dinner. "Let's hope your sister-in-law will stay away while I'm walking around your kitchen in black lace," she said as they headed for the door.

"I'll make sure the door is double bolted."

Chapter 12

Los Angeles, California

"Wow, Emerson," Luther Carlton, second in command at Lionsgate Studios, said after watching *De Chocolat.* "This is almost porn."

"It needs editing," Emerson said.

"You think? The plot is good, a female serial killer who uses sex to get her victims. It's like a sexy *Monster.* Who is the actress? She's fine."

"Serena Jacobs. She didn't make another movie after this one was shelved. But I've been doing some research on her and she's been in the media lately. We could capitalize on her notoriety and build a buzz about the movie if we package it as an independent film," Emerson said.

"I'd be willing to take a chance on this if two things happen. We need some hard edits so we can get an R rating. Right now, this is NC-17 and no one is going to release that kind of movie nationwide. And you have to get this Serena Jacobs to sign off on the film. If she's not in Hollywood anymore, she may not want to have this film released and I don't feel like getting involved in a court battle."

Emerson nodded, all the while thinking Serena wouldn't have a problem with the movie since she'd been so happy to film it. But he admitted silently that things had been different back then. A slight smile tugged at his lips as he thought back to the last time he'd seen her.

A white robe draped haphazardly across her svelte body as she'd leaned over his shoulder, cooing in his ear. All she'd wanted then had been to make love to him in celebration of completing their movie—the movie he'd promised would make her a star.

But Emerson had had to get the film to the studio and hopefully get the green light. Then he had to pick up his tuxedo for their wedding. He'd glanced at Serena and pushed her away. They were going to have a future and he'd had plans to make her star. Making love could wait, he'd thought that night, rushing to the studio. But when he'd shown the movie to the studio heads, they'd turned him down.

Emerson had sunk into depression and threw himself into his work. He'd written *Sultry Summer* and become the toast of the town again. But by that time, he'd broken Serena's heart and she'd disappeared from his life. At first, he'd thought about seeking her out, apologizing and bringing her back to share in his success. But the trappings of Hollywood kept him away from her.

Until now. Now he could atone for his past sins and possibly even win her back and finish what he'd started five years ago.

"Then it sounds as if I'm going back East," Emerson said. "Do you have a release or something I need her to sign?"

"I'll call legal and have it sent to your office. This is going to be great. Keep in mind, we're going to do this in limited release to build a buzz, if Ms. Jacobs signs off on it."

Emerson smiled, "I'm sure Ms. Jacobs will sign off on it. If I know one thing about Serena, I know she wants to make me happy."

Luther shrugged. "Just make sure the paperwork is in order," he said as he buzzed his assistant.

Emerson nodded and headed out of the office. He pulled his cell phone from his pocket and called his travel agent. "Lydia, I need a flight to Charlotte, North Carolina," he said without saying hello.

Serena woke up in Antonio's arms smiling as she thought about the dinner they didn't cook. He'd been too distracted by the barely-there teddy she'd sauntered around the kitchen in.

As he'd sautéed green peppers and onions, Serena had wrapped her arms around his waist and stroked his smooth stomach. Antonio had dropped his spoon, turned around, and lifted Serena up on the counter. While he'd feasted on her body, the vegetables burned and the smoke alarm blared as Antonio brought her to climax with his hot tongue. They'd ended up ordering Chinese for dinner and roasting marshmallows under the stars. Their simple date had been the most fun Serena had had in a while. Maybe there was something to what Jade had said about Antonio being more than sex.

Serena gently stroked his chest, wondering if she should allow herself to believe there was more than just hot desire between them. She still had an issue with his sister-in-law and Serena knew when his son came home they wouldn't be lying in bed naked.

"Um, good morning," Antonio said as he opened his eyes.

"Morning," she replied.

He pulled her closer to his chest and kissed her forehead. "So, we're going to try this cooking lesson one more time with something simple."

"What would that be?" she asked as she toyed with a sprig of hair on his chest.

"Breakfast. Cracking a few eggs and toasting some bread. It's not that hard."

"All right," she said as she looked over at her overnight bag. "And I will put some clothes on so we don't have a repeat of last night."

"Sounds good," he said, then glanced at the

clock on his nightstand. It was five after seven. "But you don't have to put on clothes right this second."

Serena smiled, then kissed him with a deep passion that brought his body to life immediately.

Two hours later, Serena and Antonio peeled themselves out of bed and cooked breakfast. She whisked eggs for Denver omelets while Antonio placed pancake batter on the griddle.

"Chocolate chips or plain?" he asked as Serena sprinkled a handful of peppers and onions into her eggs.

"Can we have both?" she asked. "What woman in her right mind turns down chocolate?"

Antonio tossed the chips into the cakes on the griddle. "I learned a long time ago not to come between a woman and her chocolate."

Serena wanted to say something about his wife, ask him if they shared moments like this in the kitchen. Her cynical side started whispering in her ear. *He's trying to replace his dead wife with you. Sort of like your father did with the bevy of women he had in and out of the house all of those years.*

"Serena," Antonio said, breaking into her cryptic thoughts. "I think you're ready to pour."

"Oh, right," she said as she walked over to the stove. Slowly, she poured the mixture of eggs and vegetables in the heated pan.

"Now," he said as he stood beside her, "watch the edges and get ready to fold it over and flip it."

"Doesn't sound too hard," she said as she watched the edges bubble and brown.

"Fold and flip," he said.

Serena did as he said and the first omelet flipped perfectly. The second one in the pan, not so much. The egg tore and looked more like scrambled eggs. "Damn," she muttered as she flipped the other half of the omelet.

"You can have the pretty one," Antonio said with a laugh. "But this isn't bad for your first time." Serena sprinkled shredded cheese over the omelets as Antonio popped a piece of egg in his mouth. He turned back to the pancakes and flipped them, making sure they were fluffy and brown.

"All right, it's time to eat," he said as he placed the pancakes on a tray and took it into the dining room. Serena followed with the eggs.

When they sat down to eat, Antonio grabbed Serena's hand and kissed it. "I had a wonderful weekend with you."

"So did I," she said quietly.

"I really hate for it to end," he said.

"But your son will be home shortly, right?" Serena asked.

Antonio nodded. "Knowing A.J. and Norman, they're returning with a lot of fish."

"And you're going to do what with it?" she asked as he placed two pancakes on her plate with his free hand.

"Clean them and cook them," he said. "Do you even go in the kitchen at your restaurant?"

"At the end of the night when I'm heading for my car," she said with a laugh. "Maybe I'll spend a little more time there so I can surprise you with a decent meal one day."

"I'm going to hold you to that," he said, then rose from the table. "I forgot the syrup."

Serena watched him as he walked into the kitchen and smiled at his retreating figure. *Don't get too comfortable,* her cynical voice said. *Either he's going try to strap his wife's high heels on your feet or you're going to be relegated to a booty call when the little boy is asleep.*

She shook her head. "That's not going to happen," she muttered.

Antonio walked into the dining room. "Did you say something?" he asked as he set the syrup in front of her.

"Oh, nothing. Getting ready for Monday," she covered.

"Talking to yourself is never good," he teased as she poured syrup over her pancakes.

"Sometimes, all you have is yourself. My Dad always said it's fine as long as you don't answer yourself back."

"I'm going to have to remember that one."

After they finished eating breakfast and cleaning the kitchen, Antonio drove Serena home. "Let me know when you're ready for your next lesson," he said as he walked her to the front door.

She stood on her tiptoes and kissed him on the end of his nose. "I don't think that will be any time soon," Serena replied. "You're such a good cook, there's no need for me mess things up."

He stroked her arm. "How do you feel about fish? Depending on the catch, I might bring you some for lunch when A.J. gets back."

"All right, if you feel like it," she said trying to

hide her excitement at the prospect of seeing him again.

"I'll call you and let you know." Antonio pulled Serena into his arms and kissed her with a hot passion he hoped would hold him for the next few hours. When they broke the kiss and Serena unlocked her door. Antonio waved good-bye to her and headed for his truck. Serena sighed as she walked in. Already she missed him.

Looking at his watch as he drove back to his house, Antonio decided he needed to take care of the nastiness Casey had brought to his home over the weekend. The last thing he wanted or needed was for her to bring up his personal life in front of A.J. and her parents. He hooked a quick left and headed for Casey's house. As he pulled into her driveway, his cell phone rang.

"Hey, Norman," he said when he answered the phone.

"What's up, Antonio? I just want to give you a call and let you know that me and the boys are running late, so if you are having a late brunch, don't rush. We got a lot of fish to clean."

"Are you at your house?" Antonio asked. "I can come over and help clean the fish. I promised Serena I'd bring her some."

"So you did spend the weekend with her. I'm impressed. We're at home. A.J. is quite the little fisherman. He caught a striped bass that's almost as big as your head," Norman said with a laugh.

"I would really be impressed if he'd caught one as big as your head," Antonio joked. "Listen, I have to talk to Casey, but when I'm done I'll come over there."

"What's going on with Casey?"

"She saw me and Serena together at the park and then she came by the house and caught us in an extremely compromising position," Antonio said.

"I'm willing to bet that your sister-in-law was pretty upset," he said. "Now, do you believe me?"

"Unfortunately, I do. But I have to nip this in the bud."

"Are you going to tell her the truth about what was going on with you and Marian before her death?" Norman asked.

"I don't think so. But Casey has to realize that I have a life to live."

"Hey, Antonio, A.J. wants to speak to you."

"Dad," A.J. said when he got on the phone. "I had a really good time. I caught a really big fish."

"I heard," Antonio said. "I'm really glad you had a good time. I can't wait to cook those fish."

"Mr. Norman said that we're going to have a fish fry and me and Kamir can make cole slaw."

"That sounds exciting. Remember, we're going to have dinner with Grandma and Grandpa tonight so don't eat to much fish and cole slaw."

"Okay," the little boy said. "Did you have fun this weekend, too?"

"I sure did. As a matter of fact, I want to ask you if we can share some of that fish and cole slaw with a friend of mine."

"Okay."

"I'm going to be over to Norman's shortly. I love you."

"Love you, too, Daddy," the little boy said.

Antonio hung up the phone and sighed as he stepped out of the truck. Walking up to Casey's front door, he took a deep breath, then knocked. While he wasn't looking for a fight with her, he had to make it clear she had to stay out of his personal life. He knew Serena was about to become a big part of his life.

"I'm surprised to see you here without getting a phone call first," Casey said sarcastically as she opened the door.

"Casey, we need to talk and I do apologize for not calling first," he said. "But this is important."

She stepped aside and allowed him to come inside. "I don't have any naked men lying around, so I don't have a problem with *family* showing up."

Antonio rolled his eyes as he closed the door behind him. "Casey, that's what I wanted to talk to you about."

"That woman?"

"Her name is Serena, and she's going to be a part of my life so you need to respect my space."

"Your space? Is this you or *Serena* talking?" Casey stalked over to the sofa and plopped down. "When did you meet her? What do you know about the kind of woman she is? I guess you just hopped right into bed with her."

"Even though it's none of your business, Serena and I have known each other for some time. But Casey, what I do and who I spend my time with is none of your concern."

"How do you think Marian would feel knowing you're spending time with that kind of woman? A woman who lounges around naked on a man's back porch? Is that the kind of influence you want in A.J.'s life?"

"You don't know Serena or the kind of woman she is. You walked in on a very private moment—"

"A moment that your son could've easily walked in on," Casey snapped. "Is your libido more important than your son?"

"Now you're questioning how I raise my son? You have some nerve. Nothing comes before my son and you of all people should know that," he bellowed.

"Right. I guess that's why you sent him with Norman this weekend. Have you even talked to him since he's been gone?"

"What's this really about, Casey? Was my life supposed to stop when Marian died?"

"Did I say that? It's just I hoped that—"

"You hoped that what?"

"Nothing," she hissed. "That you'd always put A.J. first. That you'd try and keep the family together. All Marian ever cared about was her son."

Antonio dropped his head and fought the urge to tell her the truth about her sister. "Marian is dead and my life is going on. You don't have to like it, but you will respect it."

"What do you even know about her? Why is she all of a sudden so important?"

"I'm not going to explain what I do to you. Serena is a part of my life. Deal with it and don't ever question how I raise my son again," he said.

"Well, don't expect me to babysit while you're screwing that woman!"

Antonio shook his head and stalked over to the door. "Casey, stay out of my personal business." He slammed out of the house and hopped into his truck, heading for Norman's hoping Casey would heed his warning.

Chapter 13

Serena stretched her arms above her head as Jade rocked Jaden back and forth. Though she adored her friend, Serena wanted her to leave so she could close her eyes and relive all the sexy things she and Antonio had spent the weekend doing.

"Earth to Serena," Jade said. "Are you listening to me?"

"No."

"What has that man done to you?" Jade giggled causing her baby to do the same thing. "You look like a high school girl in love for the first time."

Serena shot Jade an icy look. "You throw the L-word around too much. I'm not in love. This is the look of a satisfied woman."

Jade gently placed her sleepy baby in his carrier seat. "Well, the love bug is going around and I can't wait until it bites you."

"Don't start this again. So, the restaurant relaunch? You were saying?"

"Maurice and the new quarterback, Marcus Hastings, are hosting our launch and a party," Jade said. "Of course Maurice is open to the media covering it."

"Of course," Serena said. "Jade, can I ask you a question?"

"Sure," she replied.

"If something happened to James, do you think Maurice would have a problem with you moving on with your life?"

Jade propped her chin on her hand and looked at Serena with questions dancing in her eyes. "What do you mean?"

Serena sighed. "Never mind. So, what else is happening with this party?"

"No," Jade said. "Why would you ask that?"

Serena told Jade about Antonio's sister-in-law's reaction to seeing the two of them together.

Jade shook her head. "Something doesn't seem right about her," she said. "Maybe she thought Antonio was going to turn to her, but that is gross. Even if Maurice wasn't married, I could never look at him in a romantic way."

"I think you're right about Casey," Serena said. "Anyway, I'm not giving her another thought. Tell me more about the party."

Jade furrowed her eyebrows, but happily began telling her more details about the party. "Well, Maurice and Marcus invited some other NFL players and guess who's singing," Jade said.

Serena cocked her head to the side. "Who?"

"Babyface!"

Serena closed her eyes and tried not to think

about the last time she was supposed to hear Babyface sing live. He'd been scheduled to sing at her ill-fated wedding. Was this some sort of sign?

"Serena," Jade said. "Kenneth 'Babyface' Edmonds. Aren't you excited?"

She shrugged her shoulders. "I guess this party is going be called 'Grown and Sexy.'"

"And here I thought you weren't listening," Jade replied. "Even Kandace and Solomon are coming to the party. Alicia thinks we should have a live show every month."

"Are we a night club or a restaurant?" Serena asked. "We need to do one thing and do it well."

"But the night life in Charlotte is so blah. We can do more than one thing. Or do you think this is going to cut into your time with Mr. Billups? Did he really fall for your meal?"

"I actually told him you cooked it. So he has decided I need cooking lessons and he's going to be my teacher," Serena said with a smile on her face.

Jade chewed her bottom lip and fought back her laughter.

Serena rolled her eyes at her friend, and snapped, "Whatever, Jade."

"I didn't say a word," Jade said as she rose to her feet. "We need to buy some radio ads about the relaunch and film a TV spot."

"Who's going to pay for all of it?" Serena asked, jumping back into business mode.

"We're going to use the money we saved since Solomon took care of the redesign. But from the way you and Antonio are getting it on, we should've let you handle it."

Serena tossed a pillow at Jade's head. "Get out."

"I was leaving anyway. James and I are having a barbeque with Kenya and Maurice. Why don't you call Antonio and join us?"

"No, his son is back from his fishing trip and he's going to bring me some of the fresh fish," she said.

"Wow. When are you going to meet his son? Do you even want to meet the little boy? Let's be real, you don't really like kids."

"I don't know," Serena said. "We're taking things slowly."

Jade raised a questioning eyebrow. "If this is taking it slow, I'd hate to see you moving quickly."

"Good-bye, Jade," Serena said as she rose from the sofa and picked up Jaden's carrier seat. She looked down at the sleeping baby and smiled. Once upon a time she dreamed of having one of her own. Those dreams had died on the altar when Emerson hadn't showed up for their wedding. It wasn't that she didn't like kids. She figured she'd never get suckered by love again and she wouldn't have a baby. She hid her dreams and wants behind a prickly exterior.

Did she really want to risk allowing Antonio to get to know the real Serena Jacobs?

She walked out to the car with Jade and handed the baby to her after Jade dropped the diaper bag and her purse on the front seat.

"See you in the morning at the restaurant," Jade said after buckling Jaden in the back seat.

Serena waved at her friend, then headed back inside to think about Antonio. But as soon as she walked through the door, her cell phone rang. "Great," she muttered as she looked down at the display. The caller was calling from an unknown number.

"Serena Jacobs," she said when she answered.

"Still Jacobs? I just knew some wise man would've made you his by now," the voice from her past said.

"Wh-who is this?" she asked even though she knew.

"Has it really been that long, Serena? It's Emerson."

She pressed the END button on the phone and dropped it on the floor. *No, no! How did he find me? What does he want?*

When the phone rang again, Serena jerked as if a brick had been tossed through her window. *Get it together,* she told herself as she picked up the phone. *You're not the little girl you were five years ago.*

"You have some nerve calling me, you selfish son of a bitch," she barked when she pressed the TALK button on her phone.

"Excuse me?" Antonio said. "Serena?"

"Oh my goodness," she said, then laughed nervously. "I didn't know it was you."

"I hope not. Who pissed you off?"

"No one important," she said. "What's going on? How's the fish cleaning coming?"

"We've cleaned and cooked it. My son is quite the fisherman. He caught about five bass—one really big one," Antonio said proudly.

Serena smiled despite herself. "Good for him."

"Are you ready to try some of this fish?" he asked.

"Yes," she replied. "And I will make it up to you for how I spoke to you when you first called."

"I like the sound of that," he said, and Serena could almost see the smile on his sexy lips. "I'll be there in about twenty minutes."

"I'll be here," she said. After hanging up, Serena turned her phone off. She couldn't risk getting another call from Emerson. As she headed upstairs to her bedroom to change out of her yoga pants and tank top and into a lacy black teddy, Serena couldn't help but wonder what was behind Emerson's call.

You've reached Serena Jacobs. Leave a message and I'll return your call. Thanks and have a great day. Her voicemail played back in Emerson's ear for the third time. He snapped his phone shut. "This is going to be harder than I thought," he groaned as he left the baggage claim of Charlotte Douglas International Airport. He wasn't surprised she'd hung up on him, but she had to know he wasn't going to be dealt with that easily. He'd found her cell phone number on her restaurant's Web site. If he had to become Hometown Delights best customer, then he'd eat breakfast, lunch, and dinner there until he got what he wanted.

If the movie turned out to be the jolt his career needed, maybe he could convince Serena to give their relationship another try. He'd make her the

star she should be and he could take his place at
the top with her by his side. *I wonder if she still has
that sex appeal she had on film,* he thought as he
walked out to an awaiting taxi cab.

"Where to, sir?" the driver asked.

Emerson looked down at his phone to pull up
his hotel reservation. "The Westin," he replied.

"All right. Welcome to Charlotte."

"Thanks," Emerson replied, then slipped his
earbuds in his ears so he wouldn't have to have a
conversation with the driver. He needed to focus
on finding Serena and getting her signature on
the movie release form.

Emerson pulled the Internet browser up on his
cell phone and typed Serena's name in again. He
didn't understand why she had abandoned her
Hollywood dreams. The acting, yes. But she was
a talented writer. She couldn't be fulfilled working at a restaurant or sitting behind a desk. She
was creative and had dreams he'd planned to
nurture. Sure, he'd planned to make himself a
success first. Then it would've been easier to get
movie executives to take a chance on Serena's
screenplays. Emerson smiled as he thought about
how she'd practically rewritten *De Chocolat.* Her
revisions had made the work come alive and he
knew she would go far.

But the movie had been shelved and his stock
in Hollywood was down to nothing. He couldn't
help Serena or himself. When a picture of Serena,
dressed in a tailored business suit, popped up on
the screen, Emerson licked his lips, remembering
how he used to wrap her around his waist and

bury all of his hopes, dreams, and problems between her thighs. Sex with Serena was damned near magical. She'd been so free and so passionate. He really missed her passion and from the slick smile on her face, it was still there.

"Sir," the driver said as the car pulled to a stop. "We're at the hotel."

Emerson looked up from his phone and offered the man an empty smile as he paid the fare and gave him a paltry tip. The driver shook his head when he took the money and made no effort to help Emerson with his bags.

It didn't faze Emerson at all. The only person he was in town to impress was Serena Jacobs.

"Daddy, where are we going?" A.J. asked as they headed uptown toward Serena's place.

"I promised a friend I'd share some of your fish with her. But we won't be there long. We have to go home and get cleaned up before we have dinner with your grandparents."

"Okay," A.J. said as Antonio pulled up to Serena's. "Daddy, I have to use the bathroom."

"All right, come on. Let's see if Miss Serena will let you use the bathroom." Antonio put the truck in park and grabbed the plate of fish, grilled corn on the cob, and cole slaw.

Antonio and A.J. dashed to the door and rang the bell. A.J. wiggled around as his urge to use the bathroom became unbearable. The door opened and their mouths dropped when they saw Serena standing there in a form hugging black teddy and fishnet thigh-high stockings.

"Oh my God," she said when she saw the little boy looking up at her. Serena quickly closed the door.

A.J. patted his father's leg. "Why did that lady answer the door in her underwear?" A.J. asked.

Of course Antonio knew the answer, but there was no way he could tell his son. "I think we caught her by surprise," he answered.

Moments later, Serena opened the door wrapped in a silk robe that hit her at her ankles. "Hi," she said with a red tint to her cheeks.

"A.J. needs to go to the bathroom," Antonio said as they stepped inside and placed the plate on a table next to the door.

"All right," she replied, then pointed the little boy to the bathroom. When he was out of ear-shot, Serena turned to Antonio and placed her hand over her mouth. "I am so sorry."

"That's all right. I had no intentions of bringing him in here, but nature called and wow."

"Wow. I guess I should strip for your grandfather or another family member next," she said with a tense smile. "I wasn't expecting to see you at the door with your son."

Antonio wrapped his arms around Serena and kissed her on the forehead. "He didn't expect to see the lady in her underwear either."

She dropped her head and squeezed the bridge of her nose. "I probably scarred the poor kid for life."

Antonio dropped his arms from her waist as

he heard the flush of the toilet. "I almost forgot the purpose of my visit." He picked up the plate he'd set on the table near the door and handed it to Serena.

"Thanks."

"I made the cole slaw," A.J. said from behind her.

Serena turned around and smiled at the little boy, who returned her smile with a wide one of his own. "Then I'm going to eat it first. I love cole slaw."

"You're pretty," he said, then skipped over to his father.

Antonio rubbed his son's head. "All right, Sport, we'd better go." He winked at Serena. A.J. bounced outside and Antonio gave Serena a quick kiss. "I have to agree with my son."

"About what?"

"You are pretty."

Serena smiled and waved as Antonio climbed into his truck.

Chapter 14

Jade laughed so hard when Serena told her about meeting Antonio's son, she nearly choked on a piece of chocolate cake. And Serena wished she hadn't joined the Goings clan for dessert.

"Okay, I want to laugh, too," Kenya said as she sat down with the two women.

"This one flashed a five-year-old," Jade said as she wiped her mouth.

Kenya raised her eyebrow and looked at Serena.

"That's not how it happened," Serena said when she caught Kenya's eye. "I just made a bad decision."

"Channeling Apollonia around a five-year-old is more than a bad decision," Jade said with another laugh.

"So, a little kid saw you in lingerie?" Kenya asked.

"Not just any little kid. Her boyfriend's son," Jade said.

Serena threw her hands up. "First of all, Antonio is not my boyfriend. And secondly, I didn't think he was going to bring the little boy with him, but he had to use the bathroom."

"Do you often answer your door in lingerie?" Kenya asked.

Serena popped a piece of cake in her mouth. "Depends on who's on the other side of the door," she replied.

Kenya and Jade laughed.

"She's a mess," Jade said. "What did the little boy say?"

"That I'm pretty," Serena revealed. "At least he has good taste."

"Well, now that you've met Antonio's son, what happens next?" Jade asked.

Before she could answer, Jaden and Nairobi began crying and Jade and Kenya slipped into mother mode. As she watched them tend to their babies, Serena wondered if she could be a mother.

Stop it, she told herself. *Don't start thinking about things that aren't going to happen.*

Kenya returned to the table with Nairobi in her arms and Jade handed Jaden off to James for a diaper change. Serena smiled at Kenya's little girl, who tugged at her mother's blouse.

"One day this child will give me my breasts back," Kenya said as she draped a nursing pad over her shoulder.

"You and Jade seem as if you were born to be moms," Serena said. "You guys are doing a great job."

"I couldn't do it without Mo. Believe it or not, he's up at the slightest sound Robi makes at night. Watching him with her, I'm amazed every day," Kenya said. "Kids change you."

Serena nodded. Seeing Antonio with his son was proof of that. He was obviously a protective father. She could tell by the way Antonio had draped his arm around the little boy's shoulders and the way he checked A.J.'s seat belt before driving off. Would she have room in his life? Fatherhood wasn't easy and Serena knew that Antonio was always going to put his son first. Was she going to be woman enough to share him? Women enough to understand broken dates because something came up with his son? *Yes, you can do this because you really care about this man,* she thought. *Wait a minute, it's not that serious.*

She looked up as Jade and James walked over to the table with Jaden.

"Serena," James said, "are you excited about tomorrow?"

"I am. It's time to reopen the restaurant and I can't wait to see the finished product."

"I imagine Antonio's going to give you guys a tour," James said knowingly. "How did your dinner turn out?"

Serena turned her head and smiled. "I confessed that I couldn't cook. But he thought Jade's meal was good."

"You actually told him she cooked it?" James asked as he cut himself a hunk of cake. "That's either some real game or you really like this guy."

"I don't make a practice of lying to nice men," she replied. "And maybe I do like him."

"Shh," James said.

Jade, Kenya, and Serena looked at him skeptically.

"What, babe?" Jade asked.

"I think I just heard hell freeze over. Serena said a man was nice."

Jade shook her head and Serena stuck her finger in the middle of James's cake.

"Now, that wasn't nice," he said as she took the cake and cut it in half and gave him the piece she didn't touch, which was a much smaller piece than James had wanted.

"I never said *I* was nice," she said. "But you already know that."

James waved his hand as he dug into the cake. "That's what you want people to think, but we all know the truth about you," he said.

Before Serena could reply, her cell phone rang. She looked down at the screen and saw it was from an unknown number and she knew it was Emerson again. She pressed the IGNORE button and tried to pretend the call was nothing.

Maurice walked into the dining room with a pint of ice cream as Serena's phone rang again. "What happened to the cake?" he asked when he saw that it was half gone. "Man, y'all are greedy."

"Y'all?" Jade said. "It was your brother who tried to eat half the cake."

Maurice opened the ice cream and shook his head. "I should've known. Mom said she sent you a cake, too, Greedy."

James looked at Jade and smirked. "I'm guessing Jaden ate most of that one."

Jade pinched him on the arm. "You know I love your mother's baking. When is she coming back to town for a visit?"

Maurice and James shrugged. "She was supposed to be going to Atlanta and packing up to move up here. But she went back to the bakery and that was all she wrote," Maurice said.

"I think she's trying to let us down gently about not moving to Charlotte," James said.

Kenya winked at her sister-in-law and said, "I know why Maryann isn't in a hurry to come back here."

Jade hid her wide smile from her husband and brother-in-law.

"Why?" Maurice asked as he cut a slice of cake and topped it with a scoop of ice cream.

"Because she's in love," Kenya said.

"Yeah, with her bakery," James interjected. "We know that. But she could bake here in Jade's kitchen. She said she was happy about doing that."

Jade placed Jaden in his carrier seat as he went to sleep. "Maybe you shouldn't tell them," Jade said.

Kenya nodded as she swiped some of Maurice's ice cream. "Right because they might end up in Atlanta in the morning," Kenya replied.

Maurice and James looked at each other, then stared at their wives. "What the hell is going on?" Maurice demanded.

"Your mother has a boyfriend," Kenya said.

"A what?" Maurice said, dropping his fork to the side of his plate.

"Why wouldn't she tell us?" James asked.

Jade placed her hand on her hip. "Because you two are the most overprotective sons in history. Don't go to Atlanta questioning her about her life. She's a grown woman and she's pretty much stayed out of your lives."

"I'm not going to Atlanta," Maurice said. "Mom should be happy."

"Yeah," James said. "Who are we to stand in the way of her happiness?"

Jade, Serena, and Kenya exchanged knowing looks. "I guess you two are going to go to Atlanta this week?" Jade said.

"The kids miss their grandmother," Maurice said with a laugh. "Maybe they should go for a visit, you know what I mean?" He looked over at James who was nodding in agreement.

"And I want some cinnamon buns and all the icing that goes along with them," James said, then smiled at Jade. Heat flushed her cheeks and Serena knew she had to ask her friend what was so special about cinnamon buns and icing.

"Well, if you all are going to go to Atlanta, please do it around our schedules," Kenya said. "I have to be in court on Tuesday."

"And we're trying to open for lunch on Thursday," Jade said. "But Maurice, you're going to have to be back by Friday to go over the invitations and your VIP guest list for your party."

"And my trial should be wrapped by Friday," Kenya said.

James and Maurice looked at each other and shrugged. "Then we leave in the morning," James said.

Serena laughed. "I know this is technically not my business, but have either of you thought your mother might be busy this week? I'm sure she didn't fall in love just holding hands and talking."

Maurice and James groaned in concert. "That's a visual I don't need," James said.

"Some old man had better not be getting it on with my mother," Maurice exclaimed.

Serena shook her head. "Who said she's with an old man? It's the age of the cougar."

James walked out of the room and Maurice continued eating his cake.

Jade gave Serena a high five and laughed. "I'm going to nurse my husband now," she said. "You know these two don't think their mother is supposed to have a life."

Kenya burped Nairobi and shook her head at Serena. "You don't know what you just started. Mo and James don't think their mother should be having s-e-x."

Maurice dropped his fork. "I'm trying to eat," he said. "If some old or young man is trying to cozy up to my mother, then he needs to meet her sons. We might not hurt him."

"Try not to beat the man up or scare him off," Serena said as she rose from the table. "I'm out of here. Kenya, I hope you will stop by for lunch soon."

"I will."

As Serena walked out the door, her cell phone rang again. She knew if she didn't answer, Emerson would keep calling. And she had to admit she was curious to find out what he wanted. "Yes?" she said when she answered the phone.

"Serena, this is Emerson and we need to talk," he stated in a tone that would've had her running to his side five years ago.

"You have a lot of damned nerve calling me now, Emerson. I guess it didn't cross your mind to make this call five years ago when I was standing at the altar waiting for you," she hissed into the phone as she climbed into her car.

"We should get together and talk," Emerson said.

"I don't think so. I have nothing to say to you. Don't call me again."

"Serena, I'm not going to give up that easily. I know I hurt you, but I want to make up for it. You have to give me a chance to do that."

As much as she wanted to hang up or tell him to go straight to hell, she listened to him go on about how sorry he was.

"I should've been able to come to you and tell you what was going on," he said. "But something stopped me and I have regretted that for the last five years."

"But you didn't. You're years too late for me to give a damn."

"Serena, don't do this. Give me a chance to see you and talk to you face-to-face. I'm in Charlotte. I came here just to see you."

Serena's heart dropped to her feet and she

slammed on the brakes at a green light, causing the cars behind her to blast her with their horns. "You're where?"

"In Charlotte at the Westin Hotel. Can you meet me for a drink? I really want to see you. And Serena, I'm sorry."

Serena pressed the END button and tossed her phone on the floor. *Why is he here? And hell no, I am not going to have a drink with him,* she thought as she took off though the light. Her cell phone rang again and she ignored it, knowing it was Emerson.

She drove to her house trying to pretend the sound of his voice hadn't shaken her to the core. But Serena knew at some point, she'd have to see Emerson if she wanted to move on with her life.

Chapter 15

Antonio and A.J. pulled up to his in-laws' house dressed in matching khaki pants and button-down cotton shirts. Antonio's was white and A.J.'s was green and white. "Now, make sure you don't spill any gravy on Grandma's table-cloth," Antonio told his son as they headed up the steps to the front door. "Remember what happened the last time."

"She cried," A.J. said. "'Cause Mommy made that cloth for her."

Antonio leaned down and kissed the top of his son's head. "Yeah. And we don't want to make Grandma cry." Antonio sighed as he rang the doorbell and waited for the Wallace's butler, Sammy, to open the door.

When Antonio had married Marian, her family wasn't thrilled. They'd believed she was marrying beneath her class. The Wallaces were one of Charlotte's old money families and Antonio Billups was a simple man who had good looks and not much else, at least according to her mother. Mr. Wallace wasn't much easier on Antonio until the two had had a heart-to-heart talk about how much he loved his daughter. Lowell Wallace had told him all he wanted for his daughter was her happiness. If Antonio would make her happy, then he'd bless their union.

Antonio had known Marian was spoiled, but he didn't know she would always put herself first—even after they'd taken vows and had their son. When Marian had decided she wasn't happy anymore she had sought another lover.

Shaking those thoughts out of his head, Antonio nodded to Sammy as he opened the door and greeted him and A.J.

"Everyone is in the dining room, Mr. Billiups," Sammy said.

Antonio placed his hand on the older man's shoulder. "One day, you're going to call me Antonio," he said.

The older man smiled and looked down at A.J. "If you don't mind me saying, he's looking more and more like his mother," Sammy said. "He has her eyes."

"But I have Daddy's smile," A.J. said, and Sammy gave his cheek a soft pinch.

As Antonio and A.J. entered the dining room, he locked eyes with Casey, who was seated near her mother, sipping iced tea. A.J. rushed over to his grandmother and hugged her tightly.

"Glad to see you could make it, Antonio," Casey said as she set her glass on the table and rose to her feet. She moved in front of Antonio and hissed, "I guess you decided to pull yourself out of that woman."

Antonio shook his head and sidestepped Casey to greet his mother-in-law.

"You're looking well, Antonio," Beatrix said as she rubbed her hand across A.J.'s head.

"Did you enjoy Europe?" Antonio asked, just to keep up the small talk.

"Oh, Lowell and I had a wonderful time. That reminds me. A.J., I have some things for you upstairs. Let's get them before dinner, while your grandfather is outside sneaking a cigar."

A.J. crinkled his nose as his grandmother rose to her feet and grasped his hand. "Cigars are nasty."

"Yes, baby, they are," she said. Beatrix looked at Antonio and Casey. "Antonio, you don't share that nasty habit my husband has?"

"No, he has others," Casey mumbled.

Antonio shot her a warning look, then shook his head. "No, ma'am," Antonio replied. Once he and Casey were alone, he glared at her. "What's your problem?"

"I don't have a problem," she said as she returned to the table and poured herself another glass of tea. "Shocking that you didn't bring your tart with you. You two could've gotten it on in the gazebo."

Antonio folded his arms across his chest and shook his head. "Get over it, Casey. I'm seeing Serena and the last time I checked, I was an adult—entitled to do just that."

"I guess Mom and Dad have been right about

you all of these years. How could you go from a classy woman like my sister to that naked whore I found on your back porch?"

"Why do you sound as if you're jealous?" he asked.

Casey's face fell and before she could reply, A.J. ran into the dining room with a huge box. "Look Daddy and Aunt Casey. Look what Grandma gave me."

Casey crossed over to her nephew and looked in the box, which contained a train set. "That's really nice," she said. "You and your daddy are going to have a lot of fun putting this together."

"I know. Hey, Daddy do you think your new friend will help us? Then I can make some more cole slaw," A.J. said excitedly.

Casey slowly rose up and glared at Antonio. "He's met her?"

"I'm not getting into this. We're here to have dinner," Antonio said as he knelt down beside his son and looked at the train set Beatrix had given him. "What do you say we put this in the truck until after dinner?"

"All right,"

Antonio lifted the box and padded out to his truck, ignoring that Sammy would've taken the box for him. He needed to get away from Casey before he said something he would regret.

How would she feel if she knew the truth about her sister and what she'd put him through before her death? Marian had taken their marriage for a joke, as something she could step out of whenever she felt like it. He wasn't going to allow Casey to make him feel guilty about Serena. Closing his eyes, he thought about how being with Serena made him feel as if the outside world stopped and all that mattered was the two of them. He couldn't remember the last time he felt that way with a woman—not even when he and Marian had first gotten married.

As he walked back into the house, Lowell had joined the women at the table and was holding court telling a story about how beautiful Paris was at sunset. "Antonio," he said when he looked up. "You're going to have to let us take A.J. on our next European excursion."

"Yes," Beatrix said. "We can take him to Le Louvre and then a ride on the Venice Simplon-Orient-Express." She hugged A.J. tightly. "It would be so much fun. Your mother would've loved this trip."

Antonio sighed. "We'll have to see," he said. "A.J. and I were planning on going to Disney World before he starts school this year."

Lowell waved his hand as if he was swatting away annoying gnats. "You can do that any time, but a European trip will instill culture and class in the boy."

Antonio clinched his jaw and held his tongue. A.J. turned to his grandfather and said, "But I want to see Mickey Mouse. I don't want to go to the Lover."

Beatrix smiled and said, "Le Louvre. It's a wonderful museum. Your mother and Aunt Casey went there when they were about your age."

A.J. folded his arms and pouted. "I want to see Mickey Mouse."

"Buck up son," Lowell said. "Mickey Mouse isn't going anywhere. You can go to a simple playground anytime."

"Lowell," Antonio said. "If he doesn't want to go, he's not going. Are we going to eat now?"

"What's your hurry, Antonio?" Casey asked as she sat down.

He rolled his eyes at her and sat down on the other side of his son.

"Casey, Antonio probably has to be up early to finish that restaurant project. I read in the Sunday paper that it will be reopening soon with a big party some of the footballers are hosting." Beatrix looked at Antonio. "Do you think you can snag Casey an invitation?"

"Mother, I don't need Antonio to schedule my social life and I don't want to go to one of those so-called celebrity parties," Casey said as Alice, the cook, began bringing dinner into the dining room.

"But, darling," Beatrix said. "You need to socialize more. All you do is work, look after your nephew, and nothing else. Maybe you and I should take a trip to Paris. Then you can work on getting Antonio to agree to let us take A.J. to Europe. Look at us, Marian would be so happy."

Antonio averted his mother-in-law's gaze.

"Bea, let's not get caught up in sentiment," Lowell said as Alice set a prime rib in the center of the table. "It's time to eat."

Antonio had never been happier to get food on his plate. He didn't want to listen to his mother-in-law's revised history of his marriage to her daughter. It seemed Beatrix had forgotten how she'd tried to talk Marian out of marrying him. She'd also forgotten how she'd spent their wedding day crying until her eyes were red because she couldn't believe Marian was going to marry a man like Antonio. Now she wanted to rewrite history and pretend they were a close-knit family. He wished Marian was still around so she could tell her family she was planning to leave. He could take their judgment and disdain, but the act of believing he and Marian were a super happy couple was a bit much for him.

A.J. happily ate prime rib and green peas with pearl onions while Antonio picked at his food.

"Is there something wrong with your meal?" Lowell asked.

"No, sir," Antonio said. "I'm just not that hungry."

"I'll bet," Casey sniped.

Antonio shot Casey a cold look that Beatrix noticed. "What's going on here? You two have been sniping at one another all day. Did you have an argument while we were away?"

"Just a slight disagreement, Mother," Casey said.

"Antonio?" Beatrix asked.

"I don't want to mar this dinner, since you all wanted to spend time with A.J.," he said. "Casey and I are adults. We can work this out."

"I certainly hope so. We're all family here," Lowell said. "All we have left is right around this table."

Casey smiled at Antonio, but beneath her

smile, he could see she was still holding on to her displeasure for him being with Serena.

Dinner ended without any more drama or more talk about the cause of his disagreement with Casey. Lowell and Beatrix showed pictures of the places they'd toured over their three months in Europe. When Antonio saw that A.J. was struggling to stay awake, he bid his in-laws good-bye, lifted his son up from the table, and headed to his truck.

Casey followed him and grabbed his elbow. "Antonio," she said. "I'm sorry."

"Whatever, Casey. I don't understand why you would try to bring any of that up tonight at dinner," he said as he placed A.J. in the truck.

"You're a man and you have needs. You had a free weekend and you took advantage of it. I don't know why I felt like I should judge you."

Antonio shook his head and crossed over to the driver's side of the truck. "You don't get it. I have a right to move on with my life."

"But is she the woman you want to move on with?" Casey asked. "Never mind, do what you want to do."

Antonio shot Casey a wary look and then got into the truck and drove off.

Monday was a day full of surprises for Serena. When she went to the restaurant, there was a bouquet of roses waiting for her. She didn't even look at the card. She knew they were from Antonio. Smiling, she thought about the last time she saw him and how he'd told her she was pretty. That man was melting her in ways she'd vowed she'd never let happen again.

"What's with the grin?" a voice said. Serena turned to her left and saw Kandace standing beside her.

"I thought you were on your honeymoon," she said as she hugged her friend.

"Well, my husband said we couldn't miss the reveal of the restaurant since he feels so bad about what happened here. Then we're finishing our final week of honeymoon bliss in Atlanta," Kandace said with a huge smile on her face.

Serena squeezed her friend's hand. "You look really happy."

"I am and you have a certain glow about you. Anything to do with these flowers?" Kandace asked as she snatched the card from the bouquet. "Who's Emerson?"

"What?" Serena asked as Kandace handed her the card. "I can't believe that asshole had the nerve to send these flowers."

"Who is this *asshole*?" Kandace asked. "What's going on?"

"Nothing," Serena said as she lifted the roses from the bar and dumped them in the trash can. "So, tell me about your honeymoon and where you guys went."

Kandace smacked her friend on the shoulder. "Don't try and change the subject. What's the deal with the flowers?"

Serena shrugged and tried to act casual. "They're from a man I have no interest in who can't take no for an answer," she covered as she stepped behind the bar. "Doesn't this place look great?"

Kandace looked over the marble floors and the red walls with lace borders. "It does look good," she said. "Are you still seeing Antonio or have you gotten rid of him already?"

"Actually," Serena said with a gleam in her eyes, "Antonio will be here to detail all the changes he and his crew made."

Kandace started humming "Wedding March."

Serena shook her head. "You and Jade think everybody is walking down the aisle because you two did it. I am never getting married."

The front door of the restaurant opened and Kandace's husband, Solomon Crawford, strode in as if he owned the place. "You guys finished talking about me, yet?" he joked as he walked over to his wife, pulled her into his arms, and kissed her as if they were the only ones in the world.

"I'm sorry," Serena said when Solomon and Kandace broke their kiss. "Who are you, again?"

He frowned at Serena and shook his head. "I swear, you're going to be nice to me one day . . ."

"And hell will freeze over," Serena said.

Kandace threw her hand up. "Y'all need to stop it. I believe you two are related. Just cocky and mean people."

Solomon pulled Kandace closer to his chest. "You know I'm not mean. Your friend over here is the poster child for mean. I came bearing gifts."

Serena rolled her eyes and laughed. She did like Solomon, despite his playboy reputation. Even with her jaded outlook on love, she knew he only had eyes for his wife. Watching them together would've made another woman believe she could meet her soul mate, too. Just when Serena's thoughts were about to wander to whether Antonio was her soul mate or not, he walked though the door and her breath caught in her chest. "Good morning," she said to him, smiling brightly.

"Morning," he said as he strode over to her and nodded at Solomon and Kandace.

Kandace nudged Solomon and whispered something to him. "Good luck," Solomon murmured as he and Kandace headed to the back office.

Serena lifted her eyebrow, but focused on Antonio's smiling face.

"How was the fish?" Antonio asked.

"It was great. Tell your son I loved the cole slaw," Serena said.

"He'll be glad to hear that. I would've called you last night, but A.J. and I ended up putting his train set together." He held up a Starbucks bag. "I brought you a breakfast treat. Coffee cake."

Serena took the bag and set it on the bar. "I know a better treat than coffee cake." She closed the space between them and brought her lips to his, kissing him slowly, savoring his sweet taste and relishing his hands stroking her back. When they heard the restaurant door open, the duo broke their kiss.

"Well, good morning," Jade said as she and Alicia walked in. "It's good to see you, Mr. Billups."

Alicia smiled as Antonio said, "Good morning, ladies."

"Morning," Alicia said. "Are we early for the tour?"

Serena rolled her eyes at her friend. "I'm surprised you made it here. Are you done trying to prove to everybody you're a success without your family's help?"

"Not by a long shot. That's why I'm back," Alicia said, then turned to Antonio. "Do you know what you're getting into with this evil woman?"

"Evil woman?" Antonio asked. "Serena?"

Alicia nodded. "She drinks the blood of the young. Watch your back."

"I wish I had something to throw at you," Serena said.

Jade linked her arm with Antonio's. "Pay them no attention. They're like the sisters they never wanted. I have to say, I am impressed with what I'm seeing."

"Thank you," Antonio said. "Norman suggested the lace on the walls."

The women looked at the trimming. "This is nice," Jade said as she released Antonio's arm and walked around the dining room. "It doesn't look anything like—" Jade stopped talking when she saw Kandace and Solomon step into the dining room.

"It's all right," Kandace said. "You can talk about what happened."

"Why relive the past? What are you doing here?" Jade asked as she walked over to Kandace and hugged the newlyweds.

"Taking a short break," Solomon said. "We're heading to Atlanta after the festivities are over here."

"Where are you guys staying?" Alicia asked.

"A Loft," Kandace said. "Since there isn't a Crawford Hotel in Charlotte."

"Yet," Solomon said. "But I do know who to call when we start building one. This is some nice work."

"Thank you," Antonio said.

Solomon walked over to him and extended his hand. "I have a resort in Sugar Mountain that is in need of a makeover as well. Give me your card and we can discuss it," Solomon said.

"All right." Antonio reached into his pocket and handed Solomon his business card. "I guess I'll hear from you after your honeymoon ends?"

"The honeymoon will never end," Kandace chimed in. "But this workaholic will be back in the office soon enough."

Solomon pulled his wife against his hip. "As long as you plan to come to work with me," he said in a loud whisper.

"Aww," Serena said. "Aren't you two just sickening."

Antonio laughed with Jade and Alicia as Solomon made a show of kissing his wife.

"Are you guys ready to see the restaurant?" Antonio asked. "As you know, we didn't do anything to the kitchen or the back offices, but the dining room has been revamped. If you like what you've seen so far, be ready to be amazed."

As Antonio spoke, Serena thought about how he had already amazed her and made her think she could have her cake and eat it, too. But when her cell phone vibrated in her pocket, she realized that before she could think about the future, she was going to have to kill the past.

"Guys," Serena said. "I need to take this call. And I might have to step out to talk to the food editor at *Creative Loafing* about the story they're working on."

"All right," Kandace said. "Thanks for doing that. I know that's my area."

Serena dashed out the door and answered the phone. Though it came from an unknown number, she knew it was Emerson.

"Didn't I tell you to stop calling me? What part of that didn't you understand?" she snapped when she answered.

"I was just making sure you received the flowers I sent," Emerson said.

"Yes, they look lovely in my trash can," Serena said. "Here's what you're going to do. Stop sending me roses and stop calling me."

"Serena, we need to talk and I'm not leaving this place until we do. I didn't fly across the country to give up easily," Emerson said. "We have to put behind us what happened in the past."

"Do you think it's that simple?" Serena asked. "What are you here for, my forgiveness? You wasted your airfare. That's something you will never get."

"Why not?" he asked. "Serena, I'm sorry that I

did what—I want to explain everything to you face-to-face."

"No. I don't want to see your damn face," she snapped as she got into her car.

"Then I'm going to keep calling and keep sending flowers. At some point, you're going to have to talk to me."

"Well, let's get it over with. Meet me Wednesday at Starbucks in the Independence Center," she said.

"Where is that?"

"Google it," Serena snapped, then hung up. She drove to her place and stormed inside. She should've just ignored Emerson. Not only had he broken her heart, but she wanted to show him she was doing just fine without his wedding ring. And she wanted to know what was so damned important that he flew to Charlotte from Los Angeles.

Chapter 16

Serena should've known that not showing up at the restaurant after a few hours meant she was going to receive a visit from her girls. So, when the doorbell rang at five after two, she knew who was there.

She opened the door and Kandace, Alicia, and Jade walked in with food from the restaurant, courtesy of the *Devon Harris Show.*

"What's going on?" Alicia asked as they bum-rushed Serena.

"I'm just a little tired," she lied.

"No, you're not," Jade said. "Yesterday, you were happy until your cell phone started ringing."

"And then you tossed out those roses," Kandace said.

Serena shot her a look that meant *you talk too much.*

"Who is Emerson?" Alicia asked as she began unpacking the food.

Serena grabbed Alicia's hand. "Look, ladies, I

appreciate the lunch, but there is no need for your intervention. I'm fine."

Jade rolled her eyes at Serena and headed to the kitchen to get ice and glasses for the fresh brewed tea she'd brought along with her.

"Serena, you're not fine. If you were, you would've come back to the restaurant to flirt with Antonio," Kandace said. "After everything we've been through, we're going to head this problem off before things get out of hand again."

"Don't you think you should be with your husband instead of here?" Serena asked.

"My husband understands that I need to find out what's going on with you," Kandace replied. "Besides, he's meeting with James about some property."

"Great, so I'm stuck with you all for how long?" Serena asked as she pulled her oversized throw pillows from the sofa and placed them around the table. When they were students at Spelman, the four women would get together and lament their love lives with Japanese food and sake. They'd sit on the floor and eat and drink until they felt they'd solved their problems.

Serena didn't have time for that kind of sentiment today. "Guys, please, I have some things I need to take care of, so can we just eat?"

"No," Alicia said. "You're going to tell us what's going on."

Serena sighed as she watched Kandace pile her plate with jasmine rice and green peas. She'd never told her friends about her life in L.A.

After graduation, they'd all tried to live their

dreams. Kandace had gone off to graduate school in Wisconsin, Alicia and Jade had stayed in Atlanta. Alicia took an internship with an event planning company. Jade became a CPA and fell in love with the wrong man. Serena had gone to L.A.

When Jade returned to the living room with a tray of glasses, Serena knew she had to come clean. She sat down and looked at her friends as they focused on her. "Well," Serena began. "Emerson Bradford is a movie director. We met in L.A."

"Wait," Alicia said. "The Emerson Bradford who was hot stuff a few years back? What was the name of that movie?"

"Umm, it was done around the time of *Love Jones* and *The Best Man*," Jade interjected.

"Something about Summer," Kandace chimed in. "*Hot Summer* or something like that."

"*Sultry Summer,*" Serena said.

Jade slapped her hand against her thigh. "That's right. You would not go see that movie with us."

"No. Why would I want to put money into the pocket of the man who left me at the altar?" Serena said, then popped a piece of mushroom in her mouth. While she chewed, her friends stared at her with their mouths agape.

"Altar?" Kandace said.

"Left?" Alicia inquired.

"Married? You were going to get married and you never told us?" Jade questioned.

"Or invited us," Kandace added.

"And you never thought to tell us the sorry son of a bitch left you at the altar?" Alicia snapped.

Serena nodded. "Listen, when I went to L.A., I had one goal. I wanted to get my screenplay on the big screen, then come back to Atlanta and give a chance to the young writers I'd met in college—get some quality black films out there."

Alicia nodded. "That's what you said about why you went to Los Angeles, but I thought you were going to be a star."

"That too," Serena said. "I had been taking a writing class and at the end of one of my sessions, Emerson showed up with this slick talk about him wanting to put me in front of the camera."

"So, he was scamming you?" Jade asked.

"And you fell for it?" Alicia asked. "That—"

Serena held up her hands. "I didn't fall for anything. Emerson was who he said he was. He opened a few doors for me, we made a film, and I fell head over heels in love with him."

Again, three mouths dropped as they heard words from Serena none of them ever expected to hear.

"L-love?" Kandace asked. "You?"

Serena picked up another mushroom and popped it in her mouth.

Jade shook her head. "Why didn't you ever tell us this?"

Serena shrugged her shoulders. "What was the point? When I came back to Atlanta, it didn't seem important. But now, he's back."

"What the hell is he back for?" Alicia asked. "I

mean, he broke your heart, obviously made you a bitter woman and distrustful of all men—"

"That's a bit much," Serena chimed in.

"Whatever," Jade said. "When you came back to Atlanta five years ago, you were different and bitter."

"Well, Jade, how did you feel when you saw Stephen in the paper with that Barbie doll?"

Jade rolled her eyes. "But you guys were there for me and we would've been there for you."

"Where is this bastard?" Kandace asked. "We can roll over there now and do what should've been done five years ago."

"There's no need for that," Serena said. "I just want him to leave."

"Do you know why he's here?" Jade asked.

"No and I don't give a damn," Serena replied hotly.

Jade, Alicia and Kandace exchanged knowing looks.

Serena glared at them. "I know what y'all are thinking and you're wrong."

"What?" Alicia asked.

"Serena, you're not going to be at peace until you find out what he wants," Jade said. "You don't have to see the bastard alone."

Serena plucked a piece of bread from the middle of the table. "I do have to handle this alone. He's not dangerous, so this isn't another Carmen situation."

Kandace rolled her eyes. "Can we not mention that name?"

"Yes," Jade said. "Let's focus on Emerson."

"There's nothing to focus on," Serena said. "Why would he come back now after all this time?"

"I say find out and cuss him out. Then maybe you can be nicer to Antonio," Alicia said.

Jade and Kandace laughed. "Oh," Jade said. "She's plenty nice to Antonio."

Serena tossed her half-eaten roll at Jade. "Shut up."

"You should've seen them kissing earlier," Kandace said. "Wait a minute, when your phone rang at the restaurant; that was Emerson and not a reporter, wasn't it?"

"Yes, that was him," she answered. While the women ate in silence for a few minutes, Serena wondered what she'd feel if she saw Emerson? Would old feelings resurface? Would she fly into a fit of rage?

"Serena?" Jade asked.

"What?"

"I said, what are you going to do about this guy?"

"The only thing I can do. Confront him, and move on with my life."

"And does that include Antonio?" Kandace asked.

"We'll just have to see," Serena replied. "Now, can we eat so you all can get out of here and I can get some work done?"

Emerson walked down to the bar in the Westin Hotel and ordered a scotch and soda. He found Charlotte boring as hell and wanted to see

Serena sooner rather than later. He turned his back to the bar after the bartender handed him his drink and watched the people as they milled around, with drinks in their hands and newspapers underneath their arms.

It was nothing like Los Angeles where sitting in a bar meant watching some of the town's most beautiful people. *Charlotte is very average,* Emerson thought as he sipped his scotch. Then he saw her walk across the bar and to his surprise, she took a seat beside him. Emerson glanced at her. She was curvy in all the right places and had steller legs he wanted to feel wrapped around his waist. He could see her in a movie, or at least in his bed for the night.

"Hello there," he said to her.

She turned to him and smiled. "Hi."

Emerson extended his hand to her. "I'm Emerson."

"Casey," she replied.

"What are you drinking?" he asked. "I'm willing to buy if you tell why you're looking so sad."

Casey rolled her eyes, then smiled. "Am I that transparent?"

Emerson held his index finger a couple of inches above his thumb. "Just a little bit."

"I'm just upset by something I found out this weekend," she said. "And there doesn't seem to be anything I can do about it."

"Cheating lover?" Emerson probed.

"No," she said as the bartender walked over to the bar.

"What are you having, Miss Casey?" he asked.

Emerson looked from Casey to the bartender.

Was she one of those women who hung around in hotel bars looking to catch a business man to take care of her? Then Emerson noticed her $5,000 Birkin bag. Since he wasn't in Nevada, he figured she wasn't a hooker.

"I want an apple martini," she replied. "And why don't you give my friend a refill on whatever he's drinking."

"Scotch and an apple martini coming right up," he said.

Emerson turned to Casey and smiled.

"I buy my own drinks," she said. "And because you seem like a nice guy, I'm going to buy you one, too."

Emerson nodded. Maybe he was wrong about Charlotte. *I have to focus,* he thought. *Casey can be fun later but first I have to get Serena to sign the release form.*

The bartender set their drinks in front of them and turned to his other customers.

"Cheers," Emerson said as he tilted his drink to Casey. She tilted her drink back to him and then took a big sip.

"Is it really that bad?" he asked.

Casey smirked and grabbed a handful of nuts from the basket on the bar. She shook them in her hand. "Kind of. Have you ever watched someone walking into a snake pit, but when you try to stop them, they make it seem as if you're the one with the problem?"

"You have to allow people to make their own mistakes. How do you know this person doesn't like snake bites?"

"Because I know this person can do so much better," Casey said as she gritted her teeth.

"Better as in you?" he asked, starting to lose interest in talking to a woman hung up on another man.

"I just know that a woman who lays around a man's house naked isn't someone worthy of anything more than a booty call."

Emerson took another sip of scotch. "Why not show him that you don't care? Men hate to see women we've taken for granted happy with someone else."

"I don't think Antonio would care if I walked into the next family gathering with Denzel Washington," she said, then drained her drink.

"Well, Antonio is a fool."

"Great observation." Casey gave Emerson a cool once over. "You're not from Charlotte, are you?"

"Not at all. I'm visiting from Los Angeles. I have some business here."

"Banker?"

"No. I'm a filmmaker. If we were in L.A., I'd probably try and talk you into a screen test." Emerson finished his drink.

Casey laughed. "I'm guessing that line works better in L.A."

"Touché. But since I'm not doing anything tonight, what do you say you give me a tour of your fair city?" he suggested.

"All right. Since I picked up the tab for the drinks, why don't you buy me dinner at Hometown Delights?"

At the mention of Serena's restaurant, Emerson smiled widely. "I've been meaning to go there."

"Then let's do it. I wouldn't be surprised if Antonio is there."

"And why would he be there? Is the food that good?"

"The food is probably the last thing on his mind, but that's a story for another day." Casey reached into her purse and pulled out her credit card to pay for the drinks. "So, tell me about your films. Are you an artsy guy or a Spike Lee type?"

"I'm an Emerson Bradford type," he said with a smirk. "Have you ever seen *Sultry Summer*?"

"Oh my goodness. I love that movie."

"I wrote and directed it," he replied proudly.

"Wow! But what are you doing in Charlotte? This is as far away from Hollywood as you can get."

"Well, I have a new project I want to release, but I have to get my star to sign off on it."

"She's here in Charlotte?" Casey asked. "I can't see why she'd have a problem with you making her a star. Everybody in Charlotte wants to rise above the skyline and this star of yours can't be much different."

"That's a movie in itself," Emerson said as he stood up and held out his hand to Casey.

She placed her hand in his palm and looked him in the eye. "What's this movie about?"

"A sexy serial killer who uses her body to get what she wants and to hide her murders. It's like nothing anyone has ever seen—a smart and erotic thriller." Emerson's eyes glossed over as he thought about how close he and Serena had been when they made that movie. How sweet she'd tasted after he watched her do those things on screen all day. Looking at Casey, Emerson had a brain storm. What if the public demanded to see the movie? If he built a buzz, leaked pieces of the film on the Internet and got people talking, the studio would put the film on the big screen and it wouldn't matter if Serena signed off on the film or not.

"Are you ready for dinner?" he asked.

"Yes," Casey replied and they headed out the door.

Serena walked into the dining room of Hometown Delights just to make sure she hadn't been seeing things. Yes, the restaurant was full and there were people willing to wait an hour for a table. Alicia's idea for a soft launch of the restaurant reopening was paying off. Serena didn't expect the crowd to return so quickly, though. However, she couldn't be happier. Well, she could've been happier if she and Antonio were lying naked across her bed.

Smiling, she wiped down the bar. She couldn't wait until they hired a bartender so she could stop spending her evenings working. The bar was full because people were nosy, Serena surmised. They wanted to see if there were any signs of the horror that had happened at the restaurant. As she handed a patron a three-dollar draft, she wondered if Antonio was at home. *Maybe I should call him and see if he would like some dessert,* she thought as she remembered the special chocolate cake Devon had made to celebrate the reopening.

"Hey there, hot lips," a man said, interrupting her thoughts. "How are you doing tonight?" He eased onto a stool and smiled at Serena.

She pretended not to notice the tan ring of flesh on the ring finger of his left hand. Since she was bored, Serena decided to indulge her portly customer. "What can I get for you, sweetheart?" She leaned over the bar and offered him a seductive grin.

"Your phone number for starters and a gin and tonic with a twist of lime."

"I can get you the drink, but no on the phone number unless you can get your wife to join in," she said as she stroked his ring finger.

The man laughed and dropped his hand in his lap.

Serena fixed his drink and as she put it in front of him, she saw Emerson walk in the restaurant with Antonio's sister-in-law, Casey. "What in the hell?" she mumbled.

"You say something, baby?" the man asked.

Serena focused on the customer, hoping Emerson wouldn't see her—or that she was mistaken he'd walked into the restaurant. "Seven-fifty," Serena said. "Do you want to start a tab?"

"What time do you get off?" he asked with a wide smile.

"In about ten minutes," she said, glancing over his shoulder, watching the hostess seat Emerson and Casey.

"Then, I'll just pay for this and watch you until you go home."

Serena took the man's money and stood at the register where she had a clear view of Emerson and Casey. *I have to get out of here,* she thought as she rang up the drink. Profits be damned, she wasn't going to spend another minute in Emerson's presence.

As she was about to shut down the bar, she and Emerson locked eyes. A feeling rushed through her system that caught her off guard. Seeing him after all of those years stirred old emotions that had been long buried. Then there was anger. What the hell was he doing in her restaurant?

She broke the eye contact and snatched her apron off. Stalking from behind the bar she headed to the office. She paced back and forth, wondering if she should say something to him, but quickly decided against it. What she wanted to say to Emerson would do nothing but cause a scene and that was the last thing that needed to happen. Especially in front of Casey.

"Why is he with her?" she whispered as she picked up the phone to call Alicia.

"Hello, Serena," Emerson said from the doorway of the office.

She dropped the phone and glared at him. "Customers aren't allowed back here," she snapped. "And when I find out who allowed you back here, they're going to be fired."

"That's not nice," he said as he crossed over to her and stopped in front of the desk.

"Emerson, what the hell do you want?" she

said, struggling to keep her voice underneath a scream.

"Tonight, I just want to say hello. Are we still meeting this week?"

She glared at him. Memories of kissing him and making love to him fought with the fantasies she'd had over the last five years about killing him, pushing him over a high cliff, and watching his body fall to a rocky death.

"Don't you have a date to return to? I have work to do. Get out of my office," Serena said. Her voice was cold, despite the heated anger flowing inside her.

"All right," he said as he turned to leave. "It was really good to see you. You look great as usual."

"You should have seen me on my wedding day, you son of bitch," she snapped as she stomped from behind the desk and slammed the door behind him.

Chapter 17

Antonio tucked A.J. into bed and kissed his sleeping son on the forehead. Since he was finished with his work on the restaurant, he'd been able to spend the day with his son. They'd started their day with a pancake and banana breakfast, then headed to the Aquatic Center to play in the pool for a few hours.

After swimming, A.J. and Antonio headed to Fuel Pizza and talked about the upcoming school year. A.J. was excited about starting First Ward Elementary School in the fall.

"Are we still going to see Mickey Mouse?" A.J. had asked as he and his father shared a cheese pizza.

"Sure," Antonio had replied. "We can go next month."

"I wish Mommy was here to go with us. She liked Mickey Mouse too, didn't she?"

Antonio had nodded and wished he had fonder memories of his wife. Looking down at his son, he knew he would have to keep his negative thoughts about Marian hidden. She'd loved her son and that's all A.J. needed to know about his mom.

He quietly walked out of A.J.'s room and headed into the den to catch *SportsCenter*. As he sat on the sofa, his mind turned to Serena. Antonio silently admitted he was very taken with the sultry woman. She was seductive and sweet and if he had his way, he'd be with her every minute of the day. But was that what she wanted? Could they have more than sizzling sex between the sheets? Could they develop something meaningful?

Antonio sincerely hoped so. Glancing at the clock, he decided to call her before it got too late.

"Hello?" Serena seemingly sang when she answered the phone.

"Good evening, beautiful," he said.

"Hi, Antonio."

"How was your day?"

"A little long. We need a bartender and until we get one, I'm moonlighting. You should let me make you a drink one night."

"How about tonight?" he asked.

"Where's your son?"

"Upstairs, asleep. You can come over if you aren't too tired."

"I think I will. Do you have a blender? I can bring the ingredients for my Serena punch," she said with a hint of laughter in her voice.

"Sounds good to me."

"Then I'll see you in about twenty minutes," Serena said.

When they hung up the phone, Antonio excitedly began counting down the minutes until Serena would arrive.

Emerson sat in silence as Casey ate. His mind went back to the desire he'd felt when he saw Serena standing behind that desk. Her body was more sensual than he remembered, despite the fact that she was fully dressed. The way her blouse hugged her breasts gave him an erection he wanted to bury deep inside her just like he'd done so many times when they were together in Los Angeles.

And those lips. Thick, pouty and luscious. He wanted to kiss her and see if she still had the same sweet taste he used to crave. *That's not why you're here,* he thought as he toyed with the green beans on his plate.

"Is something wrong with the food?" Casey asked, breaking into his thoughts. He looked at her, remembering for the first time since he saw Serena that Casey was there.

"No, I think I'm full. I hope you don't mind if I take off early," he said.

"Did something happen when you went to the bathroom?" Casey asked as she dropped her fork.

"No, just jet lag. The time difference is catching up with me." He stood up and placed the money for dinner on the table. "I'm going to call a cab and head back to the hotel. Why don't we get together tomorrow afternoon for lunch?"

Casey raised her right eyebrow and scowled at

him. "I don't think so," she said tersely. "Have a good night." Casey rose from her seat and stormed out of the restaurant.

Emerson walked over to the hostess and asked her to phone for a cab. As he waited for the car to show up, he thought about Serena and wondered if he should've pressed her to sign the release and then focus the rest of his time in Charlotte on her seduction. He knew she still wanted him and the anger he'd seen on her face had only been a mask.

It had been five years since they'd seen each other, but Emerson was sure he could still read her. Just as he read her the first day they'd met. She didn't belong in that restaurant. He was still going to make her a star.

As she drove to Antonio's house, Serena thought of Emerson Bradford. Seeing him made her realize she did have some unfinished business with him. She needed to slap him with the fury she'd been holding back for five years. "He has a damned nerve, smug bastard," she cursed as she pulled up to a stop light. When her phone rang, Serena prayed that it wasn't Emerson.

"What?" she asked when she answered the phone.

"That's some way to answer the phone," Jade said. "Is that guy calling you again?"

"No, he's just showing up at the restaurant," Serena said. "I shut the bar down and went to the office. He had the nerve to come back there."

"Did you kick him in the family jewels?" Jade asked.

"No. The last thing we need is more bad press, so I just left," Serena said.

"Are you all right?" Jade asked. "It has to be hard to see him. Did he give you any clue as to what he wants?"

"No, and I don't give a damn. Since he likes to leave people hanging, I'm not going to show up at Starbucks. Let him sit there and stew."

"Where are you now? James said he passed the restaurant and it was closed."

Serena smiled despite herself. "I'm going to see Antonio."

"Really?" Jade said. "Let me guess. You're dressed in something short for easy access. I hope his little boy isn't going to answer the door."

"Oh, shut up, Jade." Serena glanced at the clock on her radio. "I'm sure his son is sound asleep by now."

"Serena, are you going to admit that you really like this guy?"

"Good-bye, Jade. Go do something with your husband and your son," she said, then clicked the phone off as she pulled into Antonio's driveway.

Serena got out of the car and grabbed her bag filled with coconut rum, pineapple juice, limes, and lemons. She was sure Antonio had ice for her treat. She looked up at the front porch and saw him standing there dressed in a pair of basketball shorts and a white tank top that highlighted his smooth brown skin and displayed his rippling muscles. Her breath caught in her chest as she recalled how she felt with those strong arms wrapped around her. Walking toward him, Serena felt a throbbing between her thighs she couldn't wait for Antonio to tame.

"Hello, beautiful," he said as he walked down the steps and met her.

"Hi," Serena replied with a smile and handed him her tote bag.

Antonio gently set the bag on the porch, then wrapped his arms around her. In a quick motion, he captured her lips, kissing her with an intense passion that made her swoon. He held her tighter.

Serena moaned, thinking how much she needed that kiss, his touch, and his heat.

Antonio pulled back and licked his lips. "I've been thinking about doing that all day," he whispered.

"What else has been on your mind?" she said with a wicked gleam in her eye.

He led her into the house. When he closed the door he slipped his hand between her thighs and stroked her gently. "Let's just say, I'd rather show than tell," he said as he placed her hand on his thick erection.

"And I thought I was going to have to get all liquored up before I could take advantage of you," Serena quipped.

"Never that." Pressing her against the wall he kissed her again, hot, wet, and filled with passion.

She ran her hand across his chest as his lips danced down her neck. He pulled back and watched as she unbuttoned her blouse, revealing another lacy piece of lingerie—gold with black lace accenting it. She shrugged her shoulders to allow her shirt to fall down.

Antonio helped her out of her mini skirt and released an appreciative sigh as she stood in black strappy sandals and that gold and black teddy. He couldn't wait to peel it off her body and kiss every inch the sexy garment covered. "Just one question," he whispered. "Are you always this sexy?"

"Only for you," she replied, then pressed her body against his and licked his lips.

He shuddered with desire. Lifting her up in his arms he headed to the back porch. Being outside with her was thrilling and added to their passion. As their lips met the world seemed to melt away, the earth stood still, and the only thing that mattered was the taste of her lips and the feel of his arms around her body.

Antonio laid Serena on the wicker sofa and covered her lithe body with his. She flicked her tongue across his neck and he shivered. Serena tugged at his shorts, wanting him deep inside her, but Antonio took her wrists in his hands and lifted her arms above her head.

"Remember those thoughts, I was telling you about? I'm about to show you one of them," he said as he unsnapped the crotch of her teddy and buried his lips in her wet folds of flesh.

Serena moaned in delight as his tongue brushed across her tingling bud. She balanced her leg on his shoulder and stroked the back of his neck as he licked and sucked her until she felt as if she was about to explode. She threw her head back as he alternated teasing her clitoris with his tongue and his finger. "Antonio," she moaned, "Antonio." Her body began to twitch as her orgasm gripped her senses and sent spasms of pleasure throughout her body.

Antonio pulled back and watched her chest rise and fall. "Are you all right?" he asked as he stroked her cheek.

"More than all right," she replied in a husky voice. She grabbed his hand and kissed his palm. "So, what other thoughts have you had today?"

Antonio stood up and smiled at her. "When I get back, I'll show you even more."

She smiled as she watched him dash inside. Then her mind flashed back to his crazy sister-in-law finding her outside naked the other week. Grabbing the blanket from the back of the sofa she wrapped up in it. The next thing she knew, she was sleeping.

Antonio walked into his bedroom, grabbed a few condoms, then headed down the hall and looked in on A.J. His little boy was sleeping soundly, but had kicked out from underneath his blanket, something he'd been doing since he was a baby. Antonio pulled the blanket around him, then kissed him on the forehead. The little boy stirred slightly but didn't wake up.

Slipping quietly out of his son's room he headed back outside to Serena. Wrapped in the blanket she looked like an angel as she slept. He lifted her into his arms and took her into the house. As soon as he laid her against the soft cotton sheets of his king sized bed, Serena's eyes fluttered open.

"What's going on?" she mumbled.

"You went to sleep. It's obvious you're tired. Go ahead and rest," he said as he eased into bed beside her. "I'll be right here when you wake up."

She snuggled against him and Antonio fingered her silky hair. It wasn't long before they were sound asleep.

As the sun began to peek over the horizon, Serena stirred in Antonio's arms. Had they simply slept all night? Yes, and she felt so good waking up in his arms. She ran her finger down his arm. So, maybe Jade was right. She did like Antonio. She liked him a lot and she was scared as hell because this was the time when things went bad. What if Antonio only wanted sex?

That's not even the case. If it was, he wouldn't have allowed you to sleep last night. Stop being an idiot. He's not Emerson and you don't have worry about him walking out on you, she thought as she watched him sleep.

Antonio woke up and smiled when he saw Serena watching him. "Morning," he said.

"I'm sorry I went to sleep on you last night."

"It happens to the best of us. I figured you needed your rest."

Serena rolled over on top of him and straddled his body. "Well, now that I've had my rest, what are you going to do about it?" She ground against him and he was instantly aroused.

Antonio gripped her hips, resisting the urge to dive into her wetness without protection. He slipped his hand underneath his pillow and retrieved one of the condoms he'd placed there last night. Serena took the package from his hand and eased down his body.

"One thing I want to do before we strap up," she said as she hovered over his erection.

Antonio's body tingled with anticipation as he felt the heat from her breath across the tip of his penis. When Serena took him into her mouth, he struggled not to come immediately. Her mouth was so hot and wet and when her tongue danced up and down the length of him, he groaned in pleasure. She took him to the brink and just as Antonio felt as if he couldn't hold back any more, Serena ended her sweet torture and rolled the condom in place. He pulled her hips forward and eased into the wetness between her thighs.

"Yes," he moaned as she rode him slowly, grinding and twisting her body in a sensual dance that sent waves of pleasure thoughout his body. But the greatest pleasure he received was watching the satisfied look on Serena's face. She was feeling as good as he was and that was all he wanted. He wanted to please her just like she was pleasing him.

Antonio gripped her hips as the explosion built inside him. Serena arched her back giving him deeper access to her desire. He released himself and she collapsed against his chest as she reached her own climax. "Amazing," she whispered.

"That's one way to describe it," Antonio said as he kissed her cheek. "I can't get enough of you, baby."

"Me either," she said as she snuggled against him.

"As much as I wish we could just lie here naked, we'd better put some clothes on before A.J. wakes up."

"Well, that's easier for you than me since my clothes are downstairs," she said as she pulled the sheet around her body.

Antonio pulled on his boxers and nodded. "I'll go get them for you," he said, then headed out the door.

While she lay in the bed, Serena looked around Antonio's bedroom, realizing that was the first time she'd been in his bed. She was struck by the fact that there didn't seem to be a trace of his dead wife in the room, which was decorated in deep earth tones, giving it a decidedly masculine feel. On his dresser, she half expected to see a picture of him and his wife, but there wasn't one—just a few bottles of cologne and deodorant. Was he truly over his wife? Her mind wandered to what they'd meant to each other. What if she was his one true love?

Why does it even matter? I'm not trying to slip into those shoes, Serena thought. But she was trying to downplay the fact that her feelings for Antonio were growing into something bigger than sex. She did want more from him, but she was afraid she'd find herself on the wrong side of love again.

As much as she wanted to forget that Emerson Bradford was in Charlotte, his image crept into her mind as she waited for Antonio. She had to find out what Emerson wanted, and get rid of him and the ghost of his heartbreak if she was to ever be able to truly open up to Antonio.

The bedroom door opened and Antonio walked in with her clothes and purse. "Here you go," he said as he crossed over to her and handed her the items. "I think you've missed some calls because your purse was beeping. Since my son might get up and head for the TV, I put your bag with the drinks in it underneath the sink."

"Good thinking," she said as she put her blouse on. Antonio climbed into the bed with her and pulled her against his chest.

"But, when I looked in on the little boy, he was still sound asleep," Antonio said. "So, don't button that up just yet." As he was about to bring his lips to hers, Serena's cell phone sounded.

"Damn it," she muttered.

"Ignore it," Antonio intoned as he stroked the tops of her breasts.

Moaning, she was poised to ignore the phone when a small voice called out.

"Daddy."

"That you can't ignore," she said.

Antonio hopped off the bed and headed down the hall to his son's bedroom. While he was gone, Serena grabbed her phone and looked at the missed calls log. There were six, all from an unknown number, but she knew who the caller was.

Emerson.

Emerson glanced at his cell phone. It was after seven and he still hadn't been able to reach

Serena. He figured she wasn't at the restaurant since she'd been there the night before. Sure, she could be sleeping, but he remembered she woke up at the same time every morning, despite what she'd done the night before. That's why he'd loved working with her on the set. She had been a professional, unlike some of the other actresses he'd worked with. But there was more that he missed about her. Seeing her had fired up emotions he'd tried to bury with their film.

Damn, she was still as sexy as he remembered. His dreams had been tortured with memories and fantasies of Serena. The feel of her supple body against his and the sweet taste of her lips kept him tossing and turning all night.

Focus, he thought. *She needs to sign the release. Anything else that happens is gravy. I can't let lust get in the way again. But hot damn she looked so good. Knowing Serena the way I do, she's never going to love anyone the way she loved me.*

He dialed her number again.

"Stop calling me," she snapped after picking up on the first ring.

"Serena, we need to talk."

"No, we don't," she replied.

"Yes, we do. Serena?" When he didn't get a response, he moved the phone from his ear and saw that she'd hung up on him. He started to call her back, but decided he needed to see her in person. The only way he could do that would be to wait her out at her restaurant. From the tone of her voice, he figured she wouldn't show up to their scheduled meeting.

Chapter 18

Serena smiled as A.J. set her plate of turkey bacon, eggs, and banana pancakes in front of her like a perfect gentleman.

"Thank you, A.J.," she said.

"You're welcome," he replied with a smile as he pulled up a chair beside her at the dining room table. "Did you and my daddy have a sleepover?"

"A.J.," Antonio called out from the kitchen. "Eat."

"Yes, sir," he replied, then cut into his pancakes with the side of his fork. Before stuffing a huge piece of food into his mouth, he turned to Serena and whispered. "Well, did you?"

"Yes," she whispered back.

A.J. smiled, then packed his mouth with food. After chewing, he asked Serena, "Are you going to sleep over more? Maybe next time we can all watch a movie instead of just you and Daddy."

Antonio walked into the dining room with his

plate and shook his head. "A.J., please allow Miss Serena to eat before her food gets cold."

"Yes, sir."

"He's fine," she said. "And a sweet little boy, too."

A.J. beamed at her compliment and ate his food in silence. When A.J. finished his breakfast, he took his plate into the kitchen, then asked if he and Serena could watch cartoons. She looked down at her half-empty plate.

"She hasn't finished eating yet," Antonio said, trying to hide his smile. "And you know the rules. No one leaves the table until they're finished eating."

Serena nodded. "I have to follow the rules, but you find some SpongeBob and I'll come watch it with you as soon as I'm finished."

"Okay," A.J. said excitedly, then dashed into the den to turn on the TV.

Antonio turned to Serena. "Somebody likes you," he said with a smile.

"He's a nice kid."

"He doesn't usually take to strangers. Then again, he's never seen me have a sleepover. I'm sorry he asked you all those questions."

"There's no need to apologize. He's a curious kid. I can't tell you how many times I had this same conversation with my dad and his women," she said, then cringed.

"I remember you telling me about that."

She nodded. "Yeah. Breakfasts like this were a common occurrence with Dominic and his women. Only, they didn't know they were just spokes in a wheel."

"Well, that's not how I do things around here," Antonio said. "To be honest, I haven't had a *sleepover*, ever."

Serena shot him a look that said *yeah, right.*

Noting the look on her face, Antonio leaned over and placed his hand on top of hers. "I'm serious. When my wife died, A.J. became my focus. The last thing I wanted or needed was some woman coming into my life trying to be A.J.'s mother."

"So, you still love your wife? Do you think anyone will ever mean as much to you as she did?" she asked. *Where the hell did that come from?*

"That's a topic for a day when A.J. isn't within earshot. But I will say this. I don't go to sleep with ghosts at night," he said, then took his plate into the kitchen.

Serena wondered if there was more behind what he said. Why did she care? *Because you care about this man,* Jade's voice whispered in her ear. Serena picked up her plate and followed Antonio into the kitchen.

"Listen," she said as she met him at the sink. "I wasn't trying to suggest that you parade women around your son. Whatever you do really isn't my business."

"What do you mean it isn't your business?" he asked as he turned around and looked at her. "Here's what you need to understand about me. I don't sleep around, I don't play with people's emotions, and I want you to know what I do. You're a part of my life now."

"Antonio," she said.

He stroked her cheek. "Serena, life is too short for me to beat around the bush. As much as I enjoy making love to you, I want more than that."

She wanted more as well. It was on the tip of her tongue to tell him but she just looked at him, afraid. She didn't want another heartbreak.

"Miss Serena, I found SpongeBob," A.J. called out.

Glad for the chance to walk away, she nearly sprinted into the den to watch cartoons with A.J.

Way to be an adult, hiding behind SpongeBob, she thought as she took a seat on the sofa and smiled at a beaming A.J.

Antonio washed dishes and thought about the look in Serena's eyes when he told her he wanted more. Was it fear? Was it disinterest? He'd spent his time with a woman who didn't want to be with him and he was not going to do it again. Still, he needed a better feel of what Serena was really thinking. If she didn't want to be with him, he knew Serena wouldn't have a problem saying so. If she was interested in a physical relationship only, why was she in the den laughing with his son?

Drying his hands, Antonio decided he'd give her a little time to determine what she wanted, but he knew exactly what he wanted. He was falling hard and fast for Serena Jacobs.

"Antonio," she said as she walked into the kitchen.

"What's up?" he asked as he turned around and faced her.

She sighed and walked over to him. "I can sometimes be a bit of a punk. I can say just about anything I want to say except for how I feel about things some—most—of the time. I want more," she said. "I like being with you in and out of the bed."

"I'm glad to hear that. I don't want you to be afraid to open up to me. I want to know everything about you, what makes you happy, your fears, your joys. I plan to share the same things with you."

Serena hugged him tightly. "I'm going to work on sharing everything with you. But I have to tell you that I'm carrying some serious scars."

"Then let's get together later tonight and compare wounds. Because we have company right now."

Serena turned around and saw A.J. standing in the doorway of the kitchen. "May I have some juice?" he asked with a smile.

"Sure," Antonio said. "There is a juice box in the refrigerator."

"Miss Serena, would you like some juice, too?"

"No, thank you, A.J. I'd rather have some coffee."

Antonio handed her a mug and pointed her to the coffee maker. "I know you can make coffee."

"What self-respecting, moonlighting bartender can't make coffee?" she asked as she pulled out the coffee filters.

A.J. took his juice box into the living room and Antonio turned to Serena with a smile on his face. "I want you to know that A.J. doesn't share his juice, so you've obviously impressed him."

"Good," she said as she waited for the coffee carafe to fill. "Because I want to finish watching SpongeBob with him."

Antonio laughed, happily surprised Serena was interested in spending time with his son.

After fixing coffee for herself and Antonio, they headed into the living room and laughed at the antics of SpongeBob with A.J. until mid-afternoon when Serena had to leave and head into the restaurant.

"Bye, Miss Serena," A.J. said from the door as Antonio walked her outside.

"Bye A.J.," she replied and blew him a kiss.

At her car, Antonio wrapped his arms around Serena's neck and brought her against his chest. "This was nice," he said.

"It was," she said as she stroked his back.

"What are you doing after work? You still owe me that drink," he said, flashing her a slick smile.

"Well, I think I can make that happen, but keep in mind, the Serena punch is powerful."

Antonio winked at her. "I can handle it. I'd better let you go," he said as he dropped his arms from around her.

"Yeah," she said, but neither one of them made an effort to move. "Jade, Alicia, and Kandace are waiting."

"Duty calls."

She stood on her tiptoes and kissed his lips. "I just don't want to answer."

Antonio cupped her booty and smiled. "I don't want you to either, but I have some calls I need to make for a project we're starting next week."

Sighing, Serena let him go and unlocked her car. "All right, we're going to be adults and go to work. I'll see you later."

When she got in her car and backed out of the driveway, Antonio could do nothing but smile. He headed inside and saw A.J. had been watching him and Serena.

"Daddy," the little boy said, "is Miss Serena our girlfriend?"

"Our girlfriend?" Antonio asked with a smile.

"Well, I like her too," he said.

"She's our friend, but possibly my girlfriend," Antonio said, then scooped his son up into his arms. "Listen, are you okay with Miss Serena spending more time with us?"

"I guess," A.J. said with a shoulder shrug. "She likes SpongeBob and she doesn't want to drink all my juice."

"Right," Antonio replied. "There may be more sleepovers, but know that you're still the most important person in my world."

"Do you think Mommy would like her?" A.J. asked innocently.

"I don't know. It's just important to me that you like her."

"I like her," A.J. said. "She makes you smile."

Antonio tussled his son's hair and sat him

on the sofa. "What do you say we go to the lake in University City after I take care of some business?"

"Okay," A.J. said excitedly. Antonio headed to his home office to get some work done, but all he could think about was Serena and how easy things were between them. He was happy for the first time in a long time.

Chapter 19

As Serena sat in the office of the restaurant with Jade, Alicia, and Kandace, the smile on her face spoke volumes to everyone. Though they were supposed to be meeting about the relaunch event, the topic of conversation quickly turned to Serena.

"Your smile is creeping me out," Alicia said when she looked over at Serena.

"What?" Serena said, the smile not leaving her face.

"This new and improved Serena is a bit much to take," Alicia said. "But I don't have to ask why you're so happy."

"That's all Antonio Billups's doing," Jade said knowingly. "I know this has to do with more than just good sex."

Kandace grinned. "Yep. That's the same look Solomon had when we woke up this morning."

Serena rolled her eyes. "Okay, Antonio and I are together and we're very happy."

"What about his son?" Jade asked.

"He's a sweet little boy. He even offered me a juice box this morning. For a little kid, that says a lot."

Kandace turned to Serena and asked, "Wedding bells?"

"See, I knew you guys were going to take things too far. Antonio and I are not close to getting married. We're just enjoying being around each other."

"I never thought I'd see the day," Alicia said, beaming. "The Ice Queen has melted."

Serena tossed a pencil at her friend. "I was never the Ice Queen," she snapped.

There was a knock at the door and Devon peeked his head in. "You ladies decent?" he asked as he walked in with a tray of desserts.

"Well, if we weren't, you're in here now," Alicia joked.

"When I heard your voices all the way down the hall, I thought I'd bring you some samples for the dessert party we're having on the show next week."

"Really?" Serena grabbed a red velvet cupcake. "You know, we should tie some of your shows to our menu."

"That's a good idea," Kandace said as she grabbed a chocolate bar. "Antonio has your brain working, too."

"Somebody needs to work around here," Serena said. "Our general manager is slack since she's a mom now, the PR guru is still on her honeymoon, and I don't know what Alicia has going on."

"And you've just been working so hard seducing our contractor," Alicia quipped.

Devon cleared his throat and set the desserts on the center of the desk. "I got to go," he said. "Y'all are crazy."

"Did you just meet us?" Serena called out as Devon left.

"Is that weird for you?" Jade whispered to Kandace.

"What?" she asked.

"Devon still being here."

Kandace shook her head and took another bite of her chocolate. "That's over and done with," she said dismissively. "Maybe it would be hard if I wasn't married to the love of my life."

Serena nodded. "I'm proud of you, Kandace. You've handled working with Devon like a real woman."

"Was there ever any doubt that I wouldn't?" Kandace asked, then burst out laughing.

"Plenty," Jade and Alicia said in concert. The women broke into laughter and sampled more of Devon's desserts.

"So, Serena," Alicia said. "Since you and Antonio have been spending all this time together, what have you done about the man from California?"

Pouting, Serena shook her head. "Nothing. He came in here last night."

"What?" the other women exclaimed.

"And you didn't beat him down?" Kandace asked.

"Or at least toss a drink in his face?" Alicia inquired.

Serena shook her head. "I wanted to but I couldn't for two big reasons. One, we just reopened and the last thing we need is more bad press, and two, he was with Antonio's sister-in-law."

"Sister-in-law? Antonio's married?" Alicia asked.

"He's a widower," Serena said. "Come on, I'm not *that woman*. If his wife were alive, I hope he wouldn't be bringing me into his home, bed, and around his son. I can't believe you'd think I'd be a part of something like that."

"Just had to check. I'd hate to find out this guy is Tiger Woods," Alicia joked. "But seriously, what does Emerson Bradford want? Are you going to find out?"

Serena took another bite of her red velvet cupcake and shook her head. "I don't care what Emerson wants. He can kiss my ass."

"Serena," Devon called out. "Someone is here to see you."

The four women stood up at the same time. "Do you think it's Antonio?" Jade asked with a smile.

"What if it's Emerson?" Kandace asked.

Serena looked at the door and shook her head. "Why are we acting like children?"

"Because if it's Emerson, we're going to kick his ass," Alicia said.

Serena opened the office door and Devon

pointed her to the dining room. Her friends followed her closely and stood behind her like sentinels. When he turned around, decked out in an Italian suit holding a dozen yellow roses, Serena wanted to slap Emerson until his face turned beet red.

"I had no idea we'd have an audience," Emerson said with a slick smile. "Serena, you and I need to talk."

Glaring at him, Serena was glad the restaurant was closed so Devon could film his show. The last thing she needed was for customers to hear what she was about to say. "I don't have a damned thing to say to you," she snapped as she took the flowers from his outstretched hands and tossed them in his face.

"That's the Serena I know and love," Alicia whispered.

Emerson stepped closer to Serena as he brushed away rose petals. She didn't move. Anger kept her rooted in place.

"Serena, is there some place where we can speak in private?" he asked.

"Hell no," Kandace exclaimed. "Why don't you just get out of here?"

Emerson glanced at Kandace and smiled. "Ladies, I don't mean your friend any harm, but we have some private matters to discuss."

"Maybe you should've had this conversation five years ago, jerk," Alicia snapped. "Your movies suck."

A flash of anger crossed Emerson's face, then he masked it with a false Hollywood smile. "I'm sorry you feel that way. But I want to talk to Serena about a movie."

Serena bristled. "Oh, you have got to be kidding me. You came all this way about that damned movie?"

"That's one reason," he said. "But I had to see you, Serena."

Jade touched Serena's shoulder. "Do you want me to call the police?"

Emerson held up his hands, "Ladies, I didn't come here to cause problems, but I want to talk business with you, Serena. If you and your friends will calm down and hear me out, this could benefit all of us."

"Where was this concern when you left Serena at the altar?" Alicia asked.

Serena turned to her friends and mouthed, *I can handle this.* Then she turned to face Emerson. "Get out, Emerson. You can take that movie and shove it where the sun doesn't shine."

"Serena," he murmured in a voice that used to send her heart into overdrive. "Please. Do you remember what it was like when we made the movie?"

"Yeah, I do," she said. "We wrapped, I went to the church the next day and you never showed up."

"I regret that and I—"

Serena closed the space between them and slapped him as hard as she could. "Get out of here and don't come back. I don't give a damn about your movie."

"You're telling me this is enough for you?

Working in a restaurant?" Emerson said with sarcastic laugh.

"I don't simply work here, you jackass. I own this place with my friends," Serena's friends grumbled in the background about him belittling their investment.

"Fine," Emerson said. "But the movie is art and I'm going to release it."

"Over my dead body! Let's be real. That movie wouldn't be spit had I not rewritten the script. But those days are behind me and I will not have you putting that movie on the big screen so you can make a profit."

"Serena, maybe when you calm down, we can talk about this," he said. "I understand you have to put on your little show for your girlfriends."

"I'm not putting on a show, Emerson. When I first met you, I told you that I was not an actress and I'm not acting now, you slimy bastard."

"You should reconsider," Emerson said. "I know what happened here. This movie would give you all some needed *good* publicity."

"Thanks, but no thanks. Now get the hell out of here!"

Emerson nodded and smiled. "It was good to see you again." He turned and walked out the door.

"I should've known," Serena groaned once she and her girls were alone. "He's trying to revive his dying career with the movie he claimed would make me a star."

"What are you going to do now?" Alicia asked. "How are you going to stop him?"

"You should call Kenya," Jade suggested.

Serena nodded as she thought about the movie. It was very sexy, damned near pornographic, and nothing that she wanted to see on the big screen. Five years ago when she thought her life was going to be in Hollywood, that would've been fine. But she was a business woman and it was not the kind of attention she wanted.

What would Antonio think if he saw her on screen doing those things? "Yeah, I'd better do that," Serena said. "I really don't need this right now."

Jade pulled her cell phone from her pocket and called Kenya, then handed the phone to Serena.

When Emerson slammed into his hotel room, he knew what he had to do. He pulled out his MacBook Pro, jammed in the DVD of *De Chocolat*, and forwarded the movie to one of the hotter love scenes where Serena was prominently featured. He'd always loved the scene where she'd been in bed with the police detective investigating the string of murders her character had committed. Every inch of her supple body was highlighted. Looking at her breasts on the screen made his mouth water. Then, she turned from sexy to dangerous as she slipped her hand underneath the pillow, grabbed a knife, and jabbed it into the man's chest as she continued to ride him.

"Well," she said, her voice husky and seductive. "You can say you got fucked to death, Detective."

Emerson edited the clip and prepared to leak it on YouTube and some other sites. But first, he had to set up a false account. *I tried to work with you, Serena. You brought this on yourself,* he thought as he uploaded the scene and called his assistant in L.A.

"Emerson Bradford's office, how may I help you?"

"Annette, I need you to draft a press release about scenes from my upcoming movie being leaked on the Internet."

"Yes, sir," she said. "Is this the *De Chocolat* movie?"

"You got it. Make sure you include some information about Serena Jacobs, the star of the movie who is now a restaurant owner in North Carolina."

"All right."

"And include something about the violence that happened at her restaurant last year, and Solomon Crawford."

"Got it."

"E-mail me a copy when you're done."

"Yes, sir," Annette said.

Emerson hung up the phone and kicked back on the bed. He was going to build a buzz for this movie and his career was going to be on the upswing again.

Antonio watched A.J. as he flipped turkey burgers on the grill. "I'm a chef, Daddy," the little boy said.

"You're on your way," Antonio replied. "But be careful. You don't want to burn yourself."

"Is Miss Serena going to come over and eat with us?"

"She's at work. Maybe tomorrow we'll go eat at her restaurant. I think those burgers are done now," Antonio said as he took the spatula from A.J. and loaded the burgers on a tray. "Ready to eat?"

"Yes. May I call Aunt Casey and invite her over?"

"If you want to, go ahead. Make sure you wash your hands before you get the phone," Antonio said. He really didn't feel like dealing with Casey, but he wasn't going to keep A.J. away from his aunt.

He walked into the house and placed the burgers on the stovetop. A.J. turned to him and said, "Aunt Casey wants to speak to you."

"Thanks," Antonio said as he took the phone. "Hello?"

"I was just making sure you're all right with me coming over there," Casey said.

"It's fine, Case."

"I wanted to check, because you haven't been wanting me around lately."

"Casey, can we table this for another time? A.J. is looking forward to seeing you," Antonio said.

"Is that woman going to be there or is this just a family meal?" Casey asked.

Antonio gritted his teeth and groaned inwardly. "All right, Case, we'll see you when you get here." He hung up the phone and turned to A.J. "Ready to make that cole slaw you're so famous for?"

"Yeah," the little boy said. "Daddy, what's a derelict?"

"Where did you hear that word? It's not a nice thing to say about someone," Antonio said, sure that Casey was the culprit.

"Well, Aunt Casey asked if you were still hanging out with a derelict."

"Derelict is a fancy way of saying someone is bad news, but we don't know any derelicts. Okay?"

"Okay."

Antonio seethed with anger as they chopped cabbage, carrots, and onions. Casey had some nerve. He didn't care how she felt about Serena, but she was not going to draw A.J. into her battle. A battle that she had no footing in. It wasn't as if Antonio was having an affair with Serena while Marian was alive. No, he'd been the one to keep his marriage vows and Antonio was not going to allow Casey to make him feel guilty about moving on with his life.

As Antonio watched A.J. mix the slaw, the doorbell rang. "Be careful with the mixing and I'll go get the door," Antonio told his son. He looked out the window and saw Casey standing on the porch with a box of cupcakes. Antonio opened the door and stepped out.

"Am I uninvited?" Casey asked, noting the look of disgust on his face.

"Casey, I don't appreciate you bad-mouthing Serena to A.J. He's a child and doesn't need to be drawn into your beef with her. I'm still trying to understand why you can't respect the fact that I'm moving on with my life."

"Because that woman is not good enough for you," Casey snapped.

Antonio laughed. "It wasn't too long ago your parents felt that way about me. But guess what—that's not your call to make. What I do and who I do it with is none of your concern. I care about Serena and she is going to be a part of my life."

"She's not good enough for you. I–I love you, Tonio." Casey sighed and dropped her head. "There, I said it."

Antonio shook his head. Casey placed her hand on his shoulder. "I know what was going on with you and Marian before she died and how she was going to leave you for Brandon."

Antonio shrugged her off. "And you thought what? After she died that I'd be so devastated I'd turn to you? Is that why you tried to move in here? Casey, I don't see you as anything more than a sister."

"That's because you didn't give me a chance," she said. "We could be good together and we could raise A.J."

"No, we're not. Now, you can go inside and have dinner with your nephew, but you need to get it out of your head that you and I will ever have that kind of relationship."

Tears welled up in Casey's eyes. "So, you want to be with that slut? A whore who sits around your house naked so you can have your way with her? That's what you want? What is it, you can't handle a real woman? Maybe that's why my sister cheated on you."

Antonio balled his hands into fists and shook

his head. All of Casey's talk about her sister's memory had been nothing but bull. He glared at her. "How can you disrespect your sister's memory like this? You claimed you loved Marian. If she had lived, we'd probably be divorced. Do you think you and I would be dating then? As far as your sister cheating, that speaks to her character—not mine."

"But . . . but . . ."

Antonio pointed to the door. "A.J. is waiting for you and I don't want to have this conversation again—ever."

"Fine, Antonio. But I thought you should know."

I wish you didn't feel that way, he thought as he watched Casey walk into the house.

Chapter 20

Serena woke up after a restless night of sleep. She'd never thought *that movie* would come back to bite her after all these years

As a business woman, that sexy movie wouldn't play well in Charlotte or with the people in her life. Antonio popped into her mind. What would he think if he saw that movie?

Shaking her head, she looked at the clock on her nightstand and saw that it was five after seven. She needed to get out of the bed and get ready for her meeting with Kenya. Serena was thankful that Jade's sister-in-law had agreed to meet with her, and hoped Kenya would be able to make the movie disappear. Slowly rising from the bed, Serena lumbered to the shower and hopped underneath the warm spray. She closed her eyes and thought about what her life had been like when she made that movie with Emerson.

She'd been ready to make a name for herself with the sexy thriller. That movie had been poised to launch her, and especially Emerson, into the upper echelon of Hollywood royalty. At the time she hadn't minded being his arm candy. She hadn't cared that people were going to look at her and pay more attention to her body than her brain.

Serena wasn't that woman anymore. She wanted people to take her seriously. They'd just gotten through bad press at Hometown Delight and the movie was going to make things worse.

Or is it? she thought. *You wanted to write a movie. You basically rewrote the screenplay. Maybe you should just make him reshoot it and take the money. No, I'm not going to have my hard work put Emerson back on the map. Why would he do this? Why now?*

Serena shut the shower off and hopped out. As she toweled herself dry, she heard her phone ring. Dashing into the bedroom, she grabbed her cell phone without looking at the CALLER ID. "Hello?"

"Good morning, Serena. Have you thought about my offer?" Emerson asked.

"Didn't I tell you to stop calling me? That movie is not going to be released, so why don't you go back to Hollywood and find another student to lie to and leave at the altar."

"I've regretted that day for the longest time, but you don't understand what I was dealing with," he said.

"Emerson, I don't give a damn. When I made that movie, I thought I was going to be your wife and we were going to be players in Hollywood.

That part of my life is behind me. You're behind me and I wish you would just disappear."

"Maybe I could do that if I thought this was the life you really wanted. Serena, are you happy in this small town with no passion?" Emerson asked.

She laughed sardonically, realizing Emerson never knew who she really was. "You don't know a damned thing about my life. If you did, you'd know that I don't need the Hollyweird spotlight to be happy."

"No, but I know I can make you happy. Tell me that you don't miss *us*," he said, his voice thick and seductive.

Serena wasn't falling for it. She wasn't going to be Emerson Bradford's victim again. "You know what," she said, her voice cool and calm. "I do miss you, Emerson. I miss your ego. I miss how everything revolves around you. See, I now know what it is like to be important in someone's life and not treated as a lump of clay to make them famous. That's all I ever was to you, Emerson. Those days are over and whatever plans you have or wanted to make with that movie, forget them."

"Serena, I was trying to make things better for both of us," he said. "When the studio decided they weren't going to release the movie, I felt as if I let you down. Now, I have a chance to right that."

"No, you had a chance to right that on our wedding day. You could've come to me and told me what was going on. Back then, I was stupid enough to give a damn and would've done anything to make you happy. So, I don't want to hear your sob story. It's five years too late."

"The movie's coming out," Emerson said with finality. "The public's already buzzing about it."

"What?"

"Somehow," he said, "a few scenes have been leaked on the Internet."

"Son of a—" Serena snapped her phone shut and released a string of expletives as she stomped over to her laptop. She typed in Emerson's name in the Google toolbar. When the video clip showed her scene from the movie, she called Kenya immediately.

Antonio kissed A.J.'s cheek as he dropped his son off for his first day of day camp at Discovery Place in Uptown Charlotte. "Have a good day, son."

"Bye, Daddy." A.J. ran toward his friend Kashim Richardson.

Antonio headed to Ray's Splash Planet to meet with county park and recreation officials about a renovation project. When he arrived at the location, Norman was standing outside waiting for him. Antonio pulled his truck into an empty parking spot and prayed the meeting didn't last long. He wanted to surprise Serena with lunch. He'd missed her last night as he'd shared an uncomfortable dinner with Casey. He'd tried to put on a front for A.J's sake, but he couldn't get Casey's confession out of his mind. What had she expected to gain by telling him that she was in love with him? Did she think he had those same feelings? Had he done something to lead her on?

"Antonio, are you all right?" Norman asked as his friend approached him.

"Yeah, just thinking about something that happened last night," he said.

"Am I going to be jealous if I ask for details?" Norman quipped.

Antonio smiled, knowing Norman was talking about Serena. "I wish," he said, growing serious again. "Remember what you've been telling me about Casey all this time?"

The older man nodded.

Antonio shook his head and closed his eyes. "Well, you were right, my friend."

"She made a move on you?"

"Last night A.J. and I grilled some turkey burgers and he wanted to invite his aunt. When he spoke to her on the phone, she said something derogatory about Serena and when I confronted her on it, she confessed that she is in love with me."

"Can't say that I'm surprised. What are you going to do about it?" Norman asked.

"I don't know. A.J. loves his aunt and I don't want him to lose another person he loves. But I'm not comfortable."

"Did you tell Serena?"

"Hell no," Antonio said. "They already had a run-in and I am trying not to have that happen again."

"Besides," Norman said with a smile, "you don't

want to do anything to mess up what you have going on with Miss Serena. Don't tell her."

Antonio closed his hand on Norman's shoulder. "She's really special." His face lit up with happiness.

"I haven't seen you this happy in a long time, so whatever she's doing to you, let her keep doing it."

The men headed into the building and sought out Torrey James, Ray's Splash Planet director. When they reached his office, his secretary guided them inside. Antonio looked at the young man staring at the computer screen wondering why he was being so unprofessional. Norman cleared his throat. "Excuse me, are you Mr. James?"

The man looked up and pulled his glasses from the top of his head. "Yes, sorry about that," he said as he rose to his feet and extended his hand to Antonio and Norman. "A friend of mine in Los Angeles sent me a movie clip and it's unbelievable. I apologize, gentlemen, let's get started."

Antonio smiled at the man, knowing that working with the county would bring more money into his business in the fall and winter when contracts usually dried up, but he couldn't help asking, "What kind of movie clip is it?"

"I'm not even sure, but the actress is hot! Detrick was telling me she lives in Charlotte and I'm trying to figure out why I've never met her. It's an Emerson Bradford production. If he'd released this instead of those last few movies he made, he'd be cool again."

"This I have to see," Norman said, never one to turn down looking at a pretty woman. Torrey turned his monitor toward the men and logged on to the Web site.

Despite himself, Antonio watched the clip and when he saw who the actress was, he nearly dropped to the floor. Norman's mouth dropped and he turned toward Antonio. "Is that . . . ?" he asked quietly.

Antonio shook his head and Torrey looked from Norman to Antonio. "Do you know her? Can I get an introduction?"

"Norman, can you handle this meeting?" Antonio asked. "I have to go take care of something." He tore out of the office confused by what he saw on the Internet. Was that Serena and was that simply acting? Why didn't she give him the details of the movie when he'd asked her about her life in Los Angeles?

I'm tripping. Everyone has a past and this is just a movie, he thought as he got into his truck and started it up. Still, Antonio didn't like what he was feeling. How was he going to explain it to A.J. if this movie gained a lot of publicity?

He drove to the restaurant, but when he didn't see Serena's car in the parking lot, he headed to her townhouse. She wasn't at home. He wondered if she even knew what was going on.

"Kenya, you're telling me there's nothing I can do?" Serena groaned. "This is all over the Internet and it isn't going to take long for some reporter to link this movie to the restaurant."

Kenya pulled her reading glasses off and gave Serena a solemn look. "I wish I had better news for you, but from what I've uncovered, no studio has purchased the rights to this movie. Emerson is more than likely the leak."

"That filthy bastard," Serena swore as she slammed her hand against Kenya's desk. "I'm sorry."

"That desk has been hit before. Let me ask you this, other than starring in the movie, what else did you do?"

"I did a lot of rewriting on the script, but that was when I thought Emerson and I were going to get married, so I didn't press for credit."

"But you do have a right for compensation," Kenya said, then pressed the CALL button on her phone and called her assistant, Talisha. "T, I need you to look up some telephone numbers for me."

"Yes, ma'am," she said.

Kenya rattled off the names of some major studios in Hollywood and Emerson Bradford. "I need these as soon as possible."

"All right. Don't forget, your husband is coming by at eleven," Talisha said.

"Thanks."

Serena recognized the smile on her attorney's face. That's how she felt when she thought about Antonio or knew she was going to see him. But what if he saw that movie clip? What would he think?

"Are you all right?" Kenya asked when she noticed the frown on Serena's face.

"No. What if Antonio sees this?"

Kenya shrugged. "Here's the one thing that you have in your favor. It's not as if this is some sex tape. It is a movie. You were acting."

"But I'm not some celebutant trying to get her face on *E!* Even if it is a movie everyone in my life might not see it that way," Serena said, then dropped her head in her hands.

"We're going to see if we can stop this, but I don't want you to get your hopes up. If nothing else, we can get you a piece of the box office."

Serena rose to her feet as her cell phone vibrated in her pocket. She pulled the phone out and saw that it was Antonio calling her. "Kenya, I'm going to take this. Call me if you find out anything."

"All right."

Serena stepped into the hallway and answered the phone. "Hello?"

"Serena, where are you?" Antonio asked.

"I'm about to head home. Is everything all right?"

"You tell me," he said. "I saw something on the Internet that—"

"Damn it," Serena muttered. "Antonio, I wanted to tell you about that. Will you meet me at my place so we can talk?"

"Sure," he said.

Serena rushed to her car and sped home, hoping she would be able to explain the movie away and Antonio would be understanding about it. *And if he isn't, what am I going to do about it?* she thought as she pulled up to her townhouse and saw Antonio leaning against his truck.

She placed the car in PARK and hopped out. She half expected to see anger in Antonio's eyes, but instead, he opened his arms to her and gave her a big hug.

"Are you all right?" he asked.

Serena looked up at him and smiled. "Thank you," she said.

"For what?"

"I just knew that you were going to be upset about this. Hell, I'm upset about this. But . . ."

"It was a little off-putting to see that," he said. "Did you know this movie was going to be released?"

"It hasn't been released," she said with a groan. "But the vindictive son of a bitch who is doing this is trying to rebuild his career on something I did when I was young and stupid."

"Are you going to sue?"

"I was talking to a lawyer earlier today," she said as she held on tighter to Antonio. "You know what makes this tougher?"

He looked down at her and asked, "What?"

"At one time, I thought I was going to marry this guy."

"Whoa."

"Can we go inside?" she asked. Serena knew she had to come clean about everything.

"All right," he said as he dropped his arms from around her. Once inside, Serena headed for the kitchen and made a pot of coffee while Antonio sat on a bar stool and watched her. He could tell Serena was trying to find the courage to tell him what was going on. As the coffee brewed, she turned to him and offered up a weak smile.

She placed her hand on top of his. "When I went to Los Angeles, I wanted to write. I took classes at UCLA and I met Emerson Bradford."

"He did *Sultry Summer,* right?"

Serena nodded. "But before that he was trying to come up with his breakout hit. He said I belonged in front of the camera. He wooed me and talked me into starring in this movie. Since I was in love with the man and wearing his engagement ring, I jumped at the chance. But things didn't work out and the movie disappeared. I found myself standing at the altar alone on my wedding day."

Antonio took her hand in his and brought it to his lips. "That had to hurt," he said. "What was his excuse for leaving you there?"

"He has no excuse," she said. "Until he showed up in Charlotte about a week ago, I hadn't heard a word from that sorry piece of . . . for five years, I hadn't heard a word from him and all he could say about not showing up for our wedding was that the studio declined to release the film and he felt as if he let me down."

"Sounds like a damned coward," Antonio said, thinking that nothing would've caused him to leave Serena standing alone at the altar. Emerson Bradford was the biggest fool he'd ever heard of.

"He is. And his career has been in a steady decline," she said. "This is a very sexy movie and I guess Emerson thinks it will put him back on top."

"You don't want the movie to be released?" Antonio asked.

Serena shook her head furiously. "It reminds me of one of the worst times in my life. It reminds me how I allowed someone else to take my dreams and turn them into mush. I wanted Emerson to succeed more than I wanted to build my career. Once I took up with him, I dropped out of school, fell into what he thought I should do, and lost Serena for a while."

Antonio cocked his head to the side and looked at her. "I never would've guessed that," he said. "I took you for the kind of woman who always did what she wanted to do."

"That's me now," she said. "Because I learned the hard way that love hurts a lot."

Antonio walked over to her and pulled her against his chest. "Real love doesn't hurt," he said, then lifted her chin. "When you're with the right person and everything is right, you're not going to feel any pain."

"I guess that's how it was with you and your wife?" Serena questioned.

Antonio ran his index finger down her cheek. "No. I wish I could say that it was, but it wasn't."

She stared at him. All the thoughts she'd had about Antonio and his dead wife danced in her mind. He seemed to notice what she was thinking.

"At first, it seemed as if it was going to be that way, but by the time Marian died, our marriage was over. She was having an affair and had served me with divorce papers. After everything was said and done, I knew I would never allow anyone else to get close to me. Then you walked into my life and I was powerless to resist you."

"Antonio," she said.

"Listen to me," he said. "I'm falling for you and I thought three things when I saw that video clip. One, this had better be a movie—because I didn't want to think about another man touching you and kissing you. That's my job and mine alone. Two, as I drove around looking for you, I started thinking this was something that you probably didn't want out in public, and three, I was worried when I couldn't find you, thinking what is Serena going to do when she finds out about this?"

Tears sprang into her eyes and Antonio brought his lips down on top of hers, kissing her gently. Pulling back, he looked up at her. "Serena," he murmured, "I'm falling in love with you."

"Antonio," she said, tears falling down her cheeks.

"You don't have to respond right now, but I want you to know that I'm going stand beside you while you fight this. If Emerson Bradford is behind this, he'd better get out of town because I might have to hurt than man for doing this to you."

"Thank you," she said as she hugged him tightly. "I thought I was going to lose you."

"It's going to take more than this for you to get rid of me."

Chapter 21

Since the news of the leaked movie clip got out, Emerson's phone hadn't stopped ringing. L.A. movie critics wanted to know when the film was coming out and who the actress was.

Of course, Emerson pretended to be shocked that scenes from his movie had been leaked, then he answered their questions. No, he didn't have a studio backing him. Yes, he was surprised the clip had been viewed about a half-million times in the few hours it had been online. Yes, he wants the public to get a chance to experience the entire movie and not just some of the sexiest scenes.

The next few calls he took were from Lionsgate. They wanted to know how the movie got online as well. Emerson blamed his assistant.

"But," he'd said to Luther, "the people want to see this movie."

"Have you talked to Serena Jacobs? Did she sign off on it?"

"I don't think we need her to sign off on it. Technically, her signature isn't needed since I own the rights to the movie. The public has spoken. We need to hammer out a deal and make this happen. You know what I've been doing all morning? Fielding calls from the press. They wouldn't do that if they weren't interested."

"Well, I got a call from a lawyer representing Serena Jacobs," Luther said.

"Really? All this will turn into is free publicity."

"Or an ugly lawsuit."

Emerson slapped his hand against his forehead. "Luther, this movie will be a hit. Are we going to make it happen or do I need to go to another studio?"

"Shake the lawyers, get those edits done, and we will make this movie happen," Luther said.

Emerson pumped his fist like Tiger Woods, but calmly said, "All right. Thanks, Luther."

"Make this happen. If we're going to capitalize on this buzz we have to get it going. When will you back in L.A.?"

"I need a few more days here," he said, thinking he could focus on one last tango with Serena before the movie was released. He didn't care what she said. He knew she still wanted fame and this movie was going to skyrocket her image.

"See me as soon as you get back," Luther said.

Emerson hung up the phone and kicked back on his bed. *Serena, my muse, we will be together again and you're going to leave this banker town as soon as you get a taste of fame.*

* * *

Serena nestled her head against Antonio's chest and stroked his arm. This wasn't how she expected the day to go. But she was lying in bed with Antonio, feeling safe in his arms. When he'd kissed her and told her he loved her, Serena had melted like ice on a hot summer's day.

She was a little apprehensive about opening her heart again, but as she snuggled against Antonio while he slept, she knew not allowing love to come into her life would be the biggest mistake she could ever make. Antonio was nothing like Emerson. He was unselfish, and her happiness was just as important to him as his own.

Antonio stirred and turned into Serena. His eyes fluttered open and she smiled at him. "I hope I'm not keeping you from your work," she said as his hand slid down the small of her back.

"Not at all. I had been planning all morning to steal you away," he said, then brushed his lips against her neck.

"Umm, I would've been excited to get away with you," she said as she straddled his body. "I really missed you last night."

"Show me again." He smiled as he recalled the lovemaking session they'd finished an hour ago.

She started with a slow kiss as she ground against him, causing his manhood to spring to life. Slowly, she inched down his body, kissing and licking his smooth skin until she hovered over his erection. Serena ran her tongue up and down the length of him making him shiver with delight. As she took him into her mouth, Antonio shuddered as waves of hot pleasure roamed throughout his body. He buried his hands in her soft hair as she took him to the brink of exploding. Serena pulled back and looked at him with smoldering passion in her eyes. Reaching underneath her pillow, she retrieved a condom, opened it, and rolled it on top of Antonio's pulsating member. Parting her legs, she mounted him, taking him deep inside her wet valley. Throwing her head back as Antonio thrust his hips, she placed her hands on his chest and rode him slow and deep. He gripped her hips, making sure she felt every burning inch of him as their bodies meshed into one. She rotated her hips against his, their breath seemingly becoming one as they moaned. Serena began to tremble as she felt her orgasm building and when Antonio palmed her breasts, his thumbs brushing against her nipples, she exploded from the inside out and he followed her with his own climax. She collapsed against his chest and Antonio kissed her on the top of her head.

"Damn, woman," he moaned as he wrapped his arms around her. "Let me never allow you to miss me that much again."

"You know what they say about absence," Serena replied breathlessly.

"And now I see that it's true." His fingers danced up and down her spine, sending tingles throughout her body.

"Ooh, I wish we could just stay here for the rest of the year," she said.

Antonio glanced at the clock on Serena's nightstand and groaned. "As much as I'd like to do the same thing, I have to go pick up A.J. from camp."

"All right," she said, reluctantly letting him go.

Antonio glanced at her as he rose from the bed and grabbed his pants. "Why don't you join A.J. and me for dinner tonight?" Antonio said as pulled on his pants.

"I wish I could, but I'm stuck working the bar for one more night. But tomorrow, I'll bring dinner over. And yes, it will be from the restaurant." Serena climbed out of the bed and stood in front of Antonio.

His eyes traveled down her naked body and he was tempted to climb back into bed with her for just five more minutes. Instead, he placed his hands on her shoulders and kneaded them gently. "Come over after your shift and we can have French toast for breakfast before A.J. goes off to camp. Then I'm free for the rest of the day. I want you to wait for me in my bed. If you have another one of those lacy numbers, you can be wearing it when I return," he said, then kissed her with a smoldering heat that buckled her knees.

"I can do that," she said when they broke their kiss. "I'd be more than happy to do that."

Serena pulled on her robe and walked Antonio to the front door, hating to see him go but excited that Emerson's leak hadn't changed anything between her and Antonio. But he hadn't had to explain it to his son yet.

Stop tripping, she thought. *I'm sure that little boy*

isn't going to go online and look up that movie clip. Maybe this isn't going to be as bad as I think. As long as Kenya and I can block the release of this movie, everything will be all right. Serena bounded up the stairs with a smile on her face and headed for the shower. She had hope and Antonio's support. She could face this and bring Emerson down where he belonged.

As he drove to Discovery Place to pick up A.J., Antonio called Norman realizing that he never checked with him about the Ray's Splash Planet deal.

"I was wondering what happened to you," Norman said when he answered the call.

"I went to see Serena to make sure she was all right. And she wasn't. She was very upset about that movie clip being released online."

"Then why did she make it? How long ago was it made?" Norman asked.

"Five years ago. She was actually engaged to the director and that sorry son of a bitch left her at the altar," Antonio said.

"Wow," Norman said. "So, she's a real actress?"

"She said she did the movie because she thought they were going to be married and she thought it would make him happy. Instead, he just tossed her aside and now he's trying to use this movie to rebuild his career."

"And she doesn't want it released? What is she going to do about it?"

"She's going to try and block it."

"That's good. I'm proud of you," Norman said.

"For what?"

"Sticking by that woman. I can imagine this is hard for her. There was a story about it on the noon news."

Antonio swore under his breath. "Then I guess the whole city knows about it."

"Yeah. Casey called me looking for you. She had some unkind things to say about Serena."

"That's just what I need. I'm about to pick up A.J. What happened at Ray's?"

"We got the deal," Norman said. "We can get started next week. Do you want to call the regular crew?"

"Sure." Antonio brought his truck to a stop in front of Discovery Place. He groaned when he saw Casey standing outside with A.J. "Norman, I'm going to have to call you back."

Antonio hopped out of the truck and A.J. rushed over to him. "Daddy," he said. "I had so much fun today. We got to see the snakes."

"That sounds like a lot of fun," he said, then glanced at Casey, who had a scowl on her face.

"We drew pictures of snakes, too," A.J. chattered, ignoring the looks between his aunt and his father.

"I can't wait to see them. Hop in the truck. I need to talk to Aunt Casey." A.J. got into the truck and Antonio turned to Casey. "What are you doing here?"

"I assume you've seen the news and heard

about your special little friend and the near porno she's the star of," Casey spat.

"Casey, I know about Serena's movie and I know that she made it when she was young."

"Do you know that the man she made the movie for is in Charlotte and has been hanging around her restaurant? Do you know that she's going milk this and be seen all over town in that movie? How is A.J. going to react to that?"

Antonio folded his arms across his chest. "Is that all you have, Case?"

"I told you she wasn't the kind of woman you needed to have around my nephew. Now the world will know. I guess that's why she didn't mind lying around your house naked."

"Casey, stay out of my business," Antonio said. "We've all made mistakes."

"Yes, but our mistakes aren't all over the Internet and the news. Wait until Mom and Dad find out about this."

"Your family doesn't run my life."

"This isn't about you. It's about what's best for A.J. If Serena is the kind of woman you're going to have influence him, then maybe it's best that he's not with you."

Anger flowed through Antonio as Casey's words registered with him. "Are you out of your damned mind? No one is taking my son away from me. You're using the fact that I don't want anything to do with you romantically cloud your judgment. But if you think I'm afraid of your family, you're dead wrong." Antonio stalked over to his truck and pulled out without looking back at Casey.

When Serena arrived at the restaurant that evening, she was ticked off to find two of the local news trucks camped out in the parking lot. "Not this again," she muttered as she circled the parking lot, then parked a half block away from the restaurant. She wished she had a hat in the back seat so that she could hide her face from the reporters. The last thing the restaurant needed was more bad publicity.

"I could kill Emerson," she muttered as she walked up to the back of the restaurant. "This is the last thing we need right now."

Though Serena wished people were coming to Hometown Delights for the food or for a chance to see Devon Harris, she couldn't deny that the press was drawing people in. The restaurant was packed again. With the economy the way it was, she had to be thankful for that. Still, as she walked behind the bar, she couldn't help but feel that everyone was looking at her.

"I'm glad you finally made it," Alicia said as she stalked over to the bar. "Reporters have been in and out of here all day. Kandace told me that one of her friends in Los Angeles who does a lot of work in Hollywood said she has documented proof that Emerson leaked this himself."

Serena slapped her hand against the bar and swore under her breath. "I knew it."

"I still say we should go kick his ass," Alicia said.

Serena shook her head. "He's not worth all of us getting in trouble over. I'm tired of him toying with my life and I'm going to put a stop to it. Can you cover me for about an hour?"

Alicia nodded. "I can stay for the rest of your shift if you need me to."

"I'll be back. I don't plan to give him that much of my time." She headed out the front of the restaurant, ignoring the calls from the reporters who had been sitting in the parking lot. Serena dashed to her car and headed for the Westin where Emerson was staying. He was going to stop messing with her life and it was going to stop tonight.

Walking into the bar at the Westin, Emerson was riding high. His movie was going to be released and thanks to Serena's scene on the Internet, *De Chocolat* had a buzz that money couldn't buy. Even if Serena tried to sue him, the movie would be released because he owned the rights. All she would do with a lawsuit was keep the publicity machine churning. Emerson took a seat at the bar with a huge smile on his face. "What can I get you?" the bartender asked.

"A scotch, neat."

The bartender nodded and turned to fix the drink. Emerson turned his back to the bar and watched as Serena stalked over to him. *This is an interesting turn of events,* he thought as he saw her. Rising from his seat, he crossed over to her.

Serena glared at him, then hauled off and slapped him.

"You bastard," she spat. "How could you do this to me?"

"That wasn't very nice," he said as he stroked his cheek. "I've made you the star that I promised I would. You could show some appreciation."

Serena shook her head and laughed sardonically. "I made that movie when I thought you and I would be married and have a life in Hollywood. I'm not that woman anymore. If you gave a damn about me, you'd know that."

"This isn't about you."

"No, because you're a selfish bastard who still believes the sun rises and sets on you. You're all that matters in the world of Emerson Bradford. What, can't come up with anymore movies on your own? Have you forgotten that I basically rewrote that piece of crap screenplay?"

"I haven't forgotten," he said. "We were good together and when it hits the big screen, we will be good again."

Serena pushed him backwards. "There is no we, you asshole. We died when you left *me* at the altar. This movie is not going to happen."

Smiling, he nodded slowly. "Actually, it is. Lionsgate is releasing *De Chocolat*."

"Over my dead body," she shouted, not caring about the looks they were receiving from the other patrons in the bar. "Why did you come back into my life? You caused me more pain than I've ever wanted to experience. You coming back

with that damned film is a reminder of the fool I
was for you. Just drop it, Emerson."

Though her eyes flashed anger, as he looked at
her all he could think about was feeling her kiss.
She had the softest lips he'd ever tasted and he
wondered if they were still soft and sweet. He
pulled her into his arms and kissed her with a
heated urgency.

It took ten seconds for Serena to snatch away
from him, stomp on his foot and knee him in his
midsection.

"Touch me again and I swear I will drop you
where you stand! This movie is *not* going to
happen. If I were you, I'd go back to L.A. and find
another sucker to buy your brand of bullshit."
Serena swore, then stomped out of the hotel.

Emerson shook his head and smirked as
he thought about the fire in her kiss. She still
wanted him and he was going to have her.

"Well, well," Casey said as she approached him.
"That was some little show you and my brother-
in-law's girlfriend put on. So, is she the actress
you came here to find?"

"She is. I take it that you don't like her since
she's the woman keeping you from the man you
want," Emerson said as he strode over to the bar.

Casey followed him, clutching her cell phone.
"I don't like her because she's not good enough
for Antonio and she isn't the kind of woman I
want around my nephew."

Emerson held a stool out for Casey, then sat
down. "So what are you going to do about it?"
he asked.

"A picture is worth a thousand words," she said as she held up her phone and showed Emerson the image of him and Serena kissing. "When Antonio sees this, I'm sure he'll dump her. Then you can pack her up and take her to Los Angeles with you."

Emerson smiled widely. "You know, I think I like you."

"Good, then you can buy me a drink," she said as she waved for the bartender. "Thanks to me, we both should get what we want."

Chapter 22

Serena didn't want to go back to the restaurant after her confrontation with Emerson. Knowing him, he'd try to spin it for more PR for that damned movie. Besides, she figured the reporters were still camped out waiting for her and she wasn't in the mood to be photographed or talked to. She needed Antonio's arms around her.

She needed to get the thought of Emerson's kiss out of her mind. It wasn't as if she was turned on by it. He hadn't rattled her as she'd thought he might if they'd ever gotten that close again. Instead, his touch and his lips disgusted her. She couldn't believe she'd ever loved him or wanted to be his wife.

Thank God I've grown up, she thought as she pulled up to a stoplight and dialed Antonio's number.

"Hey you," he said when he answered the phone. "How's work going?"

"I left early," she said as the light turned green.

"I was wondering if I could come over. I really need to see you."

"Are you all right?" he asked.

"Not really. There are reporters stalking me at work and I had an unpleasant conversation with Emerson."

"Come on over. A.J. and I are watching *Finding Nemo* for what seems like the millionth time, and eating pizza. You can escape for as long as you need to," he said. Antonio's voice comforted her in ways he couldn't even imagine.

Serena smiled and headed to his place. "Thank you," she said. "This means a lot."

"I'm here for you, baby," he said. "See you when you get here."

Fifteen minutes later, Serena was walking up the front steps of Antonio's house and she felt a calmness take over her body as she rang the doorbell. He opened the door with smile on his face and a bit of tomato sauce on his white tank top, but Serena didn't care about the stain as he enveloped her in his arms.

"It's going to be all right," he whispered as they embraced.

"When you say it, I believe it," she said as they headed into the den.

"Miss Serena," A.J. said. "We saved you some pizza."

She crossed over to the little boy and gave him a hug. "Thank you. I'm sure it's good since your dad is wearing some of it," she joked.

Antonio looked down at his shirt and laughed.

"Just for that," he said. "I'm taking the biggest piece."

"Daddy," A.J. said. "That's not nice."

"Yeah," Serena said, placing her hand on her hip and pretending to be upset. "That's not nice when I'm so hungry."

Antonio threw his hands up, "All right, all right. I know when I'm outnumbered. The pizza's in the kitchen."

Serena followed him and leaned against the counter as he grabbed a plate for her. When he walked over to the counter and set the plate down, she wrapped her arms around his neck and brought her lips to his, kissing him slow and tenderly. Antonio's hands stroked her back gently as they kissed and she nearly melted.

She broke the kiss and stepped back. "I wouldn't want to get something started and miss the movie or have your son see me in my underwear again."

"He'll be asleep soon and you can start whatever you like," Antonio said in a husky whisper. "Tell me about the conversation you had with Emerson."

Serena rolled her eyes as she picked up her plate and placed two slices of pizza on it. "I went to the Westin and he was in the bar. I told him this movie isn't going to happen and that he's a piece of scum for using something I made when I thought we had a future, to make a name for himself. He had the unmitigated gall to say he was going to make me a star. The same lies he told five years ago."

Antonio folded his arms and studied her as she spoke. Part of him silently wondered if there was more to what she was feeling for this man. He didn't want to believe she could still have feelings for the jerk who broke her heart, but he wasn't a fool. Women didn't always get over their first love.

Serena caught his questioning gaze. "What?" she asked.

"Don't take this the wrong way. But I have to ask. Are you sure this is just about the movie?"

"Yes," she said, struggling not to raise her voice. "If this was three or four years ago, you'd have a reason to wonder. But I don't feel anything for that bastard anymore. I finally see him for what he really is."

"And what's that?"

"A selfish jackass who didn't deserve me in the first place," she said.

Antonio leaned in and kissed her on the forehead. "That's good to know."

"Guys," A.J. called out. "You're missing the movie."

Antonio and Serena headed into the den. As she chewed her pizza and watched Antonio, she wondered if she should tell him that Emerson kissed her.

It didn't mean anything and there is no need to give him a reason to think that it did, she thought.

Once the movie ended, A.J. pulled out his art book and showed Serena the snakes he'd drawn at camp.

"Wow," she said as she looked at the drawings.

"That's very realistic. Were you scared when you looked at the snakes? I know I would be."

"Nope," A.J. said proudly. "I even touched a python."

"I never would've done that," Serena exclaimed. "Do you like snakes?"

"Only the ones that won't bite me," he replied with a smile.

Serena nodded. She'd known her share of snakes and if she could, she'd chop the head off the biggest one.

Antonio walked over to A.J. and Serena with two dishes of chocolate ice cream. "All right, after dessert, you need to take your bath," Antonio told his son after handing him his ice cream.

"Yes, sir," the little boy replied before digging into his ice cream.

Serena took her dish and asked, "Where's yours?"

"You're going to eat all of that?" he asked, nodding toward the overflowing dish.

"Chocolate ice cream is my favorite," she said. "I'm not sharing."

Antonio pulled a second spoon out of his shorts pocket and dug into the dish. "That's fine," he said as he took a huge scoop. "I don't play fair."

Serena and A.J. giggled as melted ice cream dripped onto Antonio's shirt. "See what happens when you steal," she said as she wiped the spot away.

The trio ate their ice cream and laughed for another hour before Serena took the empty dishes into the kitchen while Antonio took A.J. upstairs to give him a bath.

A.J. hopped out of the tub, dripping water onto the floor as Antonio grabbed a towel and wrapped it around his son.

"Are you and Miss Serena going to have another sleepover?" he asked his father.

"Maybe," Antonio said. "Are you all right with that?"

"I like her. Do you like her too?"

"I do," Antonio said. "She's a really nice person."

A.J. nodded as he dried his head. "She's not a derelict," the little boy said.

Antonio laughed tersely. "No, she isn't."

"But she's your girlfriend, right?"

"All right, son. It's time for bed," Antonio said. "And yes, she is my girlfriend."

"I have a girlfriend too," A.J. said. "She thought I was brave because I touched the snake, but I was really scared."

Antonio laughed, thinking of all the silly things he'd done to impress a girl at that age. "Well, you'd better be careful trying to impress her. She's going to expect you to keep doing it."

"I'm really not scared of the snakes anymore," A.J. said. "I'm a big boy now."

"Well it's time for this big boy to go to bed." The two bounded down the hall to A.J.'s room. Antonio watched his son as he put on his pajamas and smiled. He was happy Serena and A.J. got along so well. He'd wondered for a while after Marian's death how dating would affect his son. What if he'd make a mistake in choosing the wrong woman? What if the woman didn't mesh with his son? He was so lucky those problems didn't exist with Serena. A.J. was comfortable around her and she hadn't tried to be his mother nor tried to tell Antonio how to raise his son.

"Daddy," A.J. said, breaking into Antonio's thoughts.

"Yes, son?"

"I said I'm a big boy. I don't need a nightlight."

Antonio walked over to A.J.'s bed and tucked him in. Kissing him on the forehead, he said, "Good night, Champ." He flipped the lamp off as A.J. closed his eyes. Then he stepped out of the room and counted to ten silently. Just as he suspected, the lamp popped back on. Antonio didn't mind because he didn't want A.J. growing up too fast anyway.

When Antonio got downstairs, he was surprised to find Serena in the kitchen drying their dishes. "You didn't have to do this," he said from the doorway. Serena turned around and flashed him a bright smile.

"I know, but I wanted to." She dried her hands on a dish towel and crossed over to Antonio. "Besides, it's the least I could do. Thank you for making tonight special and simple."

He wrapped his arms around her waist. "I'm going to have to properly thank you for your dishwashing."

Serena placed her hand on his chest and

stroked him back and forth. "How are you going to thank me?"

Antonio lifted her onto the edge of the counter. "I'm going to start with this," he said, then captured her lips in a soft, searing kiss. Glad that she'd cleared off the bar, he leaned her back as he kissed her deeper and slipped his hand underneath her shirt, touching her silky skin and filling with desire.

She moaned as Antonio kissed each inch of flesh he exposed as he lifted her shirt. His tongue danced across her flat belly, spending time around her navel causing her legs to quake with anticipation.

"Antonio," she intoned as he unsnapped the button on her pants.

He pulled them down and slipped his hand inside the barely-there lace thong that covered her mound of sexuality. Antonio stroked her and parted her wet folds of flesh with his finger seeking out her bud. When he found it, he stroked it slowly, making a circular motion with his finger.

Serena became wet like a flowing river. She gasped and moaned at the same time as his lips and tongue replaced his finger. Shifting her hips, she pressed her body into his mouth as he licked and sucked until she called out his name in a husky whisper.

He pulled back from her, his face glazed with her desire. "Let's take this out back." Lifting her off the counter he headed outside to the enclosed porch. Antonio laid Serena on the plush sofa and peeled the rest of her clothes off. Slowly, he licked and sucked her erect nipples while caressing her inner thighs, making her shiver with desire and anticipation. He moved slowly, tasting every inch of her. She was the one thing he couldn't resist. She was sweeter than honey, more addictive than chocolate. Antonio's desire grew as he inched down her body. As much as he wanted to dive into her wetness, he pulled back. "Protection," he said, then dashed inside.

While he was gone, Serena checked the back door to make sure it was locked. The last thing she wanted was to be interrupted by Antonio's psychotic sister-in-law. After checking the door, she returned to the chair and laid back just as Antonio walked out on the porch, his erection shielded by a condom.

He looked at Serena as she struck a sensual pose. "Damn," he exclaimed as he closed the space between them and pulled her against his chest.

Serena kissed him with a hot passion that took his breath away. She wrapped her legs around his waist as he lowered himself on top of her, moaning as he entered her wetness. They ground against each other slowly, their moans piercing the air as they gave each other pleasure beyond words. Antonio kneaded her breasts as she pumped her hips into his. Serena arched her back, allowing him to go deeper inside her. She reveled in every throbbing inch of him as he rolled his hips, touching every sensitive spot inside her valley.

Antonio intoned her name as Serena tightened her thighs around him and gripped his penis tightly. "You feel so good," he moaned, coming closer to his climax.

Serena was in the middle of her second orgasm as he brought his lips down on top of her nipples. "Antonio," she called out as her body shuttered with pleasure.

"Serena."

Moments later, they came together and fell into a sweaty embrace, their hearts beating in sync as they lay back on the sofa. She stroked his chest and smiled as he wrapped his arms around her.

Safe. She felt safe and comforted in his embrace. *Am I in love with this man?* she thought as she ran her index finger down his bicep.

"Are you all right?" he asked.

"I'm great," she replied.

"Yes, you are," he said, then kissed her chin. "I'm glad you came over tonight. I'm even happier that you're a part of my life."

"Not as happy as I am," she said. "I never thought I'd feel this way. Never thought I'd find someone I could really be myself with and be so comfortable with." *Or love,* she added silently as she stared into his eyes.

"I'm glad we're sharing this together," he said. "You're the kind of woman I never thought would want anything to do with me and here we are. I can't get enough of you and I don't ever want to think about what my life would be like without you in it."

"Lucky for you, you're not going to have to find out," she said, then captured his lips in a searing kiss that instantly aroused him again. When they broke the kiss, Antonio stood and scooped Serena up in his arms.

"Let's go inside," he said. "I want to make love to you until the sun comes up."

As she wrapped her arms around his neck, Serena knew that she'd fallen in love again. But this time, she knew it was real.

Chapter 23

Emerson awoke with a start when he felt the faint brush of fingers against his bicep. Looking down at Casey's sleeping face, he groaned inwardly. *Serena* had been all he thought about last night when he drunkenly stumbled into his hotel room with his arms wrapped around Casey. Kissing her had been like kissing an ice cube. She had none of Serena's fire, none of her passion and when he'd gotten her into bed, Casey had been a boring and uninspired lover. To get satisfaction he'd closed his eyes and pretended he had been diving into Serena's wetness.

Casey had pushed him back. "That hurts," she'd cried out.

When Emerson had opened his eyes and saw he was buried inside Casey and not Serena, his erection shrank. He had hopped out of bed, mumbling an apology to Casey. Then he'd gone into the bathroom and splashed water on his face. When he'd returned to the bed, Casey had been asleep and Emerson was grateful.

Why did I bring her up here? he thought as he glanced at Casey as she yawned and stretched her arms above her head.

"Morning," she said.

"Morning," he replied.

Casey propped up on her elbows and looked at Emerson. "So, last night obviously wasn't about me."

"We were drunk. I'm sorry if I hurt you."

"Were you thinking about her?"

"Let's not get into this. We both want Serena and Antonio to split up. What we did was a mistake."

Casey rolled her eyes and hopped out of the bed. "You're right. A mistake and not a good experience."

Emerson laid back and looked at her. "Let's be honest here. Last night wasn't about either one of us. You wanted me to be your brother-in-law as much as I wanted you to be Serena. So, there is no need to take this personally."

Casey pulled on her clothes and looked down at Emerson. "You're right. No one can ever know about this."

"It's already forgotten," he said.

Casey grabbed her purse and slammed out of the room.

Emerson was tempted to call Serena. He longed to hear the sound of her voice and hoped he could convince her not to fight him on the movie. She still wanted to be a star and he was determined to make her one.

Antonio quietly crept out of bed, careful not to wake Serena. She needed to rest. He knew the fight with Emerson Bradford was taking a lot out of her. Heading down the hall, he saw that A.J. was still asleep as well. Walking into his son's room, he roused the little boy. "Hey, man, time to get ready for camp."

A.J. yawned and sat up. "All right."

Antonio touched his forehead. "Are you feeling all right?"

A.J. shook his head. "I really couldn't sleep last night."

"Why not?"

He shrugged his shoulders and dropped his head. Antonio lifted his son's head. "What's wrong, son?"

"Well, when I used to go to sleep, sometimes I would dream of Mommy, but I didn't last night and I think it's because I like Serena. Aunt Casey said that I was going to let her replace Mommy in my heart."

Seething, Antonio forced a smile. "Your mother will never be replaced in your heart. When your aunt says those things, she is speaking from her own hurt and pain. We're all still kind of sad that Mommy had to go to heaven."

"But I don't want to forget Mommy like Aunt Casey said I would," A.J. said.

"That won't happen. I won't let you forget your

mom." Antonio drew his son into his arms and hugged him tightly. "I'll talk to your aunt. She shouldn't be telling you those things."

"Okay," A.J. said, his voice sounding lighter as he headed toward his closet to get dressed.

Antonio watched his son, wondering why Casey kept saying things to A.J. to upset him. That was going to stop. She needed to mind her own business and quit making A.J. feel bad about liking Antonio's girlfriend.

Moments later, A.J. was dressed. He and Antonio were heading downstairs to grab a quick breakfast of Pop Tarts and milk. As they headed for the door to leave, Antonio heard a car door close. When he opened the door, Casey was standing on the porch.

"What are you doing here?" he asked when he saw her.

"Good morning," Casey said as she looked at A.J.

Antonio turned to his son and told him to get in the truck. "Casey, you need to leave. I'm sick of you trying to poison my son," he snapped.

"I'm trying to protect my nephew since you seem to be putting your libido first these days," Casey said. "But have you thought about what you're teaching him?"

"I told you not to question how I raise my son. And stop telling him that he's going to forget his mother. Do you even care what your venom is doing to A.J.?"

"I know you're having fun with Serena and you're excited because you have someone in your bed now. But have you considered that she is sharing more than one bed?"

Antonio sidestepped her and snapped, "That's what your sister did." As he got into the truck, he forced a smile for his son and started the truck without saying a word about Casey.

After dropping A.J. off at Discovery Place, Antonio headed back home and was happy to see that Casey was gone. He was getting really tired of her drama. Despite the fact that he was allowing her to be a part of A.J.'s life out of respect for Marian's memory, if she didn't change her ways, he was going to put his foot down and she wouldn't see his son again.

"Serena," he called out as he headed upstairs to his bedroom.

"I'm in the bathroom," she replied.

Antonio opened the door and found Serena laying in the garden tub. Bubbles covered most of her body and a wide smile spread across her face as Antonio took his clothes off to join her. "Is this how you start your day?" he asked as he eased into the bathtub. The warm water seemed to get hotter as Serena stroked his thigh.

"I wish I could say it was, but your tub is so big, I wondered just how clean we could get in it," she said.

Antonio brought his lips on top of hers and kissed her gently at first, but when she flicked her tongue across his lips, his desire rose like the sun in the morning sky. She wrapped her leg around his waist and pulled him against her as their kiss deepened. He ached to be inside her, but he knew they had to be protected. Serena placed her hand on his chest and pushed him backward. When he was against the wall of the tub, she planted herself on his lap and took the soap and rubbed it across his chest, circling his nipples and sending shivers of desire up and down his spine. Then she rinsed the soap off and kissed his erect nipples while stroking his growing erection. She inched up his body, licking his neck slowly and making him cry out.

"I need to be inside you," he moaned.

"I need you inside me," she called out.

Antonio lifted Serena up as he rose slowly from the tub. It didn't matter that they were soaking wet as he led her to his bedroom and laid her across the bed. He retrieved a condom and placed it on the pillow as he stroked her damp skin. His fingers danced across her nipples as Serena writhed underneath his touch. Soon, Antonio replaced his fingers with his tongue as he sucked and licked her nipples until she released a guttural moan that let him know she was beyond ready to feel him. He slipped his hand between her thighs and stroked her until her knees quaked. Slipping his finger between the wet folds of her flesh, he sought out her throbbing bud.

"Please," Serena cried. "Need. You."

"Just let me do one thing first," he said as he spread her thighs apart and planted his face in her wet valley. Antonio licked and sucked her most sensitive parts until her desire poured on him. As hard as he was, her heat, sweetness, and wetness made him even harder. With his free hand, he reached for the condom, ripped it open and rolled it into place. Serena wrapped her legs around his waist as he lowered himself on top of her and kissed her with an urgent need. Pressing her hips into his, Antonio dove into her valley. She moaned as she ground against him. Pleasurable sensations rushed through her body as he pumped his hips in and out.

Antonio and Serena became one, their hearts pounding in sync as they rocked and rolled across the bed. When they reached their climax, Antonio thought he felt the earth pause while he released himself. Serena clung to him, shivering with pleasure. He turned on his side and held her tightly.

She kissed his cheek. "Maybe we need to start the day like this more often."

"Yes," he said, then glanced at the clock. "Although, half the morning is over."

"That just means nighttime is right around the corner," she replied with a grin. "You know, I don't know what I would do without you."

Antonio stared into her eyes and smiled. "Luckily for you, you won't have to find out."

Serena reached up and stroked his cheek. "Being in your arms makes me feel safe and I feel as if what we have is real."

"That's because it is," he said, then kissed her softly. "Being with you is easy and I'm glad you gave us a chance."

"I gave us a chance?" she asked as she propped

up on her elbow and looked down at him. "I do believe I chased you for a year."

"You did, but I'm talking about a chance to be something real. Something more than what we have between the sheets. I'm glad you let me in to get to know the real you. Every tantalizing inch," he said as he stroked her hip.

"Well," she said, "you made it easier than I thought it would've been. Antonio, I've never known anyone like you."

"That's a good thing, right?"

"Absolutely," she said as she leaned her head against his chest. "After everything that happened with Emerson, I never thought I'd allow another man to get this close to me. I didn't want to ever get hurt again. That's all I thought love was—pain and suffering."

Antonio held her face between his hands and looked down into her eyes. "Love isn't supposed to hurt. I guess we fell for the wrong people."

Serena locked her fingers with his. "I know I did. But you and your wife built a family together."

Antonio shook his head. "Still, it wasn't enough for her. Marian, as much as I loved her, showed me that she was spoiled. I think what attracted her to me was the fact that her parents didn't like me. The first few years of our marriage were good. Then after she had A.J., it seemed as if she was bored. Her family had finally accepted me and she couldn't be the princess in revolt anymore."

"How did you meet her?" Serena asked. "I

can't see you being attracted to the princess type."

"I'm not going to say I was fooled, but I was young and she was beautiful. Marian was easy to fall for and she knew that—used it to her advantage. When I fall for a woman, I fall hard. I had no idea that she was upset with her parents and wanted to prove a point. By the time I proposed, I thought we were in love and would have a happy life together."

"But you knew she was using you?"

"No. I knew that I loved her and that's why we got married. Looking back, I could've done things differently but had we never gotten married, I wouldn't have my son."

Serena nodded. "That's true," she said. "Everything happens for a reason. If I hadn't been stood up at the altar, then I would've never come back to the South and needed a contractor."

"Funny how things work out, right?" he said with a smile.

"It is," she said, then looked over at the clock on the nightstand. "Is it really that late?" Serena groaned as she realized all she had to do, including interviewing a new bartender so she could have her evenings free to be with Antonio.

"I guess neither one of us thought about work today," he said, making no effort to let her go.

"This is so much more fun," she said as she snuggled against his chest. "But the girls are going to kill me if I don't get to the restaurant soon since I'm the one screaming for a bartender."

"At least let me fix you something to eat before you leave," he said.

Though Serena knew she should've just left and headed home to get dressed, she wasn't going to pass up the chance to spend a few more minutes with Antonio. She followed him into the kitchen and watched as he moved like liquid while preparing a late breakfast. Smiling, she thought about how she needed to tell Jade that she was right about Antonio.

"Juice or coffee?" he asked, breaking into her thoughts.

"Both," she said as she hopped off the bar stool, and crossed over, and kissed him sweetly.

"Maybe I should offer you coffee and juice more often," he said after they broke the kiss.

"You're really sweet. Antonio, I never thought I'd say this again, but I'm really falling in love with you."

He brushed his lips across hers and smiled. "I'm glad to hear that."

Serena placed her hand on the flat of his chest. "I'm not going to act as if I'm good at this or that I'm not afraid. Love hasn't been that kind to me. I don't really share my feelings because I don't want to look weak. I don't want to be hurt."

"I'd never hurt you and my love won't make you weak. All I need from you is everything. I want you to be able to love me and open up to me," he said as he took her hand and brought it to his lips.

She felt as if all the fear in her eased off her

shoulders as Antonio stared into her eyes. "You can trust in me," he said.

"I know," she said, then kissed him softly.

Antonio wrapped his arms around her waist and pulled her closer to him. Feeling his thick erection against her thighs, Serena didn't want breakfast, coffee, or juice and she didn't give a damn about interviewing anyone. All she wanted was standing right in front of her.

Chapter 24

When Serena walked into Hometown Delights, the lunchtime rush was in full swing. All the tables were full and the hostess had a line of people waiting for a table at the door. As she headed for the office, Kandace grabbed her by the arm. "So nice of you to show up two hours late," she said. "No need to ask where you've been."

Serena didn't even try to hide her smile or deny that she'd been with Antonio. "Well, how did the interviews go?"

"Who cares? I want to know if this man knows what he's done for you? Serena, I can't remember seeing you smile this much—ever."

"Well, I haven't had much reason to smile," Serena said, then she turned and faced Kandace. "I'm going to tell you something and I'd appreciated it if you kept it to yourself."

"You're pregnant?" Kandace asked.

Serena pursed her lips and rolled her eyes at her friend. "You're just being silly now."

"What is it, then?"

"I told Antonio that I love him,"

Kandace waved her hand. "I thought you were going to tell me something I didn't know. We all knew that."

"Whatever. How could you all know any such thing?"

"Serena, all anyone had to do was watch you two together and they knew you had fallen hard for that man. I'm just glad you admitted it to yourself without the need for an intervention. You know how hardheaded you can be."

"Where are Jade and Alicia?"

"In the office waiting for you. I won the bet," Kandace said.

"What bet?" Serena asked as they walked out of the dining room.

"That you would get here around one-thirty," she said as she looked down at her watch. "It's one-fifteen. Jade and Alicia had you in around three. Actually, Jade said you weren't going to let that poor man up for air."

"She's one to talk," Serena said. "Why are you still here?"

"Because Alicia roped Solomon into headlining her business conference and he's about to close a deal with James and Maurice's company for a new hotel on Lake Norman."

"So, how are you going to finish your honeymoon?"

Kandace smiled. "He's the boss, so he doesn't work twenty-four hours a day. You're not the only one having fun."

"Excuse me. I'm just glad he's making you happy."

Kandace opened the door to the office and all eyes focused on Serena.

"Damn," Jade said. "I lose."

"I don't appreciate you heffas betting on my love life," Serena said as she walked over to Alicia and pushed her off the chair in front of the computer.

"Hey," Alicia said as she laughed. "Jade's idea. We just went along with it."

Serena took Alicia's seat as Alicia took a seat on the sofa. "Well, do we have a bartender?" Serena asked.

"Yes, no thanks to you," Jade said. "He starts tonight."

"Great," Serena replied with a big smile.

Alicia looked from Serena to Kandace and then to Jade. "Did y'all see that?"

"What?" Serena asked.

"That big Kool-Aid grin on your face."

"And it has nothing to do with a bartender," Jade said. "That's all about Antonio Billups."

"So what? Now we can spend more time together since I won't be chained to the bar."

"This thing is getting serious," Alicia said.

"Getting?" Kandace said. "Already there."

Serena smacked her lips. "You can't keep anything to yourself."

"Please, like we didn't know you were head over heels for that man," Jade said.

Serena smoothed her hair. "He knows, too."

"What?" Alicia asked. "You told him?"

Serena nodded and smiled. "Antonio is special. I think he could be the one."

Alicia grabbed her chest as if she were Fred Sanford. "Hell has surely frozen over," she said, then fell into a fit of laughter.

Serena balled up a scrap of paper and tossed it at Alicia. "Oh, shut up."

"This calls for drinks," Jade said. "The Ice Queen has melted."

The women laughed, even Serena.

Antonio checked his watch before heading to the front porch to do some woodworking. He hadn't carved anything in a while and today he wasn't doing it because he was upset or needed to take his mind off Marian. He was carving because he wanted to make something for Serena. He'd noticed how she looked at the woodwork around his place, so he figured he'd make her a set of bookends. Since he had time before he had to pick up A.J., he could get a good start on the project. He was so engrossed in his work and thoughts of Serena he hadn't noticed Casey pull into the driveway or march up the front steps.

"Antonio," she said.

He looked up at her and cocked his head to the side as he continued carving. "Didn't I ask you to call before you show up here?" he snapped. "I've said all that I needed to say to you this morning."

Casey placed her hands on her hips and glared at him. "Yes, you said quite a few things, but you didn't let me say anything."

"Well, A.J.'s not here for you to fill with lies, so I could give a damn what you have to say, Case."

She reached into her jeans pocket and pulled out her cell phone. "Are you serious about Serena? I mean, you've only been sleeping with her. You see what she was before she came to town. Hell the whole world has seen on the Internet what you've been getting."

"Casey, you should go."

"No. You think I'm jealous or that I'm trying to put an end to some great romance but I'm really trying to look out for you."

Antonio rose to his feet. "The last thing I want or desire is you looking out for me."

"But I don't want to see you hurt again and that's what Serena is going to do to you," Casey whined.

Antonio placed his hand on his sister-in-law's shoulder. "Stay out of my life. Go home, Casey."

"Not until you see what kind of woman you're dealing with. Serena is no better than a common slut." Casey held her cell phone up to Antonio's face.

He looked at the image on the phone's screen and his heart instantly broke. There was Serena locked in a kiss with a man.

"That's the movie director."

Antonio turned his head away. "When did you—when did this happen?"

"Yesterday," she said. "I was at the Westin and there they were in the bar, looking very cozy. Then she came here. I'm sure she didn't even shower in between romps with you and him."

Antonio struggled to keep his emotions in check. He didn't want Casey to see how he really felt—on the inside, he was smashed.

How could she kiss him *and then come to my house and tell me how much she cared about me and how she didn't want to be hurt,* Antonio thought bitterly. She was the one who was hurting him. He should've known she wasn't over that guy. She'd given up too much for Emerson and no one could turn feelings off completely. With that man showing up in Charlotte, she probably didn't expect to feel anything for him, but did. *Still, she didn't have to lie to me and pretend we were going to have a chance for a future together,* he thought.

"Are you all right?" Casey asked.

"I asked you to leave."

"Look, don't kill the messenger," she said. "Wouldn't you rather find out now than get blindsided later?"

Antonio grabbed her shoulders and turned her toward the steps. "Leave," he snapped.

"I'm here for you if you need me," she said as she headed down the steps.

Antonio slammed into the house and pondered how he should handle this thing with Serena. Even more important, how was he going to tell A.J. she wasn't going to be around them any longer? He regretted ever introducing his son to Serena. As he headed for his truck, he decided to take A.J. to Disney World after all. He needed to get away.

The image of Serena kissing another man took him back to that dark place where he'd languished days before Marian died. He'd walked into his home and found her in the arms of her lover. She hadn't apologized and hadn't tried to excuse her indiscretion. In fact, she'd told Antonio that he was boring and had forced her to look outside her marriage for passion.

He in turn had told her that she could get out and he didn't give a damn if she lived or died since her world revolved around her carnal needs. Marian had laughed in his face, then tossed divorce papers at his feet as she flounced out of the house hand in hand with her lover.

He couldn't face that again. If Serena wanted to be with the man in the picture then to hell with her.

Serena was about to head home for a much deserved nap after her meeting with her friends about the upcoming relaunch party. Everything was set. She was so glad she didn't have to worry about finding a date for the party because Antonio would be by her side. As she walked out of the restaurant, she ran into Casey. Serena was about to sidestep her and head to her car, but Casey grabbed her arm.

"I hope you know that Antonio is wise to who you really are," she said smugly.

"What are you talking about?" Serena asked. "You know what, I don't even care."

Casey smirked at her and shook her head. "I knew from the moment I saw you that you weren't right for Antonio and now he knows it, too. I hope you and Emerson are happy together."

"What are you babbling about?"

"I saw you kiss him, and thanks to the fact that I captured it on my phone, Antonio knows you're a low down backstabbing slut as well." Casey flashed the image on her phone in Serena's face. "One thing Antonio won't stand for is a woman who is dishonest."

Serena blanched as she looked at the image. "Like you? If you saw what happened, then you know that I slapped Emerson seconds after he kissed me!"

"So? All that matters is what Antonio thought when he saw this picture. He's through with you."

Serena pushed past Casey and dashed to her car. She had to get to Antonio and tell him that kiss wasn't anything. As she drove, all she could think about was how he must have felt when he saw that picture. *Why didn't I just tell him everything last night? Then Casey would've been looking like the fool. Maybe he saw through her façade and knows the picture didn't mean a thing.*

When she pulled up to Antonio's house, she saw that his truck was gone. Serena pulled out her cell phone and dialed Antonio's number. The voicemail picked up immediately and a feeling of icy dread crept up and down her spine. "Antonio, it's Serena. Please give me a call when you get this." She thought about sitting in his driveway and waiting for him, but she was sure that when he returned home he'd be with A.J. and she didn't want to cause a scene in front of the little boy. Backing out of the driveway, she headed home to wait—silently praying Antonio would call her.

When she arrived at home, Serena paced back and forth in the living room looking at her phone every few minutes to see if Antonio had called. After twenty minutes of silence, she called him again and once again her call went directly to voicemail. She didn't leave another message. She simply got into her car and drove back to Antonio's house. She was not going to let Casey ruin the best thing that ever happened to her.

Serena sped to Antonio's house and hoped he would hear her out. She imagined that seeing her kissing Emerson flooded Antonio with memories of his cheating wife. He had to know Serena wouldn't betray him like that. *Please,* she thought, *if I saw a picture like that, I wouldn't believe it didn't mean anything.* For one second, Serena wished she was as smooth as her father. Then she realized she had the truth on her side. All she needed to do was find Antonio and get him to listen to her.

Arriving at his house, she saw Antonio and A.J. carrying luggage to the truck. Serena slammed the car in PARK behind his truck and rushed over to him. "Antonio," she said breathlessly.

"Hey, Miss Serena," A.J. said brightly, the exact opposite of the dark look that Antonio gave her as he opened the driver's side door and angrily tossed his bag inside.

"Hi, A.J.," she said, never taking her eyes off Antonio.

"Son, get in the truck," Antonio said through clenched teeth. He turned to Serena. "What do you want?"

"Can we talk for a moment?" she asked.

"Actually, no. We're about to leave," he said as he placed his hand on the door handle.

"I know what your sister-in-law showed you, but I can explain."

He rolled his eyes and opened the door. "I think the picture said enough. Move your car."

Serena folded her arms and stomped her foot like a petulant child about to have a temper tantrum. "Not until you listen to what I have to say. That picture isn't what it seems and I'm not moving until you listen to me."

"There's nothing you can say that I want to hear. You sat in my house and said all of that flowery bullshit about falling in love with me and not wanting to be hurt when you'd been kissing the guy who you claim to hate. This, I'm not going to deal with again. If you want to be with him or anyone else, don't let me stand in your way."

Serena closed the space between them and grabbed his chin, forcing him to look into her eyes. "You are all that I want."

"I'm sure you said the same thing to him before you shoved your tongue down his throat," he said as he pulled away from her. "My son and I have a reservation to make. Move your car."

"Antonio, he kissed me and I slapped him,

kicked him in his nuts, and pushed him away. You don't see that in Casey's picture, do you?"

"What I see is you kissing a man you're supposed to hate just moments before you came here. You lied to me and that's what I see when I look at that picture."

"It didn't mean anything and that's why I didn't tell you about it. It was five seconds of my life. Are you going to throw away what we feel for each other because of a five second kiss that I didn't want?"

"I'm taking my son to Disney World and you're in my way."

Serena glared at him. "So, this is how it's going to be? You're going to go away and just toss aside what we have? What I thought we were trying to build?"

"I'm not throwing anything away because it's obvious we don't have anything if you found it so easy to lie to me."

Tears welled up in Serena's eyes and she fled to her car. If that was how Antonio wanted things to be, then fine. She could walk away. She had a life before him and it was waiting for her in Atlanta. Serena cursed herself for falling in love when she knew it would only end in heartache. As she took off down the road, her cell phone rang and for a moment, she wished it was Antonio, but she saw that it was Kenya.

"Hello," she said.

"Serena, I have some good news," Kenya said. "We've gotten a fifteen-day injunction against the studio that's scheduled to release Emerson's movie."

"Great," she said flatly.

"I thought you'd be happier," Kenya said, confusion dancing in her voice.

"Please don't think I don't appreciate your hard work. Today has just been very crappy."

"Sorry to hear that. But we have a lot of work to do if we're going to keep this movie from being released," she said. "Can you meet me at my office?"

"Yeah," Serena said with a sigh, "I'm on my way."

Chapter 25

Antonio gripped his steering wheel so tight his knuckles turned white.

"Daddy, are you mad at Miss Serena?" A.J. asked.

"Son, I don't want to talk about Miss Serena. We're going to see Mickey Mouse," Antonio said with forced gaiety in his voice.

"But I thought you liked her," A.J. said.

"Let's get some McDonald's before we get on the highway." Antonio hoped the promise of forbidden fast food would take his son's mind off Serena. Even if it worked for A.J., Antonio couldn't get the image of Serena's tears out of his head. Had he judged her too harshly? Should he have given her a chance to explain? He knew she wasn't Marian, but couldn't help compare the situations. When she'd first started having her affairs, Marian denied them with the same voracity Serena had just shown. *But she'd never shown that kind of emotion,* he thought as he pulled into the drive-through.

"May I get a Happy Meal?" A.J. asked excitedly as Antonio pulled up to the speaker box.

"Sure," Antonio said as he lowered the window to order the food for his son. Since he wasn't a fan of McDonald's nor hungry, Antonio ordered himself a large iced tea. All he wanted to do was to put miles between himself and Serena.

But it's not going to be that easy to push her out of my heart, he thought as he paid for the food.

Sitting in Kenya's office, Serena struggled to focus on what her lawyer was explaining. All she could think about was Antonio's coldness and total disregard for her feelings and her explanation. Even if he thought history was repeating itself, didn't he owe it to what they had to listen to her?

"Serena, did you hear me?" Kenya asked.

Serena looked up at her, tears gleaming in her eyes.

"What's wrong?"

Serena squeezed the bridge of her nose. "I'm sorry. I can't really focus right now."

"What happened?" Kenya asked, pulling her reading glasses off her face. "Does it have anything to do with Emerson?"

Serena nodded, feeling weak and just like those girls from college who'd cried over a man. But she wasn't wrong about Antonio, was she? Had he just said those things to her because he thought that's what she wanted to hear? Thought that dropping the L-word would get her to do what? Sleep with him? They'd been there and done that numerous times. Maybe he just needed to know he was still appealing to women and she was the conduit to him jumping back into the dating game. His very own good-time girl and now he was done with her.

"What did he do?" Kenya asked when Serena fell silent.

"He kissed me," Serena said. "And I kicked him, but it wasn't before someone snapped a picture and showed it to Antonio."

"And the picture only showed the kiss. So then Antonio overreacted about it," Kenya said as she shook her head. "I've been there, in Antonio's shoes."

"Really?" Serena asked, furrowing her eyebrows in confusion.

Kenya nodded. "Before Maurice and I got married, there was a video that seemed to show Maurice cheating on me with his ex. It turned out to be fake, but it nearly ended what we had."

"How did you get through it?"

"Maurice wouldn't let me walk away. If you love Antonio, then you're going to have force him to face the truth."

"How am I going to do that? He left town with his son. When I tried to talk to him, he was so angry. His wife cheated on him and I'm guessing that photo brought back the pain he felt with her."

"It's not a lost cause if what you have is real. Maurice cheated on me when we were in college and was going to marry that tramp. Then after I saw the video, which was supposed to be of him and her, I tried to seduce James."

Serena's mouth fell open. "Seriously? I never would've thought you all had that kind of drama going on in your lives."

"You have to get through a lot of storms before you get to the happily ever after. But all the rain, thunder, and wind is worth it if this is what both of you want," Kenya said.

"I know it's what I want. I thought it was what Antonio wanted. Now I'm not so sure."

Emerson slammed his cell phone on the bed in his hotel room. A damned injunction! Serena wasn't playing about trying to keep the movie from restarting his career. When Luther had called him and told him about the injunction, all Emerson could think about was how much money he was poised to lose. Studios didn't like to have lawsuits floating around unproven movies. He had lost much of his audience after his last two films and *De Chocolat* didn't have a big star attached to it, just a great story and steamy sex scenes. Still, if the studio had to spend its money defending the film in court, what would be left for marketing? *I can't let you ruin this for me,* he thought selfishly. *Besides, this movie is going to bring us back together, especially if Casey has her way. Serena will have no choice but to promote this movie and we can have the life we would've had five years ago.*

Emerson decided to go to Serena's restaurant and try to talk some sense into her. Once he got her to drop the lawsuit, they could celebrate in style. He was confident that her whatever with Antonio was over. He could imagine the yarn Casey had spun about that brief kiss. Though Serena's lips had only been pressed against Emerson's for a couple seconds, he could still taste their sweetness. He needed more and he would get it. While Serena nursed her broken heart, he'd remind her how good they were together.

He rose from the bed and headed into the bathroom to shower. Once he was showered, shaved, and dressed, he headed to Hometown Delights and took a seat at the bar to wait for his muse.

Just after he ordered, a woman wearing a scowl walked over to the bar and stopped the bartender from pouring Emerson a drink. "You're not welcome here," she hissed at him.

"Excuse me?" Emerson said.

"Get out," she snapped. "Serena doesn't need you in her life."

"And how do you know what Serena needs?" he asked as he stared at the chocolate brown woman. "All I want to do is make her a star."

"Don't you see that you're making her life miserable? Just like you did when you left her at the altar. If you were a real man, you'd leave. Have some class about this situation."

"What makes you the expert on what Serena wants? She didn't even invite you to the wedding."

"She probably knew what a mistake she was making when she said yes to your arrogant ass."

She turned to the bartender. "Don't serve this man and if he isn't gone in five minutes, call the police."

"Yes, Miss Alicia," the bartender replied.

Alicia shot Emerson a cold look that would've made him shiver if he gave a damn about her opinion.

"All right, *Miss Alicia,* I will leave, but what are you going to do when Serena decides she wants the life you claim she doesn't want—when this movie hits the big screen."

"Being that it's one of your movies, it's going to suck and no one will even notice it." Alicia looked down at her watch. "You have four minutes to get out of here. I *will* call the police, if you don't leave."

Emerson rose from the stool, bit back a few sarcastic retorts, and headed out of the restaurant. When he saw Serena on her way in, he was happy he'd been kicked out. "Serena," he said as she walked toward him. "We need to talk."

"Go to hell, Emerson."

"Why don't you come with me? This lawsuit is going to be hell on both of us."

Serena glared at him as he allowed the door to close behind him. "Let me tell you one thing, you slimy bastard. Stay away from me and my business. I don't give a damn about that movie and before I see it released, I will tie you up in so many lawsuits and red tape you will have to release the entire feature online. I know you're behind that scene making the rounds on the Internet," she hissed. "That movie reflects who I used to be, a stupid, weak-willed woman who sacrificed what she wanted and needed to make you happy. That crap won't see the light of day as long as I have breath in my body and the power to fight you."

Emerson wrapped her arm around Serena's waist and pulled her to his chest. "That's a lot of energy to spend when you could just go along with me and be the star that I crafted you to be."

Serena pushed Emerson with such force he tumbled to the ground. She stood over him and said, "That's the last time you put your damned hands on me. I don't care if I'm in court until I'm ninety years old, you're not going to put that movie on the big screen. You can kiss my ass good-bye."

She lifted her foot as if she was going to kick him, but changed her mind. She lowered her foot and shot him a cold look. "You're not even worth me soiling my shoe." She stormed into the restaurant.

Emerson rose to his feet, feeling embarrassed as a few people sidestepped him to enter the restaurant. If she wanted things to get ugly, he was going to make sure she didn't know what hit her.

Antonio stopped in Savannah, Georgia. A.J. was sound asleep in the passenger seat and he felt as if he was drifting off to sleep. Rather than continue on, he decided to pull into a motor lodge for the night. While A.J. slept soundly, not even waking up when Antonio had carried him into the room, Antonio couldn't sleep. His mind kept going back to Serena. He wavered between anger and sadness. Perhaps he'd overacted and judged her harshly because of what he'd been though with Marian. Easing out of the bed, Antonio walked into the bathroom and splashed water on his face. "What am I doing? I should hear her out," he whispered, then headed back to the bed. He reached for his cell phone and dialed Serena's number before lying down.

You've reached Serena Jacobs. Please leave a message and I'll return your call, her voicemail played back. Antonio hung up the phone without leaving a message. He couldn't help but wonder if she was with Emerson.

But Serena isn't that type of woman, is she? he thought as he lay down on the bed again.

"Are you dense?" Jade snapped as she stared at Serena. "That was Antonio, wasn't it?"

Serena shrugged her shoulders. "I tried to talk to him and he was so cold to me. I'm not going to answer that phone and beg him to listen to me. I've decided to go back to Atlanta. You guys don't need me around here."

"But what about the relaunch party?" Alicia asked.

Serena rolled her eyes, trying to forget that she'd bought a slick outfit for the party and had hoped to have Antonio by her side. She was definitely going to return the jumpsuit and shoes she'd purchased from SouthPark mall. "I'm in no mood to party. Kenya and I have to get this suit rolling and I don't want to be here anymore."

"Well," Kandace said as she picked up a mug of tea from the desk, "My honeymoon's not over yet and you said you would stay until I was working full-time again."

Serena glared at her friends, ready to curse them out. Instead, she folded her arms and said, "Fine. I'll stay, but I am not coming to the damned party and I don't want to talk to Antonio."

"I can't believe you're going to give up on him after you spent all this time—" Jade said before Serena held her hand up and cut her off.

"I blame myself for this madness. I looked at you and Kandace and saw this love thing blooming. I thought I could have it, too. But love hurts and I'm done with it," Serena said, then rose to her feet. "I'll be at home if you need me."

When she tore out of the office, she didn't notice her cell phone was still on the desk.

Chapter 26

Antonio had drifted off to sleep. The chime of his cell phone woke him. His heart jumped when he saw that Serena was calling him back. He'd been wrong. The call signaled to him that she wasn't with Emerson. He grabbed the phone and headed in the bathroom so he wouldn't wake his son.

"Hello?"

"Antonio." It was a female voice, but wasn't Serena's.

"Who is this?"

"This is Jade Goings and I want to apologize in advance for making this call, but it had to be done."

"Did something happen to Serena?" Antonio asked, his voice filled with concern. What if she'd been in a car accident and was lost to him forever?

"Something is happening to Serena and you're

the cause of it," Jade said. "She's miserable, but has too much pride to admit it."

"Listen, what's going on with me and Serena is really none of your business. Why did she give you her phone to call me? I tried to reach out to her today and—"

"Wait a minute, buddy," Jade snapped. "Serena doesn't know I'm calling you. She was so upset when she left the restaurant that she left her phone here. I didn't call to argue with you. Serena is in love with you. She doesn't show her emotions easily, and she also doesn't lie. Unfortunately, she's the most honest person I know— whether the truth hurts or not."

"Then why am I hearing from you and not her?" Antonio asked, frustrated with the conversation.

"Because you two are the most stubborn people I know and if I didn't make this call, you were going to miss out on her. Serena is ready to move back to Atlanta because of what happened between the two of you."

"What?"

"Yes," Jade said. "So, if you still care about her then you'd better do something about it."

"How am I going to call her if you have her phone?"

"I'm going to take this phone to her in about an hour. I suggest you call her and make this right. Serena is the best woman you will ever meet. When she loves, she loves all the way. That woman loves you and you're a fool if you let her go."

"Thanks for the call, but if Serena and I are to have a future, I'd appreciate it if you allowed us to work out our problems on our own." Antonio could've sworn he heard Jade chuckle.

"Since you and Serena are more than likely going to have a future, I'll tell you this—we're family and this is how we roll. But only in extreme circumstances. Just don't throw away what you two have. You're good for Serena, otherwise I never would've made this call."

"All right," he said. Once they hung up, Antonio was relieved that his call went unanswered because Serena had been with her girlfriends and not Emerson. Still, did he have it inside him to move past this?

Serena kicked back on the sofa and turned the television on. But she didn't watch whatever was showing. She wasn't interested in anything. Except leaving.

"Why did I agree to stay here?" she muttered as she reached for her purse and fumbled for her cell phone. Serena smacked her hand against her forehead. Her phone was at the restaurant. There was no way she was going back there. She would call the movers tomorrow.

Tonight, she was going to veg out and make her mind forget Antonio Billups. She had to forget how he kissed her and how he made her legs shiver with the touch of his skilled fingers. She had to forget how safe she felt when he held her in his strong arms and how his smile made her heart melt. Closing her eyes, she forced herself to remember the cold look he'd given her the last time she'd seen him. Just as she was about to drift off to sleep, Serena heard a knock at the door.

"Antonio," she murmured as she leaped off the sofa and dashed to the door. When she opened it and saw Jade, her heart dropped to the bottoms of her feet. Serena opened the door and didn't hide the fact that she wasn't excited to see Jade. "What's up, Jade?" she asked flatly.

"Well, I'm happy to see you, too," Jade replied. "You left your cell phone at the restaurant."

"Thanks." Serena took the phone from her friend's hand.

"Everything is going to be all right," Jade said. "You want to talk?"

"No. Besides, you have a family to get to. I don't want to hold you up."

Jade stepped inside the foyer. "All right. You are my family and I don't want you to do this again."

"Do what?" Serena asked as she padded to the sofa and plopped down on the cushions.

Jade sat across from her friend and looked at her watch. "Shut yourself off from love. You did that after L.A. and you can't do it again. If I were you, I wouldn't give up on Antonio." She glanced down at her watch again.

"Don't you have some place you need to be?" Serena asked. "Because you can go."

Jade rose to her feet and shook her head.

"Keep being sour and I'll send Kandace and Alicia over."

Serena waved her hand as she stretched out on the sofa. "You know your way out. And Jade." Her friend turned around and looked at her. "Thanks for caring about me, but I'm not the one who gave up on Antonio. He gave up on me and I'm not going to allow my feelings to get hurt again."

Before Jade could reply, Serena's cell phone rang. "Yes?" she said without looking at the CALLER ID.

"Serena, it's Antonio."

"Antonio," she said as she heard the front door close. "I'm surprised to hear from you."

"I know," he said. "Listen, I owe you a chance to explain that picture and I want to hear what you have to say."

Serena closed her eyes and expelled a breath. "It's not something I think we should discuss over the phone," she said.

"Neither do I. A.J. and I will be in Orlando at Disney World for three days and when I return, we should meet."

"If I'm still here, then that will be fine," she said, knowing that she'd be right there waiting for his return.

"Are you planning a trip?" he asked.

"I'm going back to Atlanta. I've done all I need to do at the restaurant and it doesn't seem as if I have a reason to stay in Charlotte."

"If that's what you want to do," he said.

Serena felt a chill tear through her system.

"That's what I want to do," she snapped. "I can tell from your tone you don't really want to work this thing out."

"Really? Since you can read my mind over the phone, tell me why I would've called you if I didn't want to work things out? Serena, I've been cheated on before and yes, I allowed my past to cloud what I saw. But I'm not going to pressure you into doing something you don't want to do."

All I want is to be with you, she thought but held her tongue. "I haven't made any plans so, I can wait. It's not a problem."

"Serena, I . . . I'll see you when I get back," he said bringing their tense conversation to an end.

"All right. I hope you and A.J. have a good time at Disney World," she said with tears welling up in her eyes. Serena could feel things were coming to an end between them. When he returned to Charlotte, it would be official.

Antonio looked at his cell phone and shook his head. Was what he'd found in Serena worth saving? *Hell yes,* a voice inside him screamed. *She's a woman who has been hurt so I shouldn't have expected that she was sitting around waiting for me to call her.* He climbed into bed beside his son and closed his eyes. He loved Serena and he couldn't let her go. He wasn't going to let her walk away and go back to Atlanta. But what about that kiss with Emerson? Was it just as she said it was and Casey was using it to her advantage?

Damn, I should've known better than to take Casey

at her word. I know she doesn't like Serena and she wants to be with me. What was I thinking? By the time he drifted off to sleep, Antonio knew he had to make things right with Serena. He didn't want to have a life without her in it.

Early the next morning, A.J. woke up and poked his father in the arm until Antonio sat up. "Are we there yet?" A.J. asked. "Are we going to see Mickey Mouse today?"

"We sure are. But first, let's get out of here and get some breakfast." Antonio was glad to have his bubbly son with him. It forced him not to think about Serena that much. When they checked out of the hotel and got on the highway, Antonio stopped at a Waffle House on the Florida/Georgia border. A.J. talked about Mickey Mouse and how many pictures he wanted to take with his favorite cartoon character. As the waitress brought their waffles and eggs over, A.J. said, "I wish Miss Serena could've come with us. Do you think she likes Mickey Mouse?"

"I'm sure she does," Antonio said, masking his hurt with a smile. "Everyone loves Mickey Mouse." *And I love Serena. That's why I'm not going to let anything come between us when she has shown me that I can and should love again. I can trust her because she isn't Marian.*

"Did you hear me, Daddy?" A.J. asked.

"No, what did you say?"

"I said you can take some Mickey Mouse ears back to Miss Serena," the little boy said with a laugh.

"We can do that," Antonio said as he and A.J. dug into their breakfast.

After eating, Antonio and A.J. drove nonstop to Disney World. While he was focused on the road, every now and then he thought about Serena and how his son really liked her. Allowing her to move back to Atlanta wouldn't just hurt Antonio, but A.J. as well. He couldn't and wouldn't let that happen. He knew that when he got back to Charlotte, the first thing he was going to do was tell Serena in no uncertain terms that she was a habit he couldn't let go. He wasn't going to allow her to leave when he loved her so much.

Serena woke up still sprawled on her sofa with an ache in her lower back. Rolling her eyes, she sat up and ran her hand across her face. She hadn't liked the way she and Antonio ended their conversation. Had she been wrong about his feelings for her or was she overreacting? He had said he wanted to see her when he returned but she felt there was still an accusatory tone in his voice. She wanted to bash Emerson and Casey until they were bad memories. But as much as she wanted to blame them for Antonio's change of heart, she had to accept that he was a grown man and if he wanted to forgive her, it would be his choice.

"Just what in the hell is he forgiving *me* for?" she mumbled. "*I* didn't do anything wrong and have no reason to kiss his behind."

She rose from the sofa and started upstairs to take a shower when her cell phone rang. Serena nearly tripped over her feet rushing back to the sofa to grab it, hoping Antonio was on the other end. "Hello?" she said.

"Serena, it's Kenya."

"Hi, Kenya," she replied, struggling to keep the disappointment out of her voice.

"I have some good news and some bad news," her attorney said.

"Why am I not surprised?" Serena muttered. "Just lay it out for me."

"Well," Kenya began. "We can't stop the release of the movie because Emerson has all the rights to the film. However, Lionsgate is starting to back away because a few women's groups are calling it a sexist film."

Serena chewed on her bottom lip not knowing if she agreed with that assessment of the movie, but if protest would keep it off the big screen then she was all for it. "I guess that is good news," she replied finally.

"That's not the good news," Kenya said and Serena could almost hear her smile though the phone. "I spoke with the credited screenwriter and he confirmed that more than ninety percent of the screenplay's rewrites were done by you. That means if the movie is released you will be paid for it."

"I don't want his money," Serena said.

"It's not about his money. It's about getting what you are due for all of your hard work," Kenya said. "It won't be his money. Unfortunately, the

movie will be a hit. I saw a rough cut of it and it's
pretty good."

"Damn it."

"Emerson will profit from it and leave you
alone. He wants to get his career back on track,
but I have enough media contacts to spread the
true story about him."

"No," Serena snapped. "I don't want any press
and I don't want credit for the screenplay. Just
the money, since that seems as if it's the only
thing I can get from this. It's not as if I'm trying
to become a screenwriter anymore."

"All right, but you should let image-conscious
Hollywood know what kind of snake he is and
how little talent he has."

Serena paused and considered it, but then Antonio flashed in her mind. How would he feel
about that? *What does it matter?* Serena's cynical
side said. *He's not worried about my feelings right
now.* "I'll let you know about that. I just want this
to go away."

"Well, for good measure and possibly to keep
the studio even more leery about releasing this
movie, I'm going to file another injunction and
an intent to sue," Kenya said.

"Thanks."

"Antonio will understand what this is really
about," Kenya said as if she read Serena's mind.

"Not that it matters," Serena said in a near whisper that Kenya didn't hear. "Thanks for everything."

"I was glad to help. If it makes you feel any

better, I'll be sure to tell everyone I know not to go see the movie."

Serena smiled despite herself, then said good-bye. Feeling a little less depressed, Serena headed upstairs to take her shower and prepare for her day. She was going to go into the restaurant, then prepare for her move back to Atlanta. *Should I at least hear Antonio out before I go back to Atlanta?* she thought as the warm shower spray poured over her. Before she knew it, Serena was thinking of the moments when Antonio kissed her the way the water rained down on her. She remembered how tenderly he made love to her and how seeing his face sent her heart into overdrive.

Serena shut the water off as it became ice cold. She could give up those desires and the passion she shared with him. After all, he was only a man.

The man you love, she heard Jade's voice telling her. *And if you try to pretend that you can walk away from this man and be fine with it then you're a damned fool.* Serena stepped out of the shower and toweled herself dry trying to remember the woman she was before Antonio. The Ice Queen.

Serena soon realized the Ice Queen had melted. In her wake was a blubbering, emotional woman who wasn't going to allow the man she loved to get away from her that easily.

Chapter 27

Though Antonio enjoyed seeing Disney World through A.J.'s eyes, he was ready to get back to Charlotte and talk to Serena. A.J. was talking a mile a minute about how much fun he had and how cool it was to finally see Mickey Mouse. Antonio noticed that A.J. held Serena's mouse ears carefully as they drove.

"We had so much fun," A.J. said. "Can we do this every summer?"

"I think we can," Antonio said. "Maybe next year we'll stay at the Animal Kingdom."

"Anywhere but Cinderella's castle. That's for girls." A.J. made a face as if he'd tasted sour milk.

"All right, no Cinderella's palace," Antonio said with a laugh.

"Dad, can we stop and get McDonald's?"

"No. We can stop at Subway and get some veggies today."

"Aww man," A.J. said as Antonio took a highway exit.

When they made it to the restaurant, Antonio's cell phone rang. He hoped it was Serena, but when he saw it was Casey, he groaned. "Yeah?" he said into the phone.

"Is everything all right? Mother has been looking for you and A.J.," she said frantically. "Where are you guys?"

"A.J. and I are fine. We're actually on our way back to Charlotte from Disney World."

"I thought you were . . . Did you take Serena with you?"

"Casey, I'm not going to talk to you about Serena. You've done enough."

"Would you rather not know what kind of woman you were dealing with? I know how hurt you were when you found out about Marian and her affairs."

"I don't want to have this conversation with you. Be aware, Serena will still have a place in my life."

"How do you know she isn't with Emerson Bradford right now?"

"Good-bye, Casey." Antonio hung up and turned back to his sandwich.

A.J. looked up at his father. "Are you and Aunt Casey still fighting?"

"No, just having a disagreement. Adults do that sometimes," Antonio replied. "Come on and eat up." The last thing he wanted to do was put his son in the middle of what was going on between himself and Casey. At the end of the day she was still A.J.'s aunt. No matter what Antonio thought about her, his son loved her.

"Do you think Aunt Casey is going to be upset because we didn't bring her some Mickey Mouse ears?" A.J. asked.

"We'll make sure we get her a set next year," Antonio said in between bites of his sandwich.

After finishing their meal, they were back on the road and A.J. soon drifted off to sleep. As they crossed into South Carolina, Antonio smiled. There were less than one hundred miles between him and Serena. His mind was conflicted as he wondered if she had spent the last few days alone or with Emerson. Antonio forced those thoughts out of his mind and replaced them with images of Serena wrapped up in his arms. The first thing he had to do when he saw her was apologize for the way he'd acted before he left. Then he'd hope that she would accept his apology by kissing him in the way that made his libido rise like the sun in the east. He could feel the warmth of her breath dancing on his neck as she kissed him. If he was lucky and Serena was in a forgiving mood, his fantasy would become reality.

"Emerson," Luther said in an exasperated tone. "You're not listening to me. We've spent a good portion of the marketing for this film in court answering all of these motions Serena Jacobs and her attorney filed. The best thing for us to do is to either have the movie released straight to DVD or in theatres as a limited release feature."

"I'm not some chitlin' circuit director who wants to get a movie released to the masses." Emerson groaned. "You know this movie deserves to be on the big screen."

"I also know we can't go broke trying to release this movie. I implored you to get Serena Jacobs's cooperation and you did everything you could to make her want to sue you and everyone tied to your film."

"The public wants this movie," Emerson said as he looked at the YouTube clip again. "Do you know how many people have watched the movie clip on the Internet?"

"I'm well aware of that. Emerson, listen. The decision has been made. We're doing a limited release or nothing at all. You'd better hope those millions of people who watched that clip go to the theatres where the movie is going to be shown."

"You're going to regret this."

"I'm already there," Luther said, then hung up the phone.

Emerson growled like a wounded bear as he looked at his phone, realizing he wasn't going to get what he wanted. *Fine,* he thought. *If Serena wants to play it this way then I can make* her *life hell, too.*

Serena scratched her head as she looked over the press release Kandace had sent for her to approve. Tonight was the relaunch party and they had a few media outlets that wanted a statement for the evening news. Serena wasn't at all surprised they had gotten some national exposure for the party—due to Solomon Crawford and the fact that Kandace was his wife. Not to mention Maurice Goings's involvement with the party.

While she was happy they were getting so much exposure for the event and the restaurant, Serena couldn't wait until the party was over and she could leave. She had thought she was going to be at the party enjoying Babyface's sweet love songs with Antonio by her side, but that was looking as if it wasn't going to happen. He'd told her that when he returned to Charlotte he was going to talk to her, but she hadn't heard from him and assumed he'd changed his mind. Well, her mind was made up and she was going back to Atlanta.

"Are you excited about tonight?" Alicia asked when she burst into the office.

Serena ignored her question and handed her a letter. "This came for you."

Alicia took the letter from her friend's hand and looked at the return address. "Ugh, you should've tossed this."

"Isn't that from your high school? Either it is reunion time or they want money."

Alicia rolled her eyes. "I don't care. High school was not good to me and I'm not looking forward to going back over there."

"Then don't. Send them a fifty-cent check and

call it a day," Serena said as she watched Alicia open the letter. "Well, what is it?"

Alicia scowled. "Fifteen-year reunion. They want me to come and receive a special award."

"Are you going?"

Alicia shook her head. "I hated high school. I'm in no hurry to go back and see those people."

Serena was surprised by the venom in her usually calm friend's voice. "Who did enjoy high school? Go back and show those assholes what a success you have become."

"Let's talk about our party. Will you be attending with Antonio?"

"I'd rather talk about the guest list and who's going to be working the door," Serena said, tossing her head back.

"So, it's true?" Alicia shook her head.

"What's true? I know you heffas have not been talking about me behind my back," Serena raged.

"This is why we talk about you behind your back—because you fly off the handle. Is that what happened with you and Antonio?"

Serena eased back in the chair and tossed her feet up on the desk top. "It doesn't matter what happened between Antonio and me because he's—"

"Standing right outside the door," Alicia said as she watched Antonio walk down the hall.

"What?" Serena scrambled to her feet.

Alicia glanced at her. "Hurry up and do something with that hair—like pull it out of that ponytail."

Serena snatched her ponytail holder out of her hair and smoothed her skirt, then shook her head. "What am I doing?" she muttered as Alicia opened the office door all the way.

The moment Antonio stood in the doorway, Serena realized why she cared about her appearance.

Antonio took a deep breath as he drank in Serena's image. She looked sexy . . . and confused to see him standing there.

"Hello, Antonio," Alicia said. "Well, I have to go. Serena, we'll work on the guest list later."

"Hello, Serena," Antonio said when they were alone.

"Antonio," she said, her voice cool and detached. "I'm surprised to see you here."

He crossed over to her and stood inches from her, struggling not to pull her into his arms and kiss her until they were both dizzy from passion. "I told you I wanted to talk to you when I returned from Disney World."

She shifted as if she could feel the heat brewing between them. "This really isn't a good time for me," Serena said.

"Yes, it is. I'm going to make this quick and simple. I was a fool. I was wrong. Please forgive me and let me make up for being an asshole."

Serena's lips curved into a smile and she placed her hands on Antonio's cheeks. "Did you just come in here and apologize?"

"Yes. I was wrong for not giving you a chance

to explain that picture, especially when I know Casey has an agenda," he said.

Serena didn't reply. She leaned into him and kissed his lips with a gentle yearning that eased his tension and fears that he'd lost her. His hands snaked down her back and rested on her ample bottom as their kiss deepened and his knees quaked.

Serena broke the kiss and looked into his eyes as he smiled at her. "As much as I want to stand here and allow you to accept all the blame, I have to apologize as well. Like I said, that kiss with Emerson meant nothing, but when I told you about my day and how we'd had a run-in, I should've told you everything. However you and I were having such a wonderful night I didn't want to ruin that. When I'm with you, all I can think about is being with you and kissing you and having you wrap these arms around me." She ran her hand down his left arm and smiled, thinking how she thought she'd never feel his strength around her again.

Antonio brushed his lips against hers. "I'm always going to be here for you, no matter what."

Serena felt the warmth of joyful tears in her eyes and she blinked to hold them back. Antonio took her face into his hands and wiped away the lone tear sliding down her cheek. "Baby," he said. "What's with the tears?"

"Honestly," Serena said. "I've never gotten this far before. I can't say I'm not going to make mistakes in this relationship, but you have to know you're the only man I want. But, I can be selfish and sometimes I'm going to get on your nerves."

"And you think I'm not?" he asked as he kissed her again. "I don't expect perfection. I want you."

Serena hugged him tightly. "I'm going to hold you to that when I burn some rice."

"Please, you know we don't do much cooking in the kitchen," Antonio laughed as he cupped her bottom. "A.J. has something for you."

"Really?"

"Yes, he wanted you to come to Disney World with us. I kind of committed you for next year."

"I like the sound of that," she said. "What do you say we get out of here for a little bit?"

"All right, but don't you have some work to do?" he asked.

Serena shrugged and smiled. "You know I do my best work outside the office."

"Let's go."

Serena and Antonio rushed out of the restaurant and headed to his truck. They hopped inside like two teenagers about to skip school. "Where are we going? My place or yours?" he asked.

"My place is closer," she said as she slipped her hand between his thighs. "Unless you want to—" Before she could say anything else, someone tapped on the driver's side window. Antonio and Serena angrily looked at the person interrupting them.

"Emerson," she growled.

Antonio glared at the man who'd nearly made

him lose the best thing that had happened to him. "What do you want to do?"

"Drive off."

Antonio started the truck and they tore out of the parking lot. Neither of them looked back at Emerson as he glared angrily at them.

Chapter 28

Anger surged through Emerson's body as he stood in the parking lot of Hometown Delights. Did Serena really think she could brush him off after she'd ruined his chances for a comeback? He wanted to grab her by her throat and shake her until she got it through her head that this movie wasn't about her. If she was so happy with her new life, then she wouldn't be trying to ruin his. Despite the fact that he had other scripts and could easily abandon the project, Emerson wanted to put *this* movie on the big screen. Serena had pissed him off. All she had to do was go along with the plan. She knew what she was getting into when she made the movie.

At some point she had to know it was going to be released. Now she pretended she didn't want that to happen because of *him*. Didn't Antonio know he wasn't man enough for a muse like Serena? Emerson was going to make sure he knew it. He reached into his pocket and removed his cell phone, then dialed Casey's number.

"Yes?" she snapped.

"I thought you said you had gotten Antonio out of Serena's life? Didn't you show him the picture?"

"I did, but obviously she has cast some sort of spell on him. He's giving her another chance."

"I know. I just saw them leave together."

"Then you have to do something," Casey said. "You still want her. You know her restaurant is having a party tonight. Maybe you should make your move then."

"What about your end of the bargain?" Emerson asked. "You wanted him and you're just sitting back and letting him walk away with Serena."

"You're starting to sound as if you're obsessed. Why don't you just let it go?"

"Maybe you lay down and let people walk over you. But I didn't get to where I am today by doing that."

"And where are you, Emerson? You're on the outside looking in at Serena's life. Give it up."

"If that's what you want to do, then that's fine." Emerson clicked the phone off and headed down the street.

Serena sauntered into the kitchen, dressed only in her black thong and matching lace bra. She grabbed a bottle of water from the refrigerator and downed half of it before Antonio met her at the refrigerator and took the bottle from her hand, finishing off the rest.

"The argument, I don't like, but that was one hell of a make up," he said as he placed the bottle on the counter.

Serena tugged at the waistband of Antonio's gray boxer briefs. "We still have some more 'I'm sorries' to moan," she said seductively.

Antonio looked down at his watch and shook his head. "Rain check. I have to pick A.J. up. And you have to come over before the restaurant party because he has something special to give you."

Serena wrapped her arms around his waist and kissed his chest gently. "Then I will be there before I go to the party. Do you think you're going to be able to be my date tonight?"

"I'll have to find a babysitter."

"If you can't don't worry about it. I won't stay long and we can have our own party."

Antonio kissed her lips and smiled. "I'll look forward to it."

Serena released him, opened the refrigerator, grabbed another bottle of water, and handed it to Antonio. "Then you're going to need to be hydrated."

A few moments later, Antonio was dressed and headed out to his car. Serena watched him from the door with a smile plastered on her face. She hadn't expected things to go that way, but she was over the moon with happiness. Love hadn't hurt her as she thought it would.

* * *

Out of habit, Antonio nearly called Casey, but he closed his phone as he pulled up to Discovery Place to pick up A.J. from his last day of camp. Antonio smiled when he saw his son standing out front holding court with his friends. He knew the little boy was telling them all about Disney World and all the fun he'd had. Antonio beeped his horn and waved for A.J. to come over. The little boy waved to his friends and one little girl rushed over to him and gave him a hug. Antonio smiled as he saw the blush on A.J.'s cheeks when he walked to the truck.

"Was that your girlfriend?" he asked his son when he climbed inside.

"Yes. She really likes Mickey Mouse too."

"That's good. Serena's going to come over tonight and get your gift."

"Really? You didn't tell her what it is, did you?" A.J. asked.

"And ruin the surprise? No."

"Okay. After I give her the ears, may I go spend the night with Kamir and his granddaddy? Kamir said they're going fishing again."

"Well, son, this is kind of last minute. I'll have to call Norman and make sure that it's all right."

"I hope he says yes,"

"If he doesn't, we can take our own fishing trip next weekend. Maybe you can teach me your trick for catching big fish."

A.J. shook his head. "Mr. Norman said a real fisherman never tells his secrets."

"Not even to his dad?"

A.J. shook his head again and laughed. "Nope."

"All right, keep your secrets. But I have a few of my own, too."

When they pulled up to the house, Antonio saw Casey's car parked in the driveway and shook his head. He was not in the mood for his sister-in-law.

"Aunt Casey," A.J. said as he rushed out of the truck, spotting his aunt sitting on the edge of the porch. She enveloped A.J. in her arms and hugged him as Antonio unlocked the front door.

"How have you been?" she asked sweetly.

"Really good. Daddy took me to Disney World," A.J. replied excitedly. "I got you something."

Antonio stepped aside from the door. "Why don't you run in and get it for her?"

"Yes, sir." A.J. headed inside.

Antonio turned to Casey. "What are you doing here? I think I asked you to stop popping up at my house without calling first."

"I know, but I thought this couldn't wait. Emerson Bradford isn't done with Serena."

He shook his head and glared at Casey. "So, you're here to cause more trouble as usual. I know Emerson is done with Serena because we spent the afternoon together, so if you came here to spread lies, then you can go home."

Casey leaped to her feet and stood toe to toe with Antonio. "I know you want that woman but you need to be aware you're not the only one under her spell and I'm afraid that he may—"

"Casey, I'm done with this and you," Antonio said as he saw his son bouncing down the steps with his aunt's oversized lollypop in his hand.

"Don't say I didn't try to warn you," she snapped as A.J. reached the bottom step.

A.J. looked from his father to his aunt, then handed Casey the lollypop. She smiled sweetly at her nephew as she took the candy. "Thank you for thinking about me," she said, then pointedly glared at Antonio. "I'm glad someone does."

"Are you still mad at Daddy?" A.J. asked his aunt. "He said you guys were having a mis—"

"I'm not the one with the problem. It's your Dad," Casey said.

"Go inside, A.J.," Antonio said, then turned to Casey. "You're not going to do this. I've stood by and allowed you to say things about Serena. I tried to ignore it because you're his aunt, but I'm telling you for the last time. I'm not going to let you poison my son's mind against a woman I love. You're not going to tell him that I have a problem with you because you won't mind your damned business."

"You love her? What do you even know about her?"

"Go home, Casey," Antonio said, struggling to keep his voice down.

"Fine, if you love her and you want to be with her, then fine—but I hope you know what you're getting into." She stormed to her car and sped out of the neighborhood. Antonio simply shook his head as he watched her car disappear down the road. When he turned around and saw A.J. standing at the door, he knew he had some explaining to do.

He walked into the house and looked down at his son, who had a confused look on his face. "A.J.," he said.

"You're fighting with Aunt Casey just like the night Mommy went to heaven," A.J. said with tears welling up in his eyes.

Antonio knelt in front of his son and grasped his chin. "Listen," he began, "your aunt is going to be fine. Just because me and your aunt got into an argument doesn't mean she's going to die. What happened the night your mother died was a terrible accident."

A.J. sniffed and struggled to hold his tears back. Antonio hugged him tightly. "I know you love Casey. Right now, we're not getting along really well, but that doesn't have anything to do with you."

"Okay," the little boy said, then sighed. "I just want you and Aunt Casey to be friends again."

"We will," Antonio said, though he knew thing would never be the same between him and Casey ever again.

Serena woke up from her much needed nap when she heard a banging on her door. She groaned as she pulled herself off the sofa. Realizing she was still in her bra and panties, she called out, "Hold on," then dashed upstairs to grab her robe. She pulled the curtain back and saw Alicia and Jade standing on her front step.

"What's up, ladies?" Serena said when she opened the door.

"That's a good question," Alicia said as she and Jade walked in.

"Am I late for something?" Serena asked as she looked down at her watch and up at her friends.

"She's going to play games," Jade said as she shook her head. "You know why we're here."

"Where's Antonio?" Alicia asked. "Please tell me you didn't mess things up!"

Serena rolled her eyes, but was unable to hide her smile.

Jade clapped her hands and giggled. "It's about damned time," she said to Serena. "So, he's coming with you to the party tonight?"

"Maybe not. He has to find a babysitter. Since it's such short notice, I may see him after I leave."

"Sounds like you won't be there long," Alicia said.

"That's right, so I guess I could get there early and help set up," Serena said as she led her friends into the living room. "You guys want something to drink or have you gotten the information you wanted?"

Alicia and Jade exchanged a look that Serena didn't like. "What's going on?" she asked them.

Jade and Alicia sat down on the sofa and Serena took a seat across from them on the love seat. "I'm going to ask again, what's wrong?" Serena asked.

"After you and Antonio left, James came up and found Emerson skulking around the parking lot," Jade said. "That guy is losing his grip on reality."

Serena shrugged. "I saw Emerson when Antonio and I left. He lost his grip on reality when he tried to put that movie on the big screen after everything that happened between us. He's not a problem."

"I don't know," Alicia said. "James said he was mumbling about making you pay as he stormed away."

Serena shrugged again. "He isn't a threat. That's Emerson being Hollywood. I'm sure he's going to be leaving soon. There is nothing in Charlotte for him. He found that out when he saw his little stunt with that witch Casey didn't work."

"Stunt?" Alicia asked.

"You are always holding back information," Jade said.

"Right," Alicia agreed, "but is always front and center in our business."

Jade nodded and turned to Serena. "Spill it. And make it fast because I have to go see my husband and son before the party."

"I went to the Westin one night and confronted Emerson about the movie. That son of a—he kissed me."

"What?" Alicia and Jade exclaimed in concert.

"How did you let that happen?" Jade asked.

Serena held up her hand to silence her friends. "It lasted all of two seconds and I kneed him where it hurt. But that little twit Casey was there with her cell-phone camera and snapped a picture."

Alicia threw her hands above her head. "Some people are so lucky that we have matured. If we were still in college, Casey would catch a beat down."

"No, she wouldn't," Jade said. "We'd just flatten her tires."

The three women laughed and Serena continued with her story, telling them that Antonio had been very upset and that had been why they weren't speaking.

"Once again, holding out on us," Alicia said.

"That's why I'm happy I did what I did," Jade said with a slick smile.

"What did you do?" Serena asked. "You called him that night when I left my phone at the restaurant?"

Jade nodded and flashed Serena a look that said, *I dare you to be mad about it.*

Serena crossed over to her friend and hugged her. "Thank you for being a nosy heffa."

"That was the most backhanded thank you I've ever gotten," Jade said as she pinched Serena's shoulder.

"All right, now that you're happy again, what are you going to do about Emerson's crazy ass?" Alicia asked.

"There's nothing to do," Serena said. "I'm sure security will keep Emerson out of my way."

"But—"

Serena cut Jade off. "Stop worrying about Emerson. He isn't going to do anything. I'm telling you, he's running that Hollywood drama now, but he's lost. Knowing him, he's on his way back to L.A."

"But what if he is still here? The last thing we need is more bad press on the restaurant," Alicia said.

"Then make sure security is tight. Emerson doesn't want bad press either. It's not as if we're dealing with a psychotic stalker again," Serena said as Jade stood up and smoothed her hand across her pants.

"I'll make sure the security guards know to keep him out and if I have to ask Maurice to put a few of his football friends at the door, I will."

Serena rolled her eyes and shook her head. "You all are overreacting. By the way, where is Kandace?"

Jade and Alicia exchanged a knowing look. "She's going over the guest list in the office with Solomon."

"Ugh, that means they're having sex on the furniture again?" Serena groaned. "Solomon is going to buy us some more office furniture."

"Why, so you and Antonio can break it in?" Jade said as she and Alicia headed to the door.

"Absolutely not. We have our own special place outside of the restaurant," Serena said. "And I know you aren't talking."

"Thank you," Alicia said. "You never know what you're going to walk in on with James and Jade."

Jade smiled and shrugged her shoulders. "Whatever. He is my husband and trust me, we stay out of that office."

"We'll see you later," Alicia said. "Unless you skip the party and spend the evening in your *special place* with Antonio."

"That might not be such a bad idea," Jade said. "Lord knows you were sick over that man."

"I'm coming to the party, taking a few pictures with the other owners, and then I'm off to spend the night with my man."

The women waved good-bye to each other and Serena headed upstairs. After getting ready for the party, she went to see Antonio to make sure she hadn't spent the afternoon dreaming.

Chapter 29

Norman and Kamir sat in the living room as A.J. grabbed his fishing gear.

"Thanks for taking him with y'all," Antonio said. "But are you sure this isn't too much?"

"Not at all. I love hanging out with A.J.," Norman said. "He and Kamir are the best fishermen I know."

Kamir smiled proudly under his grandfather's compliments.

"Besides, Kamir needs to hang out with someone his age. His brothers are into other things these days and they don't want little brother hanging around.

"I don't want to play no stupid video games anyway. But they can't have my fish," Kamir said.

"That's right, no fishing, no eating," Norman said.

Before Antonio could respond, the doorbell rang. Since the door was open, he saw it was Serena and he beckoned her in. Dressed in a strapless black lace dress that hit her at her knees all the air was sucked out of the room when she walked in. Her skin seemed to glow and with her hair pulled back from her face, her eyes were expressive and shining. Antonio stood up and inhaled sharply as his eyes roamed her body. Even Kamir smiled appreciatively at Serena.

"Hi," she said as she walked over to Antonio.

"Hi," he said.

Norman cleared his throat to remind everyone that he was in the room.

Serena turned to him and smiled. "Hello, Norman, long time no see."

The older man stood up and smiled at Serena. "Yes, I see you're still wearing those sky high shoes."

"Well, when I walk in the restaurant tonight the floor will be finished. You guys did a great job," she said, then glanced at Kamir who hadn't taken his eyes off her since she walked in. "Hi, there."

"Hee-hee, hi," he giggled, then buried his face in Norman's arm.

"This is my grandson, Kamir," Norman said. "He's not usually this shy."

"Where's A.J.?" Serena asked. "I wanted to see him before I headed to the party."

"You're just in time," Norman said. "He was about to join us for a fishing trip. So, I guess I'll have to wait and go to the next party with you. Antonio will take my place tonight."

Serena and Antonio laughed as A.J. ran into the living room with his fishing gear. "Miss

Serena." He dropped his gear and hugged her around her legs. "You look pretty."

"Thank you. So, you're going fishing. Does that mean I get to eat some more cole slaw and fish?" she asked as she stroked his head.

"Yes! Tomorrow we can have a fish fry, right Mr. Norman?"

"We sure can," Norman said. "Right here in Antonio's big kitchen."

"That's fine with me," Antonio said, thinking that Serena was going to wake up at his place anyway.

Norman seemed to have the same thought. "I'll call before we bring all the fish over," he said knowingly and Antonio nodded in silent thanks.

"Ooh, Miss Serena," A.J. said. "I have a present for you." He turned and rushed upstairs.

Serena stood beside Antonio and squeezed his arm. "So, this means I have a date tonight?" she whispered.

"Yes," he replied in a low voice. "And you can help me get dressed."

"Or undressed," she said, then turned to the staircase when she heard the pitter-patter of A.J.'s feet. He stood at the bottom of the staircase proudly holding her Mickey Mouse ears. Serena headed over to him and took the ears from his hands and stuck them on her head. Antonio couldn't help but smile. Serena didn't care about messing up her hair or anything.

"It matches your dress," A.J. said.

"Then I will keep them on during the party," Serena said.

"People might laugh at you," A.J. said with a giggle of his own.

Serena shrugged. "Are you kidding me? I love Mickey Mouse and I don't care who knows. Thank you for my gift, A.J."

A.J. hugged Serena again. "You're welcome."

"All right," Norman said. "We'd better get going so we can set up camp at the lake."

A.J. picked up his gear, then he, Norman, and Kamir told Serena and Antonio good-bye.

Once they were in the house alone, Antonio grabbed Serena and pulled her against his chest. "I've been wanting to do this since you walked through the door," he said, capturing her lips in a hot wet kiss that made her swoon. A soft moan escaped her throat as Antonio's tongue danced around inside her mouth. His hands danced across her back and he felt her shiver against him.

Serena pulled back from him and placed her hand against his chest. "If we're going to go to the party, you can't kiss me again. You're going to have to go and get dressed," she said breathlessly.

He winked at her. "Too bad you've already taken your shower. I could use some help upstairs."

Serena unzipped her dress revealing she didn't have anything on underneath. "You can never be too clean," she said with a wink.

Antonio lifted her into his arms and dashed upstairs. Though they'd made love a few hours ago, feeling her soft skin underneath his fingertips and her lush lips brushing against his neck, Antonio was aroused beyond words. His erection nearly leaped from his boxers as he laid Serena against his sheets. She was a goddess, even with the Mickey Mouse ears on the top of her head. He was about to take them off when Serena locked her arms around his neck and kissed him hot and deep. With her strong legs, she pushed his pants down his thighs as they kissed and she pressed her body against him. Desire grew inside him and his erection ached for her wetness. Serena ground against him, teasing him with her wetness. Without even thinking of the protection they needed, Antonio dove inside her and Serena cried out with pleasure. She tightened her muscles around him, nearly bringing him to climax. Raw pleasure surged though his body as he and Serena rocked to the sensual rhythm of their throbbing heartbeats. She squeezed her thighs around him and Antonio dove deeper inside her, lavishing in her wetness.

"I love you," she cried as he felt her climax exploding around him.

"I love you too," he breathed into her ear. He slowed the pace of their lovemaking, in and out, in and out until her thighs shook and he released himself. Antonio's climax escaped like an atomic explosion.

They drifted off to sleep, spent from their lovemaking. It was another hour before they were up, showered, and dressed for the party.

Antonio channeled his inner Eric Benet with a pair of blue jeans, a white button down shirt, and black sports jacket. He slipped a pair of aviator sunglasses on to look cool as Serena stepped into her dress.

"Sexy," she said as she smoothed her hair, then picked up her Mickey Mouse ears.

"You don't have to wear those," he said with a smile.

"I'm going to take a few pictures in them to make A.J. smile. He looked so happy when he saw they matched my dress."

Antonio walked over to Serena as she put her shoes on and kissed her on the cheek. "Thank you."

"For what?" she asked.

"For thinking about my son. I know in the beginning you weren't sure about us dating because of my son."

"I'm the first to admit I'm glad I was wrong. I love A.J. How could I not?"

"Exactly. He's a chip off the old block," Antonio quipped. He stared into her eyes, thinking Serena was everything he and his son needed in their lives.

"What?" she asked.

"Nothing. Are you ready?"

"Yes, the sooner we get there, the sooner we can leave," she said with a wily smile. "Because I want to sleep under the stars with you on top of me."

"Then we're wasting time," Antonio said, lifting her into his arms and heading downstairs.

When Serena and Antonio arrived at Hometown Delights, Kandace met the couple at the door. "It's about time you got here," she said to her friend as she hugged her. Kandace looked up at the Mickey Mouse ears Serena was wearing. "What's up with that?"

"My son gave them to her and told her they matched her dress," Antonio said.

"Okay, so who is this woman and what have you done with my friend?" Kandace joked.

"I'll tell you who I am, as soon as you tell your husband to buy new furniture for our office."

Kandace blushed and led the couple over to the table where Solomon, Jade, James, Kenya, and Maurice were sitting. A few photographers snapped pictures of them and Serena pulled her ears off and set them on the table.

"Did you think this was a costume party?" Jade asked.

Serena rolled her eyes and kicked her friend underneath the table. "I did that for A.J."

Maurice leaned into Antonio and said, "Congrats for still being alive."

"I heard that," Serena said over Maurice and Antonio's laughter.

"Right now, I'm not scared of you," Maurice said.

Kenya pinched her husband on the arm. "Play nice," she said.

"That's right," Antonio said. "Y'all must have my lady confused with someone else."

The table erupted in laughter. James leaned over to Antonio. "There are stories that I could tell you, but I'm afraid you'd walk out the door."

Antonio took Serena's hand in his and kissed it. "That's not going to happen," he proclaimed.

"And James, I got stories too," Serena shot back with a smile on her face.

Jade shook her head. "Leave Serena alone. Antonio, ignore them."

Solomon chuckled as he sipped his drink, then glanced at his wife.

"What?" Serena asked. "No smart comment?"

"No," he replied. "I was always taught that if you can't say anything nice, wait until the ladies leave."

"Stop it, Solomon," Kandace said. "But Antonio, we're really glad that Serena met you."

"I'm the one who's glad," Serena whispered to Antonio, then slipped her hand between his thighs underneath the table.

He leaned in to her and whispered, "If you do that again, we're out of here."

"Promise?"

"Hey," Maurice said, "no whispering. Share with the class."

Kenya smacked him on the arm. "Leave them alone," she said again. "You remember when you couldn't keep your hands off me?"

"Oh yes. Every day I'm reminded." Maurice pulled his wife against his chest and kissed her forehead. "And later, I'm going to remind you how you can't keep your hands off me."

"It's getting thick at this table," James said. "Y'all could at least wait until you get home."

Maurice rolled his eyes at his brother. "Put both your hands on the table then."

"Mind your own business," Jade admonished, causing another chorus of laughter.

Alicia walked over to the table with Devon Harris, the celebrity chef who had been running the kitchen for Hometown Delights and filming his popular Food Network show there. "Hey," Alicia said as she hugged her girlfriends. Everyone noticed the coolness between Solomon and Devon but didn't acknowledge it. The two men, mostly Solomon, were leery of each other because Devon and Kandace dated in college. For a brief moment before Kandace and Solomon met in Sugar Mountain, Devon had been trying to ease his way back into Kandace's life as more than a friend and business associate. But Kandace hadn't been interested since their relationship ended badly. Since her marriage, Devon knew they'd only be friends and business associates, but Solomon didn't trust the guy. Before marrying Kandace, Solomon never allowed a wedding band to stop him from going after a woman. He couldn't help but think that Devon was harboring feelings for his wife.

"Devon has a great idea," Alicia said. "Instead of me introducing Babyface, he should do it. It would give the women a jolt and at the end of the first set, we can all get our pictures with Face."

"That is a good idea," Kandace said.

Solomon muttered, "Anything to get him out of my way."

Kandace stomped on his foot.

"Ouch," he said, then drained his drink.

Devon and Alicia ignored Solomon and ordered another round of drinks. "This is a really good crowd," Alicia said, hoping to ease the tension as she and Devon took their seats.

"Yes," Devon said. "And the menu is being executed perfectly. You ladies should be proud of what you've done here."

Jade smiled, then kissed James on the cheek. "Now all we need to do is make sure nothing happens here to put us on the evening news for all the wrong reasons."

"Exactly," Kandace said. "Because no matter what people say, all publicity is not good."

When the waiter came to the table and set everyone's drinks in front of them, Kandace tried to quietly send hers back, but soon all eyes were on her.

"What's up with that?" Jade asked.

"With what?" Kandace coyly replied.

"Oh, play if you want to," Alicia said. "You're not drinking, so does that mean you're—"

"Knocked up?" Serena said.

Solomon smiled proudly revealing the answer that Kandace was trying to avoid.

"Wow," Jade said. "This is so beautiful."

"Wait a minute, guys," Kandace said. "I don't know for sure yet, but—"

"She's pregnant," Solomon said. "I have eight home pregnancy tests to prove it."

"Oh, those things are accurate, right Jade?" Serena joked.

Jade tossed the lemon from her drink at her friend. "Shut up."

"Are you sure y'all are just friends and not family?" Antonio asked.

"That's the question we've all asked at some point," James said. "Welcome to this dysfunctional group."

"And please don't leave," Devon said. "I've never seen Serena smile this much."

"Why do they keep saying that?" Antonio asked.

"Because these losers never gave me a reason to smile," she joked, then kissed his lips gently.

Chapter 30

Emerson wasn't surprised that he'd gotten into the restaurant. The security officers at the door had abandoned the guest list and were allowing anyone with the cover charge inside the restaurant. Emerson gladly paid the fifty dollars and tipped the doorman twenty. He saw Serena and her friends sitting at a table near the stage. None of them noticed him as he slipped into the crowd near the bar. Before he'd come to the restaurant, he'd gotten a call that had put him in a sullen and angry mood. Lionsgate was passing on releasing the movie. Luther had told him he wouldn't be interested in any other future projects that Emerson was a part of.

"Basically," Luther had said, "your career is over. There's talk about you not writing your own projects and what you did to Serena Jacobs has turned many studios against you. I had no idea you were going to marry her but left her at the

altar when the movie didn't materialize. Women,
who buy most of the movie tickets, don't like that."

"Are you kidding me?" Emerson had said.

"No, I'm not. Give it a couple years and allow
this to die down. During that time, write a hit,
film a hit, and maybe you will get out of this
muck you created. All you had to do was get her
to sign off on the film and we would be getting
ready for the release."

Emerson had slammed his phone against the
wall of the hotel room and smashed it to pieces.
As he looked at Serena, his anger rose again.
He wanted to smash her as she'd done with his
career.

"What can I get for you?" the bartender asked
Emerson.

"A shot of whiskey," he said, not taking his eyes
off Serena and her friends. Somehow, he had to
get her alone. Then he'd seek his revenge.

The bartender gave Emerson his drink and
he gulped it down. Turning his back to the bar,
he pretended to be excited about the start of
Babyface's set, as Devon Harris introduced the
crooner.

Emerson's eyes were glued on Serena. He felt
as if he'd lost everything because of her. At no
point did he think his downfall was his own fault,
although he was the one who had put out crappy
movies and hadn't tried to improve his craft.

It didn't matter to him. She was the person
who had shut down the movie. The one who had
been his muse was now his enemy.

"Give me another one," he said to the bartender, as the lights dimmed, then slid a fifty dollar bill across the bar. "Keep them coming until the money is gone."

As Babyface began singing "Soon As I Get Home," Emerson saw a few couples get up and start dancing. He smiled when he saw Serena stand up and head toward the back of the restaurant. Slamming his glass on the bar, he bounced through the crowd, nearly knocking over a few couples. Finally, he made it to the back hallway just a few feet behind Serena.

He watched the sway of her hips as she walked into a door marked OFFICE. Looking over his shoulder, he didn't see a security officer or one of Serena's friends behind him, and knew it was time to make his move. Emerson walked into the office and slammed the door behind him as Serena walked out of what he assumed was a bathroom.

"Did you really think I was going to let you do this to me?" he hissed when he and Serena locked eyes.

"What are you doing in here?" Serena asked.

"What am I doing in here? You and your lawsuit sank my movie and ruined my reputation with the studios. No one wants anything to do with me."

"And that's my fault?" she snapped as she attempted to push past him.

Emerson grabbed her and pushed her against

the wall, holding her there with a hand on her chest.

"Get off me! Let me go!" Serena flailed at his hand, trying to free herself.

He caught her hand. "No, you bitch. How could you do this to me? All you had to do was sign off on the film, but you wanted to fight me," he growled as he slammed her against the wall.

Serena clawed at his face with her free hand. "Help! Somebody help me!"

He grabbed Serena's jaw and squeezed. "Shut up." Pushing her head back into the wall he leaned in close. "All I needed from you was to let this movie restart my career. You got a second chance but you destroyed mine."

"And you left me at the altar." Then she attempted to knee him in his privates. Emerson shifted his hips to avoid her blow, but didn't loosen his grip. Serena dug her nails deeper into his hand. "Let me go, fool."

Emerson flung her onto the sofa, then pounced on top of her. He held her down with his knee on her midsection. Serena struggled to push him off her, but he gripped her throat and choked her. She writhed against the sofa and Emerson tightened his grip. Her body went limp and a jolt went though Emerson's body. She was dead. He backed away from her, looking at her motionless body. He'd expected to feel satisfaction when he did to Serena what she'd done to his career. But all he felt was fear and emptiness.

* * *

"Ladies and gentlemen," Devon said from the stage. "Give it up for Babyface. He's coming back, right after dessert."

Babyface took a bow and the lights came back up in the restaurant. Antonio looked over his shoulder hoping to see Serena fighting her way through the crowd. "Do you think the bathroom line was that long?" Antonio asked.

Jade and Alicia looked at each other and shrugged. "I figured Serena would've gone into the private bathroom in the office," Jade said.

"She has been gone for a long time, though," Kenya said.

Antonio rose to his feet and studied the crowd. "I don't see her. I'm going to the office."

Alicia stood up and headed through the crowd with Antonio. More appropriately, she struggled to keep up with Antonio as he crashed through the crowd, nearly pushing people over. His mind reeled with the worst-case scenario—something bad happened to Serena. Had she drunk too much and fallen in those five-inch pumps? Maybe she had broken her leg and couldn't move.

"Antonio," Alicia said as she finally caught up to him. "I'm sure she's fine. Serena's a workaholic, so she might be in the office on the computer." She reached into her purse and pulled out the key for the office door, but the door was unlocked and cracked open.

Antonio gently pushed her aside and entered the office. Looking to his left, he saw Serena lying motionless on the sofa. He rushed to her side and felt her wrist for a pulse. He found a faint one, then yelled, "Alicia, call 9-1-1."

He turned back to Serena. "Come on, baby, wake up. Wake up." Hot tears of anger and fear poured from his eyes. Someone did this to her and his first thought was Casey. "Don't die on me, Serena. I love you." He brought her hand to his lips.

"She's dead," a voice from behind him said.

Antonio turned around and saw a figure in the darkness. Rushing the man, Antonio grabbed him by his collar and pulled him out of the shadows. When he saw it was Emerson Bradford, he knew who'd hurt Serena and began to pound him.

"You son of a bitch! You tried to kill her," Antonio swore as he punched and pounded Emerson to within an inch of his life. He hadn't noticed the police, the EMS workers, and Serena's friends had entered the office until two police officers snatched him off Emerson. "He did this to her!" Antonio barked as the officers held him back and an EMS worker checked Emerson's injuries. "To hell with him, you have to save Serena."

The EMS workers turned their attention to Serena, taking her vital signs to determine whether further action was necessary.

Jade shivered against James's shoulder as Serena was loaded onto a stretcher and wheeled out of the office.

"Let go of me," Antonio said. "I'm going with my wife."

"Sir," one of the police officers said, "we have to ask you some questions."

"Let him go with her," Solomon and Maurice yelled out.

"They're going to the hospital. You know where to find him," James added angrily. When the officers released Antonio, he tore out the door and hopped into the ambulance with Serena.

"Her airway is constricted and there may be a broken bone in her neck," one of the EMS workers said to the other as they worked on Serena. Antonio watched silently, his mind flashing back to the day when Marian was taken away in an ambulance.

The EMS worker closest to Antonio touched his shoulder. "Sir, do you know what happened? Did you do this to her?"

Antonio shook his head. "I would never hurt her. Emerson did this."

"Do you know if he used a ligature?"

Antonio looked up at the worker and wanted to say, *If I'd seen him trying to kill her, she'd be walking around and he'd be in here.* Instead, he said, "I didn't see what happened."

"She needs oxygen," one of the workers said, then placed a mask over Serena's face. Antonio stroked the back of Serena's hand and prayed she would be all right. Prayed she would wake up and he wouldn't have to tell his son that another woman they loved was gone.

Serena heard Marvin Gaye's voice—not singing but talking. "You can't leave that man. And you can't let the other man win."

What? Where am I? I thought Babyface was singing tonight, she thought as she looked around and saw nothing familiar. She wasn't in the restaurant anymore and all she saw was a bright light. And her throat ached.

Emerson. Emerson tried to kill her. Serena wanted to open her eyes, but her eyelids felt as it they were being held down by boulders. She could feel someone stroking her hand and that motion comforted her and she thought she smiled.

"Serena." Marvin Gaye was singing. "Baby, open your eyes and look at the man who loves you and wants you more than you need to go to Heaven."

I'm going to Heaven, for real? Serena thought, then her eyes fluttered open.

Antonio was standing at her bedside, holding her hand. "Thank God," he whispered, then pressed the button for the nurse.

A woman walked into the room. "Is everything all right?" she asked as she crossed over to Serena's bed.

"She opened her eyes," Antonio said.

The nurse looked at Serena. Seeing that her eyes were open she pulled out a penlight and shined it in her eyes to evaluate her pupil response. The nurse smiled when Serena's eyes followed the light. She placed her hand on Antonio's shoulder. "I'll go get her doctor."

Antonio wanted to kiss her. He prayed that Serena was coming back to him. It had been three days since he'd seen her beautiful eyes.

Three days of pure hell not knowing if Serena would wake up. He'd told A.J. that Serena wasn't feeling well. He hadn't wanted to upset his son about Serena's true condition. Antonio couldn't say that she might die—he couldn't go through the pain of losing her. Not when he loved her as much as he did. He'd spent every moment he could by her bedside.

Jade had tried to get Antonio to leave earlier to get something to eat, but he'd told her she needed to go eat more than he did. "Antonio," she'd said as she left the room. "You're not going to do her any good if you wind up in a bed beside her. Be prepared to eat when I get back."

He'd offered her a halfhearted smile. "Thanks."

Then Serena had opened her eyes and Antonio was glad he hadn't left.

The doctor walked into the room and began running a series of tests to determine if Serena was fully awake. Antonio watched with baited breath as the doctor made notes and placed his fingers on the sides of Serena's neck. "What's going on?" Antonio asked the doctor.

"Well, Mr. Jacobs, Serena's vocal cords are still swollen, so she won't be able to speak, but her vital signs are strong and she is awake. She can hear you."

Antonio smiled and returned to her bedside, seeing that Serena was following him and the doctor with her eyes. He also knew that not being able to talk was killing her. He took her hand in his and kissed it as he'd done over the last three days.

"Welcome back, beautiful," he said. "I have missed you."

She smiled at him and blinked her eyes.

"Killing you not be able to talk, huh?" Antonio asked. "Not that you talked a lot, but now I have your undivided attention and I have to say this. I never want you out of my sight ever again. When you get your voice back, we're getting married."

Serena blinked her eyes in rapid succession as if she was saying something to Antonio's declaration.

"I'll give you time to think about it," he said. "But know that I love you more than anything in my life."

Serena parted her lips and the doctor touched her foot. "Mrs. Jacobs, don't put stress on your vocal cords right now. I'll have the nurse bring you a notepad."

Serena nodded, then squeezed Antonio's hand. She mouthed, *I love you, too.*

As the doctor left the room, Jade walked in with a bag from the cafeteria. "Is she awake?" Jade asked when she saw Antonio holding Serena's hand.

"Yes," Antonio said happily. "Her doctor just left and said her vitals are looking good but she can't talk."

"She's in hell." Jade smiled at Serena as she set the bag of food on the chair next to the bed. She leaned over and kissed her cheek. "Thank you for coming back to us. You'd better keep this man around because he's the one." She glanced up at Antonio. "But I'm sure you already knew that."

Serena nodded and Jade turned to Antonio. "I'm going outside to call the girls and let them know how she's doing."

When they were alone, Antonio grabbed Serena's hand and kissed it again. "A.J. wants to see you, but I think we're going to hold off on that until you're talking again."

She nodded, but her eyes said she had so much to say.

"And when you're able to say 'I do,' I expect to walk down the aisle and make you Mrs. Antonio Billups."

A tear spilled down Serena's cheek as the nurse walked in with a pad and a pencil. Serena pressed the up button on the bed and accepted the pad and pencil. With a shaky hand, she wrote,

I love you so much and I never thought that you and I would make it this far. Marrying you would be the best decision I've ever made.

Pulling the pad toward him, Antonio read the note, then tore the piece of paper off the pad, folded it, and slipped it in his pocket. "I'm going to keep this and remind you of it when we have our first argument."

She smiled and the doctor walked into the room again. "Sir," he said to Antonio, "I need to get by you to adjust your wife's medication and take another look at her throat."

Antonio nodded. "I'll be right outside the

door," he told Serena, not correcting the doctor about their marital status.

"Is everything all right?" Jade asked as she approached Antonio.

"The doctor is examining her," he said. "But everything is fine, better than fine. Serena and I are getting married."

Jade's eyes lit up like candles. "Are you serious?"

Antonio pulled the note out of his jacket pocket and handed it to Jade. After reading the note she handed it back to Antonio and hugged him tightly.

"She is so right. Marrying you will be the best decision she ever made. Now, we have to start planning a wedding, preferably while she can't voice her opinion."

"I don't know about that," Antonio said with a chuckle. "She's going to have to have a say in this because this is her first and last marriage."

Jade patted his shoulder. "I like the way you think, brother."

When the doctor walked out of the room, Jade and Antonio returned to a find a smiling Serena sitting up in the bed. She'd written several notes for them.

Jade laughed when she read

If you think there will be pink in my wedding, you have another thing coming.

Epilogue

Three weeks after Serena had been released from the hospital, she still thought her voice was a bit raspy. Antonio told her it was sexy, but she didn't buy it. On her wedding day, however, she felt as if her voice was right back to normal.

Kandace walked into Jade's bedroom, which was doubling as Serena's dressing room since she and Antonio were getting married in a small ceremony at Jade and James's house. "Nervous?" Kandace asked as she sipped on a glass of ginger ale.

"No."

"Liar, your hands are shaking."

Serena looked in the mirror and dropped her eyeliner pencil. "Still battling morning sickness?"

Kandace nodded. "It should be called all day sickness."

Serena smoothed the lace bodice of her simple, yet sexy strapless wedding gown. The dress was snow white with red lacing in the bodice. Standing, she looked at the gown and smiled. "Thanks for helping me pick out this dress."

"Well, we couldn't have you walking down the aisle in all white," Kandace joked.

"Oh, shut up."

Jade and Alicia walked into the room with a box. "We could hear you in the hallway," Alicia said with a smile.

"I never thought I'd say it, but I'm glad to hear your evil voice so clearly now," Jade said.

"We need to hurry up and get you outside to the altar before Antonio changes his mind," Alicia said, then handed Serena the box.

"What is this?" Serena asked as she set the box on the dressing table and lifted the top. Inside was a white gold tiara with three large stones in the center of the filigree metal work. She ran her finger across the stones and smiled.

"This is the last remnant of the Ice Queen," Alicia said.

Serena laughed as she placed the bejeweled tiara on her head. "Let's get one thing straight. I'm still a queen. Just one who has a king now." She stood up and gave herself a once-over in the mirror.

"Beautiful," Jade said.

"You look great," Alicia said.

"And isn't this better than doing it without us?" Kandace added. They all looked at Jade.

"Look," Jade said. "Get over it."

"Yes, because she and James will probably do something corny like renew their vows soon any way," Serena said.

"So sarcastic and it's your wedding day," Jade said.

Serena sucked in a deep breath. "My wedding day."

"Are you all right?" Alicia asked as she touched her friend's bare shoulder. "You're sure about this, right?"

"Of course, but I guess I am a little nervous," Serena replied. "The last time I was about to get married I ended up standing at the altar alone, expecting to be married to a psycho who tried to kill me."

"Well, Antonio is outside waiting for you. Emerson is locked up and facing serious jail time since he pleaded guilty to attempted murder," Jade said.

"And Antonio proved he's no crazy killer by allowing Emerson to live when he found him in the office that night," Kandace said, then shivered. "But that's the past. Let's get you set for the future."

"That's right," Alicia said. "And no more talk about psychos or the restaurant until after your honeymoon."

Serena nodded. "That's right. I'm ready to become Antonio's wife."

Antonio accepted a can of Pepsi from Maurice as they waited for the reverend to arrive for the ceremony. "You all right, man?" Maurice asked.

"Just anxious to get this over with," Antonio said as he took a sip of the soda.

With a beer in his hand Solomon walked over

to the two men. "It's hot out here"—he looked at Antonio, who was dressed in a white linen suit with a red tie—"but it looks like a beautiful day for a wedding."

"It could be raining and it would still be a beautiful day to marry Serena," Antonio said.

Maurice and Solomon laughed. "Man, you got it bad," Maurice said.

"Really bad and thank God you're marrying her. You have transformed her," Solomon said as James and A.J. walked over to them.

"Daddy," A.J. asked, bouncing around, "is it time to get married yet?"

"Not yet," he said, then handed his son his can. "Do me a favor and put this in the recycling bin."

"Okay, but when I come back is it going to be time to get married then?"

"Almost," Antonio said.

"I can't tell who's more excited," James said. "He's a great kid."

"I can't wait until Robi is that age. Maybe she'll sleep all night then," Maurice said.

"It can't be that bad," Solomon said. "Having the baby has to be better than dealing with the pregnancy. Kandace is an emotional wreck these days and she's not that far along. Please tell me it gets better."

"It doesn't," James, Antonio, and Maurice said with a laugh.

"Damn," Solomon said. "So, you guys are telling me it's going to be a long nine months?"

Maurice nodded. "And tell her not to breast

feed," he said. "It was Kenya's idea to do that, but when she couldn't have her coffee, it was somehow my fault."

"Jade said breastfeeding made her and Jaden closer," James said. "So, you better let that woman make her own decision about that."

"Are you and Serena going to expand your family anytime soon?" Maurice asked.

"Let us get married first," Antonio said, smiling. "But I'm not going to say I wouldn't love to have a little Serena running around here someday."

"Oh, Lord," Solomon said. "I don't think the world is ready for two of them."

Antonio was about to reply when he saw A.J. and the reverend heading their way. A.J. was practically dragging the man to the altar.

"The preacher is here. It's time to get married," A.J. exclaimed when he and the older man made it to the group of men.

"Sorry I'm late. Reverend Layton Jackson." He extended his hand to James and the other men.

"Luckily, my future wife is inside with her friends and they probably have lost track of time themselves."

The reverend nodded, then turned to Maurice. "Mo Goings. You know, I'm going to have to tell my congregation that I met you, especially since during football season they spend their Sundays with you."

Maurice smiled. "Sorry about that, sir."

"It's all right. I moved the service up an hour because I like to cheer for the Panthers myself."

A.J. tugged at the reverend's pant leg. "Excuse me, sir," he said. "Can you stand up there and marry my daddy and Miss Serena?"

The men laughed as Reverend Jackson rustled A.J.'s head. "All right, son. We're going to take our places now."

Solomon knelt down in front of A.J., "Why don't you go knock on the door and tell the ladies we're ready to get this show on the road?"

"Okay." A.J. took off running.

Moments later, Antonio stood at the altar with his son by his side. Though he'd thought A.J.'s excitement about the wedding would get the best of him, his little boy stood like the perfect best man as the chords of *Wedding March* began to play. Serena appeared at the doorway leading to the backyard. Antonio didn't see anyone but her as she slowly walked down the aisle to him. She was a vision in snow white and red. The diamond-studded tiara made her look as if she'd stepped right out of Cinderella's castle. It took everything in him not to rush down the aisle and scoop her up into his arms. When she made it to the altar, Antonio took her hand in his and brought it to his lips as A.J. giggled and the reverend smiled at the couple.

The audience was intimate—Norman and his grandson, Serena's friends and their husbands as well as their little babies, and the chef from Hometown Delight. When the reverend began the ceremony, Antonio couldn't take his eyes off his future wife as they held hands and the sun beamed down on them. When he offered his vows to love and cherish her, he knew it would be the last time he ever said those words. Tears welled up Serena's eyes as she recited her vows. Antonio stroked her cheek, silently telling her she didn't have to cry.

"If there is anyone here who thinks these two should not enter into matrimony, speak now or forever hold your peace," Reverend Jackson said.

"I better not hear a word," Serena admonished, causing everyone to erupt in laughter.

"All right," the reverend said. "Then, by the power vested in me by the Lord, our heavenly father, and the state of North Carolina I now pronounce you man and wife. You may kiss . . ."

Before the reverend said *kiss the bride*, Antonio had Serena in his arms kissing her with a burning passion that caused everyone to hoot and applaud.

"I love you," he said when they broke the kiss.

"I love you, too," Serena replied, offering him a smile that nearly outshone the sun. "You've given me the greatest gift of all. You showed me that love doesn't hurt and I will always be grateful to you for that."

He kissed her again, gently brushing his lips against hers. Antonio would've lost himself in a second kiss with her if A.J. hadn't tugged at his leg. He and Serena looked down at him.

"Yes, son?" Antonio asked.

"Can we eat cake now?" the little boy asked.

Antonio and Serena smiled and nodded. "Yes," Serena replied. "We can go and eat cake."

The couple turned around and A.J. hopped in between them. They headed into the house to eat cake and start the rest of their lives together.

Dear Reader,

Behind every bad attitude, there's a reason. When I introduced Serena Jacobs in *Betting On Love*, I knew you'd either love her or hate her. I'm glad so many of you actually loved her. Serena isn't mean just because she can be, she's that way because of her past. Like many of us, myself included, Serena pushed her pain down because she never wanted to be hurt again.

But sometimes, you meet someone who reminds you that there are good people in the world, who you can believe in. That's what Serena found out when she met sexy Antonio Billups.

I hope you enjoyed the story of Antonio and Serena. It was a lot of fun to bring these opposites together. Thank you so much for supporting me and happy reading.

Cheris Hodges
P.S. You can always reach out to me: cheris87@ bellsouth.net
Follow me on Twitter, www.twitter.com/cheris hodges
Or be my friend on Facebook, www.facebook.com/cherishodges

Don't miss Solomon and Kandace in

No Other Lover Will Do

On sale now wherever books are sold.

Turn the page for an excerpt from
No Other Lover Will Do . . .

Chapter 1

Solomon Crawford turned his back to the buxom blond model lying beside him. She was on the cover of *Maxim* this month and he thought it would've taken him longer to get her in bed. In reality, it had only taken him two hours and a bottle of expensive champagne to get "what's her name" to drop her panties and give him what every man in America wanted. But for all her beauty and silicone, she was a complete bore in bed. The woman lay there just like a sack of flour and Solomon had never been more disappointed. He probably would've had more fun watching paint dry or grass grow.

The red numbers on the alarm clock next to the bed read four-thirty. *Hell, the room is paid for,* he thought as he rose from the bed. Solomon didn't even try to be gentle or quiet as he reached for his discarded Armani slacks and Italian leather loafers.

"Where are you going?" she asked, her voice deepened by sleep.

"Home," he said.

"But, I thought we could . . ."

"Listen, we're done. And honestly, there's nothing you can say or do to make me want to spend another minute with you," Solomon said as he buttoned his shirt. "The room is paid for, but checkout is at noon."

"You're going to leave me here alone?" she asked incredulously. "How can you do this to me? Do you know who I am?"

Solomon shrugged as he picked his jacket up from the armchair near the door. "Just another piece and not a very good one," he said, then walked out the door. Solomon heard a crash as he headed down the hall to the elevator. Maybe if she'd shown that kind of passion in bed he would've stayed until at least five. Solomon chuckled as he stepped onto the elevator and rode to the W Hotel's parking garage. She, like so many before her, would get over it and have a great story to tell about her night in Solomon land.

Solomon Crawford was the kind of man that women couldn't help but get naked for. He had money, power, and model good looks. To the many women he'd bedded, he was an untamable stallion they had to ride at least once. And one ride was all they'd ever gotten. Solomon didn't believe in fidelity, love, or all that other bullshit that sold greeting cards and roses. He wanted sex and it was given to him freely. The only thing he'd ever worked for was building his family's hotel empire. The Crawford chain of hotels and resorts stretched across the United States and Canada.

Three years ago, Solomon had been handed the reins to the business when Cynthia and Elliot Crawford retired from the hospitality business. His older brother, Richmond, was super pissed when he was passed over to run the business. Richmond was forty years old and thought he knew more about running a hotel business than "the little playboy."

But at age thirty-five, Solomon had been more than ready to take charge. Solomon knew the only way to shut Richmond up was to take the business to the next level and that he did with the help of his bright business partner Carmen De La Croix. Carmen talked him into investing in resorts and making the Crawford name synonymous with deluxe vacation resorts. Of course, Richmond thought this was a bad idea until they turned a million-dollar profit in the first quarter. And the money kept rolling in. Solomon knew he'd be lost without Carmen. She was the only woman he was able to talk to and trust. She didn't want anything from him and he liked that. Why couldn't the women he slept with be more like that? Solomon Crawford wasn't going to give anyone a diamond and a happily ever after—that wasn't the Crawford way.

Despite the hour, Solomon picked up his BlackBerry and dialed his business partner and best friend, Carmen De La Croix. She had to hear about his night.

* * *

Kandace Davis was tired of waking up in the cramped office of the restaurant she owned with her three best friends, Jade Christian-Goings, Serena Jacobs, and Alicia Michaels. Glancing at the clock on her computer, she saw that it was nearly six A.M. "Damn," she muttered. "I did it again."

Kandace knew she had to get out of the restaurant before Jade came in, because she wasn't in the mood for another lecture. She picked up her leather bag and was about to stand up . . . too late.

"Kandace, you'd better not be in this office," Jade said as the door swung open.

"I just got here," Kandace lied.

"Umm-hmm, wearing yesterday's clothes?" Jade shook her head as she looked at her friend. "I picked up these extra hours because you just had a baby. Why are you here?"

"Because James and Maurice are doing the 'daddy thing' today," she said referring to her husband, James and his brother. Kandace smiled remembering how Jade and James brought their son into the world just a few months after Maurice and his wife Kenya had welcomed their daughter into the family. Kandace was happy that despite the unconventional way Jade and James became husband and wife, hooking up in Las Vegas of all places, they seemed happy.

"So," Kandace asked, "since James and Maurice

have the kids, what are you and Kenya going to do with yourselves?"

Jade clasped her hands together. "Kenya and I can actually do something other than lactate for a few hours. I've never worked the breakfast shift and . . . wait, this isn't about me. You need a break." Jade perched on the edge of Kandace's desk. "You've been in Charlotte for six months and I know you love Atlanta. I've leaned on you so much, it's surprising that you haven't broken in half. This place is up and running, you've gotten us publicity all over the place. So, the girls and I decided . . ."

"Now you guys are making decisions about my life?" Kandace asked with a terse laugh.

"Yeah, because you won't," Jade shot back. "We're voting you off the island for two weeks. Go on vacation. You've got to relax. Everybody around here has noticed how tense you are. If you're trying to prove to Devon Harris that you're a capable businesswoman who no longer wants his cheating butt, mission accomplished."

Kandace stifled a yawn. "Since you chicks are making decisions, are y'all paying?"

Jade folded her arms underneath her full breasts. "Now you're just being ridiculous," she said. "I don't care where you go, but I don't want to see you for two weeks!"

Kandace knew Jade meant well and she rose to her feet and gave her friend a kiss on the cheek. "All right," she said. "But you guys are going to miss me. I'm leaving my cell phone, laptop, and everything right here."

"Good," Jade said. "Maybe while you're on vacation you'll have a little fun and get your feet wet."

"Whatever. All of us don't find Mr. Right on vacation like you did," Kandace said as she gathered her things.

Jade smiled and glanced down at her wedding band. "Yes, I was lucky in vacation love. I just hope you get lucky."

"I think I'm going to go somewhere and be pampered for two weeks. Then you all can eat your hearts out while you're here slaving away. And I don't need to get lucky, thank you very much."

Jade waved to her friend, "Kick rocks, chick," she joked.

As Kandace headed to her car, she thought about what Jade had said. Over the last six months, she had poured herself into her work because she had nothing else. Her life was all work because at home, Kandace had a big empty bed waiting for her and she was tired of it. Kandace hadn't been with a man in a year. Her last relationship ended when she decided that she'd wanted something serious. Robert Harrington was happy with the sex, the nice things that Kandace did for him, but he wasn't willing to take their relationship to the next level. After watching Jade get married, Kandace wanted her own marriage but Robert wanted no part of it.

"What's wrong with the way we are?" he'd asked when she'd broached the subject of marriage before she moved to Charlotte.

"I want to know that we're moving toward a future," she'd said. "Is that too much to ask?"

"This is just like a woman. Your girl gets married and then you think it's your turn to walk down the aisle. I don't want to get married."

"All right," Kandace had calmly replied. "If you don't want to get married, then I don't want to have sex with you. I don't want to do your damned laundry and I don't want to waste any more of my time."

Robert had promptly walked out of her penthouse. Kandace had packed for Charlotte and never looked back. If she'd been honest with herself, she would've admitted that Robert wasn't the man she needed to marry. He was selfish, he tried to be controlling, and he lacked passion in bed and in life. Of course Robert hadn't wanted things to change. He liked being in a rut, but Kandace had grown tired of it.

She knew for a while that her relationship had been a dead end, had actually realized it over a year ago. But because she had been comfortable with him, she stuck around until she saw what a real and passionate relationship looked like. Jade and James had inspired her to seek something better and real in her relationships. Maybe pressing Robert about marriage had been her way of ending the relationship.

Yeah, she needed a vacation. But more than anything else, she needed some sleep. Kandace drove to her uptown townhouse and for once, she was happy her bed was empty.